WHITE HELL

WHITE HELL

A NOVEL

SEAN TYLER

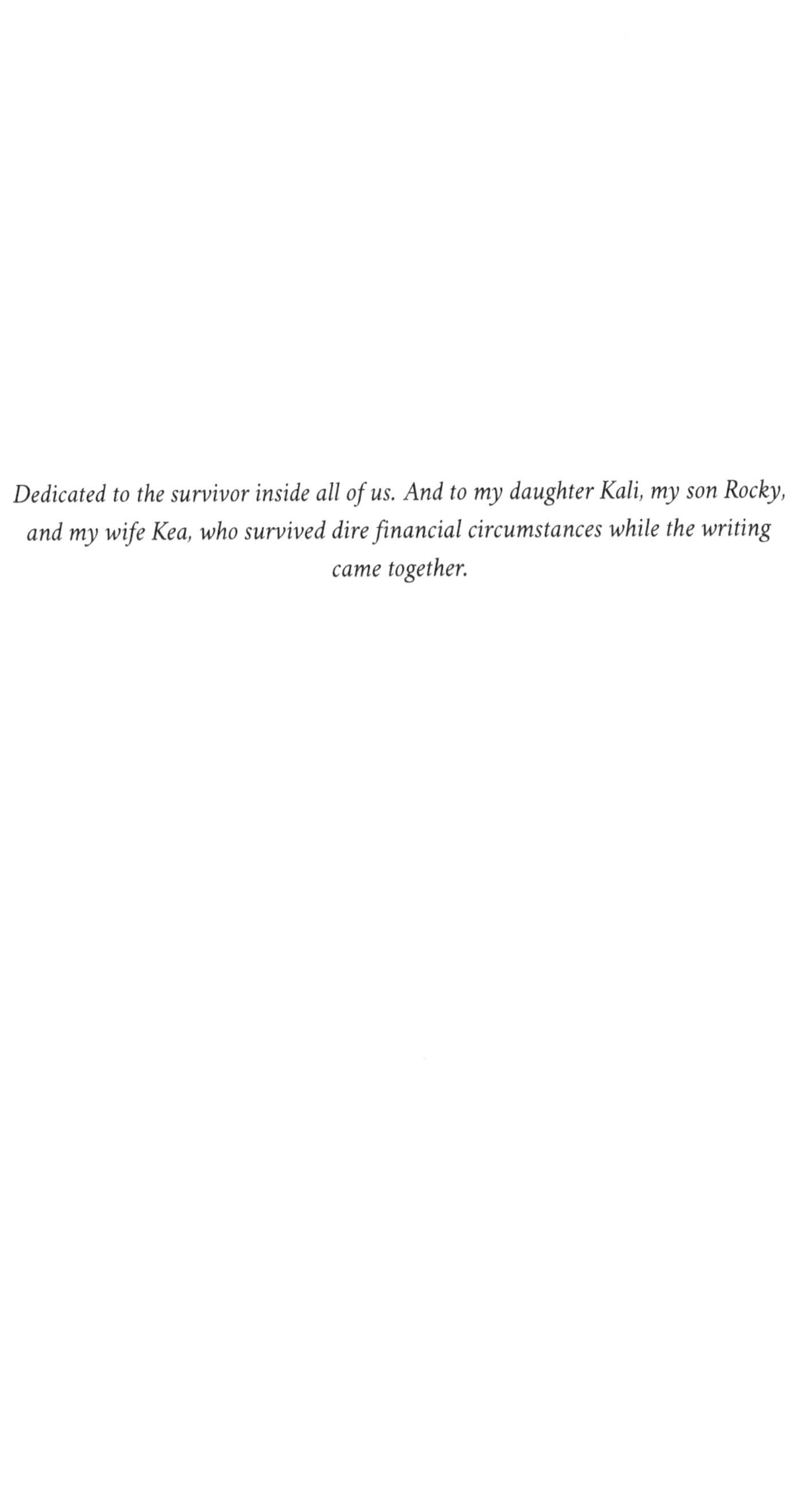

Dedicated to the survivor inside all of us. And to my daughter Kali, my son Rocky, and my wife Kea, who survived dire financial circumstances while the writing came together.

Praise for White Hell

"Debut author Sean Tyler has a unique style—like God put Cormac McCarthy and Jack London in a blender. You'll be drawn into his characters and storytelling and will find it impossible to put this book down!"—Kevin Klusener, author of *The Killer's Terms*

"*White Hell* takes you on a journey you won't soon forget. It's 1846 and you're headed west in the capable hands of Sean Tyler. He'll take you on that long desperate journey with bigots, ex-preachers drunk on trailbrew and freed (or maybe not) slaves. You may even fall in love with the beautiful Violet along the way. You never know who is following you, watching you, or waiting up ahead to ambush you. Some of you won't make it, but it's a hell of a ride."—Jenny Dandy, author of *The Brownstone on E. 83rd* and *The Penthouse on Park Avenue* (April 2025)

Prologue

In the fall of 1847, news reached the territorial lands of California that a party of American emigrants had sacrificed the lives of the African slaves among them, and eaten their flesh and bones in order to survive the winter snowbound in the Sierra Nevada Mountains.

On April 13 1847, *California Star* staff writer Samuel E. Jones published the only public report of the ordeal in a small, two-paragraph article titled 'Distressing Rumors from the Sierra Nevada.'

'We have received numerous inquiries at this paper regarding a disturbing incident among emigrant travelers who were prevented from crossing the mountains because of snow—and that these emigrant travelers may, or may not, have resorted to the cannibalism of black slaves. My investigation into the matter has led to many dead ends, closed doors, and outright denials, until I visited the saloon at Sutter's Fort and happened upon a young white man who claimed to have survived the fabled disaster party. He refused to give his name, but agreed to speak anonymously, as long as I financed him supper and a bottle of Old Crow. The young man was ragged and rough-looking, severely emaciated, and in a fragile state of mind. Extracting a coherent timeline of events proved difficult, and once the Old Crow went dry, the man abruptly stood and disappeared from the saloon, not to be seen or heard from since.

'Thereby, of the incident at large, I offer this vague abridgment: The emigrant party at issue had come from the eastern states via the regular overland migration road, a company of nine ox-drawn wagons and thirty-five ambitious souls seeking land and fortune in California under

the guidance of a prospector named Irwin McEwan. At some point along the road west, the McEwan Party had crossed paths with a group of deserted blacks, presumed to be runaway slaves, and with good intentions provided these blacks with a lift to California. The McEwan Party then suffered a series of time-consuming setbacks that delivered them upon the Sierra Nevada Mountains in the dead of winter. The emigrants became entrapped by deep snow, provisions ran out, and longing hunger made it necessary to sacrifice the lives of the blacks, so that their corpses might be used for food until the snow melted and travel was possible again. The exact number of survivors is unknown but reckoned to be less than half of the original ranks. It is of my belief that those who lasted this horrid ordeal are weary of explaining themselves, having been through hell and back, and thus the reason they remain hidden from the public eye.'

Three months later, the *California Star* seized all publication when the entire staff rushed out to the Sierra Nevada Gold Fields. And with that, the so-fabled 'McEwan Party Disaster' went unmentioned in the press for another century. Then in 1932, an anonymous donor submitted an old diary to the National Oregon/California Trail Historical Society containing a firsthand account of the disaster as written by Peter 'Peanuts' McEwan–the younger brother of Irwin McEwan. The diary was in bad shape, and many of the pages were torn or stained by what appeared to be blood, but its text confirmed the existence of five ex-slaves traveling amongst the party when the terrible snows fell and that desperately starving and hopelessly bigoted white travelers had indeed turned to cannibalism. Peter McEwan, however, was tremendously conflicted about eating black flesh, because he had fallen in love with one of the five ex-slaves to be sacrificed, a strikingly good-looking young black woman named Violet. The following story is based on Peter's diary.

Chapter One

They were…black? I counted five of them, standing in the middle of the road ahead, plus one wagon with empty hitches, and one ox lying dead and bloated behind them.

It was certainly unusual, seeing people of colour stranded along the emigrant road to California, and I wasn't sure what to make of it.

But I didn't think it was a bad thing. To blaze the trail west implies a general freedom of passage that is typically denied to black people in America, and for five of them to be stranded here, on an unmarked road through a blank space on the map, was profoundly altering to the prejudice of the norm. It meant that the new and exciting prospects of the West were enticing all kinds of Americans, not just your typical pale-skinned colonizer like myself. It meant that California was a dream shared by whites and blacks alike.

Embracing this new truth, and feeling that sudden rush of excitement that comes with helping the disadvantaged, I slammed on the brakes and brought the tall iron wheels to a skidding halt.

My brother Irwin, however, just kept leading his horse down the road without stopping. But then he turned around, reined and dismounted, and approached me in a rather aggressive manner. "Who told you to stop?!" he snapped. "There's no time for this."

"There's always time to help *fellow travelers* in need," I eagerly replied, jumping down from the schooner and beating the dust off my riding coat to look halfway presentable.

"Help them?!" Irwin scoffed. "Christ Almighty, we're not a goddamn charity."

The five blacks stood within earshot, watching us with dark, bony faces and bright, twinkling eyes. I looked at those five innocent faces and doffed my cap politely. "Excuse me, one moment," I said, then turned to Irwin to put a word in his ear. "Don't be so daft," I said, quietly. "We've got oxen to spare. Let's help these *fellow travelers* get back on the road."

Irwin folded his arms across his chest, standing tall and rigid in his dusty riding drapes, his expression entirely lacking in enthusiasm. "I have no authority over those spare oxen," he flatly said.

Feeling a touch of embarrassment over my brother's rude demeanor, I smiled at our company and courteously said, "I apologize, just one more moment, please." Then I leaned into my brother's ear and whispered, through my teeth, "The hell you don't. You're the Wagon Master. The Man in Charge…and we're driving enough oxen to fill a farm!"

Irwin raised his eyes and studied the train of eight covered wagons catching up behind us. A white-hot sun rained down from a cloudless blue sky, beating the brim of his hat. A warm wind blew gentle waves across a vast sea of tall grass surrounding the road.

"Damnit, Peter" he hissed. "Most of those oxen belong to Boggs—and I guarantee you this: A stingbum like Boggs ain't loaning his precious oxen to a bunch of ragged coloured folk."

Now, before passing judgment, let me say this about my brother Irwin: he was a good man. He'd been voted Wagon Master because of his strong mind and leadership qualities, but, indeed, he was looking and sounding like a real narrow-minded jackass in the presence of them poor blacks.

"Oh, but if they were *white*, you'd bend over backwards to help."

I looked him square in the eyes as I said this.

Irwin made a dismissive gesture with his hand, as if to say, Peter, you're being overdramatic.

The five coloured pilgrims just stood there, staring, blinking, looking like a couple of unlicked cubs desperate for our help. Two of them were young males, tall but scrawny in the cotton rags they wore, with wildly overgrown beards and heads topped with bushes of thick black hair coated in dust and pieces of dry leaves. Not that my own hygiene was any better, but the rough and wild of trailblazing had certainly left an impression on these two. The other three blacks were young females, each wearing gray-colored gowns with long sleeves, like a maid's gown without the apron, and gray sunbonnets made of canvas that shaded all but the white shine of their eyes and teeth.

"They're clearly runaway slaves," said Irwin.

"How do you figure?" I said, folding my arms across my chest.

"Well," he said. "For starters, I don't see any white men overseeing this ambitious pilgrimage of theirs."

"So what!?" I exclaimed. "Maybe they came from a free state."

"They'd need freedom papers to prove it," he declared. "And by the look of them, I doubt they're carrying any freedom papers."

I shook my head. "It's just plain ignorant," I said. "The way you talk *at* them like they're beneath us."

Irwin sighed and turned his gaze over the dead ox and the busted wagon, then out across the flat horizon of sun-soaked grasslands. His eyes turned small and distant under the brim of his hat. I could tell that he was thinking about the nature and fate of these five wayward pilgrims, wondering just what in the hell they were doing out *here*, all the way out here, in the exact middle of nowhere, but he declined to share his thoughts aloud. He was normally communicative in this unnervingly reserved way with me, as older brothers generally are, yet his blatantly prejudice attitude necessitated an explanation that suddenly poured out of him in a hideous blaze of racist gibberish: "Now look here," he said. "We're not about to get mixed up with a bunch of fugitive slaves. No, the last thing we need is *more* hungry mouths to feed…God knows we have our own problems…There ain't enough rations to spare…Nope…No way…No way in hell…Not gonna' carry a bunch of freeloaders all the way to California."

"Goddamnit, Irwin!" I snapped. "They'll starve to death if we don't help… or they'll be scalped by natives. Look at them, *brother*, they need us."

Irwin shook his head, looked away. "Goddamnit," he grumbled.

The five blacks just stared, blinking, looking lost.

I sucked my teeth and held my arms out, a gesture of my indifference with Irwin, then turned to our poor company and said this: "Sorry folks, but my brother's not feeling very charitable today. Unfortunately, he is the Wagon Master, the Man in Charge, and we *must* follow his orders, no matter how heartless and ignorant they may seem."

An impatient look flashed across Irwin's face. "I'm only doing my job," he snorted. "The Wagon Master has to make the tough calls for the greater good of the party…calls that can be unpopular with the lazy meat-beaters like *you*."

"Sorry, folks," I said, removing my hat and holding it in my hands apologetically. "Wagon Masta' Irwin has cracked his whip."

"Damn you, Peter!" he cursed. "I don't care if they're black, white, or purple. We ain't got *no food, no oxen, and no time to spare!*"

I replaced my hat and bowed my head obediently. "Yessa! Whateva you say, Wagon Masta."

"Damnit! Don't talk to me like that," he hissed, pointing the warning finger in my face. "You're completely out of order!"

"No. *You're* out of order."

"The hell you just say?!" he shouted. "You little fruit-picker! Why I *outta-*"

And our bickering may have carried on this way, back and forth for who knows how long, had a voice not interrupted.

"Excuse me…gentlemen…hello?…Excuse me…gentleman!"

One of the coloured females timidly stepped forward and lifted her sunbonnet. Thick dreadlocks of black hair fell freely down her shoulders as the sunlight came over her, and a rather pretty face was unveiled.

She was…surprisingly cute.

And her eyes were green, and big, and gorgeous, and they were staring right at me.

I was too stunned for words.

"I'm sorry to interrupt," she said, rigid and nervous. "But gentlemen, please believe that we are free people of colour. Our former Master granted our freedom—a Mister Jack Beasley of St. Louis, Missouri—and encouraged our plight to California by gifting us that wagon." She paused for a breath and nodded her softly rounded chin toward the busted wagon behind her, then continued. "But our freedom papers were lost during a river crossing, believe it or not. The river tipped the wagon sideways and washed half of everything away."

"Bullshit," muttered Irwin.

"What?" I said confusedly.

I'd grown distracted by her body, which, at second glance, was small and petite, yet curvy in a way that made her seem larger and busty. It was nothing like the thin body of your typical white woman, but an exotic thickness of eye-catching hips and thighs.

And the more I studied her, the more stunning she became.

Irwin turned his nose up at the pretty black girl. "What's your name, missy?" he grunted, folding his arms impatiently across his chest.

"Violet," she said in a voice innocent enough to tune a brass violin.

"Violet," repeated Irwin, studying her intently. "Why do I get the feeling that some Johnny Cracker cotton farmer is lookin' all over Dixie for you, right now.'"

This patronizing remark snapped me back into the conversation. "But we're a thousand miles from The South," I interrupted, glaring over the flat, featureless wasteland. "Ain't no cotton farms...no slavers out here."

Violet snapped her pretty green eyes and said, "But, sir! We's free! I swear it be the truth. We had papers...but the river—"

Irwin raised a hand to shut her off. "That's enough," he said. "The less I know, the better." He shifted his stony glare on the two boys standing behind her. "Don't they talk?" he gruffly asked.

Both boys blinked, neither one spoke.

"I do the talking for them," curtly answered Violet. "I'm best with words and all."

Irwin half-smiled and turned his eyes back on Violet. "Can they at least drive oxen?" he asked.

"No, I also do the driving," she said, justly clicking her heels together.

"You drove your last ox into the grave," said Irwin, sounding unimpressed.

Violet shook her head. "That shouldn't count against my ability. That ox was no good from the start."

"Then why try for California with a no-good ox?"

Violet looked flustered by the question and fumbled her response. "Well…sir…you see…"

Irwin waved his hand impatiently. "Keep your bucket of lies, missy," he said. "From here on out, I'm just gonna' assume ya'll telling the truth about them freedom papers getting lost in the river…and leave it at that."

Violet blinked and nodded attentively. Irwin continued. "Now I don't intend to leave ya'll here in a lurch…and seeing that it's mutually advantageous for pilgrims to congregate together, as to ward off attacks from Savages or Mexicans or Mexican Savages, I suppose I ain't got no slack in the matter, but to adopt ya'll into our party."

Violet's face warmed to a look of satisfaction. "Thank you, Mister!" she said with a clap of her hands. "We're forever in debt."

I was so shocked by everything that for a long moment I couldn't speak. My eyes were fixed on Violet, examining the way her dingy gown pressed snuggly to her lovely profile, and my thoughts were fixed on her too. I was guessing at her age, nineteen, twenty perhaps, not much younger than myself, when the gravity of the situation finally dawned on me.

"Wait a second!" I snapped, as if waking up from a dream. "So, we're gonna help them after all!?"

Irwin looked at me. "I'm already regretting this."

I clapped my hands together. "Excellent!" I shouted. "My brother will guide us to California in a jiffy…just one or two months more travelin' at the most. Now if *you people* need anything, *and I mean anything at all,* don't hesitate to knock on my schooner…I sleep inside the box at night." I was talking directly to Violet as I said this, but feeling a little intimidated by her looks, and thus lacking in eye contact. "If you get hungry," I said. "I have plenty of beans to spare. And we have salt pork too, but it's halfway rotten—"

"Alright," snapped Irwin, raising a hand to shut me off. "That's enough of that."

Violet smiled at me, a smile that can only be described as something warmer and brighter than the blazing sun overhead. Then she turned her smile on the other blacks, who each lifted from their individual despairs to smile back at her. She introduced them in the order by which they stood. "That's my brother Donavon, and my other brother Rutherford, and my sisters Daphne and Rose."

Right off, I couldn't help but notice that each sibling was a different shade of brown. The men were much darker in color than the women, with noses that were all differently shaped. Violet herself had a small and sharp nose, while the males sported wide snouts with huge flaring nostrils. I wondered if they were not genuinely blood-related, but rather connected through a previous ownership, and thus bound by the common struggle of being former slaves. Whatever the case, Violet had the greenest eyes and fullest lips of the bunch, and no doubt, she was the most brilliant flower in the garden.

After the introductions were made, my brother, the Wagon Master, gave our new trail-mates a stern lecture on the lofty expectations of our California crusade. He said things like, "Ya'll better not inconvenience me," and "I will not hesitate to leave any slacking wagon team behind." None of the blacks dared to interrupt him, and when Irwin was finished speaking, he abruptly turned on his heels and walked away as if more important matters were calling him.

* * *

Irwin's horse went by the name Ringo. Ringo was a powerful quarterhorse with a silky brown coat, a strong back, and a marvelously fast gallop. But Ringo was also a big dumb animal with a moody temper and would snap his teeth and try to bite the hands of anyone who tried to feed him, anyone not named Irwin.

I stood out of reach while Irwin fed Ringo a handful of dry apple chips. Behind us, eight high-wheeled wagons awaited, held up in a pale haze of dust and hot sunshine, while our new exotic friends hitched a new ox to their busted old wagon.

I wanted to hug my brother and sing his praises up and down the dusty road for being so kind to them black fellers, but because of Ringo, I merely slapped him on the back from a safe distance. 'It was the right thing to do," I said. "Such charitable acts only serve to ensure our good graces with the patron saints of pioneering."

Irwin made no reply to this. He merely sighed, as if the whole thing was a waste of invaluable time, then dug into his trouser pockets for another handful of apple chips. Ringo glared at me with his big dark eyes, a look that said he wanted to hurt me for no good reason at all. I took a step back.

"I saw the way you were lookin' at that coloured girl," muttered Irwin. "Staring all dewy-eyed…"

I shut my eyes and groaned, feeling my skin flush hot with embarrassment. "I was merely impressed with her vocabulary," I tried to explain. "That's all. She sounded smart for being a…well, smarter than most of these white knuckleheads you're partnered up with."

Irwin looked at me. He rarely smiled outright, he was too serious for all that, but a slight grin stretched his lips. "I believe her name is Violet," he said. "Yeah, you had that stupid look in your eyes. Like the one you have right now."

I shook my head and tried to laugh it off. It was uncomfortable to talk to my older brother about feelings of the heart, and I wanted to run away. "To be frank," I said. "She's quite a looker, wouldn't you agree?"

Irwin smirked, but his words weren't as glowing: "As Wagon Master, I order you *not* to sow oats outside of your race. Only trouble will come of it. There will be plenty of white women once we reach California."

Before I could respond to this, heavy footsteps caught my ear, and a large shadow suddenly passed over the sunlight. I swung around to see Boggs approaching, a big, ugly white man wearing a straw hat and a dusty pair of overalls.

"Get outta' my way!" he growled, swinging his large arms out and pushing me aside like a ragdoll. "Them is *my* oxen, *goddamnit!*" He shouted at the back of Irwin's head. "And them pickaninnies can't have 'em."

Irwin continued to feed his horse. "It's not up for debate," he calmly responded.

A small Mexican cigar was stuck in the corner of Boggs's mouth. He snatched the cigar, tossed it, and leaned aggressively over Irwin's backside. "To hell with that," he growled. "Them black-son-a-bitches can find their own way back to the plantation…I ain't given' my oxen to no cotton-pickers!"

Irwin rubbed his horse between the ears. "We're helping them poor blacks to California," he calmly reiterated. "And that's an order."

Boggs huffed and stared crossly at the back of Irwin's head, then rolled his mean glare in my direction. "Pee-nuts!" he croaked. "Help me out, here. Tell your goddamn brother that it's a bad idea: Given' them precious oxen away to a bunch of moochin' toads."

I shrugged and looked away. Boggs was, without a doubt, the sloppiest and dumbest member of our party. The man was more pig than human, and I hated his guts, especially when he called me Pee-nuts instead of Peter.

"Stop calling me Pee-nuts," I muttered.

Boggs snarled and turned back to Irwin.

"Oh, I get it," he groaned. "You and little Pee-nuts here done turned into a couple of fancy pants colour-lovers." He exploded with laughter and swung his huge arms in the direction of the idle wagon train, trying to draw the attention of the other drivers. "Oh, how high-n-mighty!" he roared. "We're driving West behind the great Irwin McEwan: A blue-bellied, Yankee doodle dandy! A fighter for the liberation of the cottin'-pickin' peoples! A man with the kindness of heart to guide any runaway pickaninny to freedom."

A dark look came over Irwin's face. He suddenly spun around, lashed out, and seized Boggs into a headlock, pushing him face to face. "You stupid baboon!" he shouted, staring intensely into Boggs's eyes, not blinking, nothing playful about it. "I'm the Wagon Master. And I'm givin' them blacks an ox. Now shut your fat-stinkin' mouth about it."

Boggs flailed like a chicken and jerked out of his grasp. "Alright!" he gasped. "Take my damn ox…hell…I got plenty to spare…no skin off my back, boss."

Like a grizzly bear losing interest in a fight, Boggs turned away and lumbered back towards his wagon, huffing and growling as he went.

Irwin watched him go, then fixed the ruffles in his duster and calmly returned to feeding his horse. And in this way, the matter was settled. Irwin was the Wagon Master.

* * *

We drove on. Ten wagon teams, churning up the dusty road behind the Wagon Master's lead. The drive through the unorganized territory was dull and slow going as usual, the terrain mostly flat and featureless, no trees, the sky huge and blue, the road well-used and easy to follow. Around mid-day, we forded a small river, then passed an Indian burial ground where the graves were recently dug up; the bones left scattered about by either coyotes or grave robbers.

In the late afternoon, the trail climbed an easy pass through a low range of hills before descending upon a wide basin that was evenly blanketed in purple sagebrush. Here, we came to a fork in the road that gave the Wagon Master pause. A lowly signpost was sticking out between the forks with a single piece of paper tacked to it, wavering in the low sunlight like a tiny flag.

Irwin dismounted and tore the paper from the post, and read it quietly to himself. It was a message from a dandy of a young man named Gaylord Hightower, a successful lawyer and author back east, who, by way of hounding press, had turned himself into something of a famous western adventurer. Hightower was planning his own town in California, where he envisioned himself mayor, and was hoping to attract settlers by leaving these messages along the trail, messages containing updated travel information and directions to his town.

As the ten wagon teams came to a standstill behind Irwin, I hurried over to his side to see what the holdup was about. "Well, what's the letter say?" I asked him. "Another love letter from Hightower?"

"Quiet you," he grumbled. "I'm tryin' to read."

Hightower's messages had appeared tacked upon random signposts ever since we left 'the states' behind for good, so every pilgrim heading west that summer was well acquainted with Hightower's advertising techniques. Hightower had also authored a book called *The Pilgrims' Guide to the West,* that my brother carried a copy of, and that, perhaps, was the single greatest driving force behind this entire Western movement—that would come to be known as the Great Migration of Eighteen-Forty-Six.

When Irwin was finished reading the letter, he looked up and squinted his eyes down each fork. He sighed ruefully, his face grim as usual, then handed the letter over so I could read it myself.

To all emigrants on the road to California,

As reported on page forty-five of my book, the road ahead attaches to the wide meanders of the Bear River for another hundred miles, and the river itself must be crossed several times, thus adding many extra days onto the overall trip.

Ah, but there's good news to report! For I have recently discovered a new shortcut around that blundering portion of road! Just take the left fork and continue upon a fine and level road across a dry but pleasant basin—and follow this road for a good hundred miles or so, for it reconnects with the old road just prior to the crossing of the Great Desert of the West.

I strongly encourage all California-bound wagon trains to take the new shortcut, as it is nothing but advantageous and time-saving. Rations will be spared, and the health of the oxen will be preserved ahead of the desert crossing—the final obstacle before the California border.

OK. That's all for now.

Good luck and happy trails to all,

Gaylord

P.S.—I almost forgot, I have finally decided upon a name for my newly-laid town in California...

I shall call it Gayville. It stands to be the crown jewel of the West. Hope to meet you there soon!

I snapped my head up from the letter. "*Gayville?*" I said with a laugh.

Irwin looked annoyed. "Sounds like a wonderful place," he muttered. "Can't wait to see it."

On the backside of the letter was a map, a clumsy doodling of squiggly lines and points of reference, like something an imbecile would follow in search of buried treasure or to a fabled town called *Gayville*. I told my brother that I didn't care for Hightower, or his map, and this all but cemented his frumpy mood for the remainder of the conversation.

"It's a good map," he said. "It shows a fine sense of civic duty. Who else would take the time to compose such an informative letter, but our good friend Hightower?"

"Good friend?" I disputed. "But you've never met the man."

"Oh, but he wrote me this letter."

"It's not personally addressed to you."

Irwin narrowed his eyes. "Listen here," he snapped. "This party is taking the new shortcut—and meeting Hightower at Gayville—*and that's an order.*"

"Dumbest order ever."

Irwin sighed, raised his eyes and gazed off over the long-stretching fields of sagebrush surrounding us. The land was becoming less inhabitable by the day. His patience was running thinner and thinner as the hot struggles of our westward venture mounted, though he did his best to hide his frustrations behind steely eyes. "Just tryin' to get these people to California…alive," he quietly said.

"But you're relying on directions from a man you've never met personally," I complained. "A man who, according to the bio in his book, was born in Manhattan, *New York City.* A man who attended *Harvard Law School* on his daddy's dime. A man who, in truth, is nothing but a pompous rich-kid adventurer, leaving instructions alongside the road for anyone thick enough to follow."

Irwin looked insulted. "Goddamnit!" he grumbled. "Gaylord Hightower is a *trailblazer*, a world-famous author, a lawyer, an experienced guide, and a cartographer. The man has a goddamn town named after himself. Hell, he accomplishes more in a single day than you have in an entire lifetime. Now git back to the wagon, and git movin' down the new road. We'd be fools not to take it."

"Hightower ain't shit without his daddy's money," I muttered.

Irwin snatched the letter from my hand, then abruptly turned on his heels and walked away to retrieve his horse. The discussion ended there.

I had no rational reason to dislike the lawyer/writer/adventurer Gaylord Hightower, no plausible bitch against him, but the man's bigheaded ambitions and nationwide fandom bothered me for whatever reason—perhaps jealousy, or perhaps a deeper suspicion of his true motives to be realized in time. I had read Hightower's book. It was an interesting read, its text painted lovely pictures in the mind, describing California, like some dreamland vacation spot. For example, page twenty-one, paragraph three has this to say: *'The California coast is lined with sand beaches and palm trees, with lush valleys further inland where the vegetation is always in bloom. The soil here is of the topmost quality like that of the Deep South, but with a climate that is mild year-round like in the Mediterranean...December is as pleasant as July.'*

As you can imagine, Hightower's book had sparked a nationwide frenzy, encouraging thousands of hopeful crusaders to drive across the continent in large parties of covered wagons. Here was the root of the California Dream, and though I'm reluctant to admit it, the book had made a believer out of me as well.

* * *

The story of the McEwan Party begins like so many other stories involving the American West: It starts back east, where men who live in meager shacks dream of bigger and better things. This dream gets blended with a fascination of the West and all its untapped prospects. The dreamer then acts upon this dream by selling everything he owns, just to afford the ever-rising price of covered wagons and all supplies necessary to survive the estimated five-month-long journey across the unorganized territory of the American interior.

That dreamer was my brother Irwin. Born Irwin Theodore McEwan in Boston, Massachusetts, in 1815, the elder son of Darla Jean, my sweet mother, a seamstress who died nine years ago from eating toxic fish, and of our father Raymond, a lifelong prospector who died four years ago in the bottom of a mine shaft that suddenly filled up with water. As heredities would have it, Irwin and father look remarkably alike: same reddish-brown hair, same hard jawline, broad shoulders, and cagey eyes that never lied, whereas I'm small and petite like Mother. And like Father, Irwin was a prospector, and a hard-driven one, but after years of chasing worthless prospects all over New England, Irwin got it in his mind that more lucrative outlooks were out west. Incidentally, page thirty-three of Hightower's book says this: *'The mineral prospects in California are endless. Flakes of gold flounder in the currents of the mountain streams, meaning precious metals lay abundantly just below the surface, waiting to be unearthed by any man with the tools and grit to make his own fortune.'*

That all sounded good to me, but my reasons for going west were slightly less ambitious than my brother's. Sure, I was hoping to get rich, and looking for some real adventure in the process, but mainly I just wanted out of Boston. The city is one huge disease-invested slum, covered in snow half of the year and burdened year-round by crime, violence, racism, corruption, and the good old American systematic neglect of the poor. The best hours of my day were spent working a measly job in pest control, which barely paid enough to cover my half of the rent on the one-room shack we shared. My job entailed me to walk around the city all day long with a cache of rat traps hanging from my shoulders while hollering out, 'Rat Catcher!" at every dwelling I passed. "I can catch the sneakiest...the stingiest...the nastiest rats ever! For only a half penny!"

"Rat Catcher here! Hire me for only a half penny."

I was a rat-catcher living in a one-room shack, covered in a foot of snow and surrounded by ramshackle pubs and brothels, pimps and hustlers, disease and poverty—and I just wanted to get away, plain and simple. So, when Irwin finally asked me to join his California crusade, I needed all but five minutes to decide. And that's my story in a nutshell. I had no definite plan. I was just sort of drifting on the winds of opportunity. I wasn't sure what would become of me out west, but I loved the thought of lounging on a sandy beach, with the sun bronzing my skin and the cool blue Pacific Ocean washing against my toes.

All types of men came to join my brother's crusade. Originally, our party departed Boston three months ago with only four wagons, driven by a motley crew of fortune-seekers, carpetbaggers, and general lowlifes that my brother had recruited from failed mining operations throughout New

England. These men were the whole root and branch, from honest family men to genuine losers and hopeless drifters who hardly knew anything about trail-blazing. A German emigrant who spoke not a word of English, a hard-smoking Irishman who carried two dueling pistols, a beer-bellied scoundrel named Boggs who was, at best, an unruly squatter drifting on the rumors of a golden payout.

All and all, we were just another gang of bearded white men in dusty riding clothes, bigots and drunkards and prospectors with wandering hearts and wild eyes fixated on the west, looking to get rich off the virgin lands beyond the horizon.

The final four wagons in our party belong to an elderly gentleman named Milt Crabtree, a moderately wealthy furniture maker from Ohio, who joined us in Missouri Territory, right before the jump-off across the Great Prairie. When Milt was asked why he sold his furniture store and forty-acre estate in Ohio to rough it west, he only shrugged and said this: 'for a change of scenery,' for which, to me, was completely understandable. Milt's three grown sons, Calvin, Daniel, and Ryan, separately drove wagons with wives and children in tow, while old Milt and Martha, his wife of thirty years, road comfortably inside a customized grand Conestoga with steel axles and springs, two storage compartments, two sets of cozy bunkbeds, a wood burning stove, and a cabin as big and homely as a hotel suite. The big Conestoga, or what I'd nicknamed the 'land yacht,' required four yoked pairs of oxen to pull it and two drivers to constantly lash the oxen to maintain our slow but steady pace.

And onward we trekked across the wild territory, my regular schooner driving at the head of the train, followed by the black wagon team, then my brother's men and the Crabtree brothers in the middle, with the big land yacht bringing up the rear like a giant caboose.

* * *

The new shortcut was nothing but an old Indian footpath streaking through the sagebrush that moved us ever so slowly across a great featureless expanse.

The drive was boring; my eyes grew heavy, and I nearly dozed off several times. By late afternoon, I could no longer stand it; the heat, the tedium, the same old slow going. I handed the bullwhip over to my cousin Wilbur, then climbed into the wagon bed to take a nap. Wilbur was only fifteen with a face full of big red pimples, but he was a good driver, and I felt confident enough in his abilities to knock out while the wagons trudged onward.

I was barely out for five minutes when the sudden thundering sound of a galloping horse snapped me awake. Peering through the canvas bow, I saw Boggs mounted upon his white-spotted Appaloosa and reining to a trot alongside the coloured wagon team. Sporting a beard full of trail dust, he fixed his crusty eyes upon the wagon's driver, the pretty-eyed black girl in the ragged tight summer gown.

"Hot Damn! That's one good-lookin' piece of dark meat," he loudly blurted, leaning back in his saddle to study her backside. "And how about that fanny! Looks like you're stashing two Christmas hams back there."

Violet kept her eyes trained on the road, and walked alongside the oxen with the same graceful rhythm, acting as if Boggs didn't exist, as pretty women often do when their good looks invoke unwanted attention from rough-looking men.

"You got a ripe little body," continued Boggs, plunging his hand down into his crotch and scratching at it. "It must come from all this manly work you're doing…drivin' *my oxen* and all."

The emphasis placed on *my oxen* was antagonistic, and its petty significance seemed to hang in the hot, dusty air. Violet's chin rose, and sort of traced the words back to their wretched source. She looked at Boggs and opened her lips to say something, perhaps thank him for the oxen, but then she seemed to think better of it and looked away without saying a word.

Boggs jumped at her lack of gratitude. "Oh, you'll be thanking me later on," he snorted, his hand digging vigorously into his crotch now. "When I slip this big white snake inside that blackberry pie of yours…you'll be howling thanks."

I was watching from the tailgate of my wagon and listening to every stupid thing Boggs was saying. At first, I thought he was just kidding around, rudely pestering her like he pestered the rest of us—but his last comment gave the whole thing a certain violent, rapist tone. I turned away in disgust, feeling the need to get the authorities involved, and moved to the front of the wagon to find my brother.

Irwin was riding about ten paces ahead, mounted on Ringo and looking half-asleep in the saddle.

I popped my head through the front bow and yelled at him. "Are you gonna do something, *Wagon Master*?!"

Irwin peered over his shoulder and simply regarded the situation with a drowsy, uninterested glance. "Boggs won't touch her," he said, returning his eyes back to the road and lazily kicking his horse back up to speed.

I shook my fist at him. "Damn you," I yelled, then turned and hurried back to the wagon's rear. I pressed myself against the tailgate, watching, listening, worried sincerely about the pretty-eyed coloured girl.

Boggs was still trolling his horse alongside her, but his eyes were looking distractedly at her wagon. "What's this hunk-a-shit you're drivin'?'" he asked gruffly. "The same old wagon used for cotton pickin'?"

In truth, her wagon *was* an eyesore. Its wooden wheels were terribly wobbly, the axles squeaked for grease, and the frame was warped and lopsided. Someone's stained-old bedsheet was pitched over the bed like a tent, where Violet's two sisters hid underneath from the sun while her two brothers sat lazily against the tailgate with their feet dangling over the side, looking like two farm hands catching a ride back to the barn.

"Them two boys is uglier than sin," huffed Boggs. "But you, my darling—you're as golden as a peach."

Violet rolled her eyes in disgust, saying nothing.

Boggs leaned forward in his saddle and squinted his eyes, studying her intently. "You got any white in you?" he asked.

Violet bit her bottom lip, refusing to answer, leaving Boggs to answer himself. "Yeah, you got some whiteness in you, alright," he said with a nod. "And you fixin' to get *more* white in ya' tonight, once we make camp." He laughed harshly and slapped the shoulder of his horse, then cocked his head up and sang this wretched ditty: *"Oh Yessiree...Tonight I'm gonna have me some warm blackberry pie."*

It was his singing that finally pushed me over the edge. Not metaphorically, but literally, I went flying over the tailgate, jumping feet first and hitting the ground running, stumbling, and nearly biting the dust.

I used my hands to break my fall and regain balance, then crossed intently before Boggs's white horse. The look in my eyes said this: I have come to rescue the pretty-eyed black damsel in distress.

"Get away from her!" I screamed.

"What's it any business of yours, Pee-nuts?!" Boggs howled from his mount.

"You can't talk to her like that," I protested, turning and following beside his horse with quick, angry steps.

"Why not?" he snarled. "Because you're eyeing this blackberry pie for yourself? For that limp little Pee-nut pecker of yours?"

This set my teeth on edge. "I'm warning you!" I howled, pointing the warning finger at his face. "Touch her, and I will have you brought up on assault charges extra-judicially—and you will hang from the next tree we come across. And stop calling me Pee-nuts, goddamnit."

Boggs squealed with laughter and slapped his horse again. "Assault charges?!" he gasped. "Why, you little shithead! It's not a crime for a white man to help himself to the mud pie of a negress, especially one indebted to him. Learn the rules, *Pee-nuts!"*

Boggs's fat mouth, his ignorant logic, it all seemed to trigger an awful tingling sensation in the left side of my face that made my left eye twitch uncontrollably. I felt my hands clenching into fists. I wanted so bad the courage to throw the most immaculate uppercut across his jaw and scatter his rotten yellow teeth all over the dusty road, but considering his elevated position and that he was twice my size, I only mustered this snippy retaliation: "She owes you nothing, you fat-ugly sack! And why do you keep referencing pie? Pie this and pie that? Are you so hopelessly obese that all your thoughts turn to food?"

Boggs stiffened upright in his saddle, his eyes smoldering with humiliation. He shook his head and tried to laugh it off, but it was clear that my insult about his weight landed right under his greasy skin. "Is that right, Pee-nuts?"

he hissed. "Tough talk from the scrawny afterbirth." He reached out and turned the warning finger against me. "I'd bust you one good if not for your brother," he said. "You wimpy little rat-catcher."

"That's right, boy, I heard you were a rat-catcher before Irwin became your mammy, cradling you in his arms and carrying you West like a whiny little baby."

"Now, don't make me come down from this horse and bend you over my knee and give that rear-end a good hammer spanking. You hear me, *Pee-nuts!?*"

Boggs opened his hand and flattened his palm to mimic the spanking of a buttock. "Hammer spank that rear!" he howled.

I grew timid and backed off from Boggs's horse, feeling paralyzed by the sting of his insults and doubting that I would ever recover from such a slander of my manhood in Violet's eyes, who was still driving close enough to overhear the whole thing. It was true, I had been a rat-catcher, a measly job for a measly boy, but what the hell? Look at me now, twenty-one years old and fearlessly pioneering into the Wild West, and certainly too old to be bullied.

"Fuck you, Boggs," I said. "You greasy meatbag. Your horse is dying from carrying your fat *ass—*"

That's when Boggs jumped from his horse. His big left hand lashed out, and his fingers snatched around my neck.

And suddenly, my world went black. The big fat pilgrim was over-top of me in a flash, faster than I could react, and his grip was strong enough to snap my head off.

Then I felt a hand smacking against my bottom. Sharp and punishing smacks, followed by the terrible realization that I was being spanked.

A grown man, twenty-one years old, helplessly being spanked.

And then I was that wimpy child all over again, captured on his way home from school by the neighborhood bully, my backside a punching bag for his misguided aggression. I kicked my legs in a panic and struggled to get free, screaming like a little girl desperate for help. In the process, I caught a glimpse of Violet, who appeared to be moving away from me as fast as she could, trying to disassociate herself from this terribly embarrassing nonsense. A dismayed look on her face seemed to say this: of all people, a skinny rat-catcher named Pee-nuts came to my rescue.

Terribly embarrassing. Then, from the corner of my visibility, I saw Ringo turn broadside and stop alongside the road. Irwin was sitting upright in the saddle, his hat pushed back against his forehead, his eyes wide-awake now and focused on Boggs.

"BOGGS!" he shouted over the wagon clatter. "Enough of that horsen' around. I got a job for you."

The painful smacks against my bottom abruptly ceased. The big ugly pilgrim stood upright on his heels, turning his attention on Irwin. "What job?" he grumbled.

"Ride out yonder and shoot us something to eat," commanded Irwin, nodding his head to the sagebrush desert beyond.

Boggs stiffened and shifted his crusty eyes over the flatlands. "Ain't nothing out there but jackrabbits, boss."

Irwin narrowed his eyes. "Go shoot some jackrabbits then."

Boggs tilted his head forward, hawked, and spat onto the trail ruts. His expression turned bitter. He looked ahead to Violet, who had maintained course and was far ahead now, fading behind the dust cloud generated in the wake of our passage. He looked back at me and snarled like a dog and mumbled something about my gnads being the size of two peanuts before turning to retrieve the reins of his white-spotted horse.

* * *

I was first introduced to Boggs on the very day we departed for California, so I'd only known him a few months, yet I learned to hate him with the kind of passion that normally takes years to build. This man was a real horse's ass. A devoted rumhead who drank during the daylight hours from large vats of whiskey stored in his wagon, and a drunken menace by nightfall, when he would use his formidable mass to bully food from his fellow travelers while selfishly hoarding his own rations for future consumption. He ate anything in sight, humped anything with two legs, and drank until he either vomited or passed out beside the campfire. He had a thing for Injun whores, the tawdriest and saddest and most abused-looking whores he could find along the road west. And I once saw him piss on a harmless Pawnee elder who was blind in both eyes, then kick the poor man's dog for an extra laugh.

I had never met such a malcontent, a man so bigoted, so perverted, so crude in every way. An outright jackass with the moral principles of a jackal. His reputation back in Boston was so notoriously rotten that he was banned from even the most horrible pubs and brothels, no banks would lend him money or cash his checks, and no landlords would give him tenancy. Thereby, the only thing left for a miscreant like Boggs was to take the plunge west where the natives still roamed, where personal histories could be erased, where a man could practically do as he pleased.

The Wagon Master threatened to kick Boggs out of the party almost daily, but it never amounted to anything. To actually remove Boggs from our numbers would certainly involve a confrontation that Irwin intended to avoid, because Boggs was a dangerous ruffian who carried a huge twin-barreled horse pistol on his hip.

And yet, a man like Boggs had a certain value in the Wild West. "We need him," Irwin once explained to me. "In the event of an Injun attack, a reckless nut like Boggs is essential." Irwin also believed he had Boggs under control in the way a man would tame a wild dog.

* * *

Later that evening, an underwhelming site of sand and sagebrush was circled for camp. The horses and oxen were corralled inside the circle, fed from sacks of cornmeal, and watered from storage kegs. A communal campfire went up as a huge full moon waxed over the plains. Road-weary pilgrims gathered around the fire with meager helpings of rations stirring in their frying pans, mostly beans and near-spoiled cuts of salt pork purchased in Missouri two months ago.

After dinner, it was off to my transient bed inside my schooner to rest up for another grueling day on the road.

As for the sleeping arrangements of our new trailmates, the two males joined the pile of men sleeping beside the campfire while pretty-eyed Violet and her two sisters shared the wooden bottom of their wagon. Irwin pitched a small tent near the campfire, and Boggs eventually passed out face down in the dirt like a dead monster.

Chapter Two

Since the beginning of our journey, I'd established a relatively consistent morning routine. I would sleep in as long as possible until roused from bed, usually by some terribly unsettling noise like the sharp clanking of two frying pans banging together or the rude smack of my brother's calloused palm against the side of my face. I took my coffee steaming hot and black as possible, with a usual breakfast of dried apple slices and a pan-fried biscuit. Then it was back to the wagon to secure our possessions, double-check the water level in the kegs, and help cousin Wilbur hitch up the oxen. With a few exceptions, we normally drove non-stop until sundown, then searched out a good, level campsite to circle the wagons, eat and sleep, and repeat. Progress was slow and tedious, things were often uncomfortable, and nights in the wagon bed tended to get lonely. But it was the only sensible way west. Striving for one's dream life, I reckon, was always easier said than done.

A heat wave set upon us as we continued west across the barren territory. At high noon, we rumbled down a sandy ravine and crossed a dry riverbed. It was a turbulent affair; the tall iron wheels banged and scraped against the bare white stone of the riverbed, and the oxen hobbled, and the drivers cursed and cracked whips.

We drove on through the afternoon heat with water reserves half empty and all other vital provisions dwindling faster than expected.

By and by, we came upon heaps of luggage scattered about the dusty roadside, cast off by previous travelers to lighten the load on the poor, suffering oxen. I saw cookware, stoves, furniture, mattresses, boxes of gear, a wooden rocking horse, a baby carriage, a black case shaped like a violin or guitar, heaps of family possessions left baking in the sun, casualties of a desperate odyssey.

I remember passing a tiny wooden cross staked in a crypt of stones where the journey prematurely ended for some poor traveler. Death and abandonment were the only news from this parched corner of the world.

We drove on. It took three days to cross that brutal plain of sand and sage. Eventually, the road climbed through a gap in a modest range of hills, then descended upon a low valley enclosed by red-sandstone cliffs. Fields of dry-yellow grass spanned the valley floor, divided down the middle by a green zone of foliage that lined the course of a small river—the first water source spotted in four days.

I was the first of our party to reach the river. Thirsty as a dog, I fell to my knees immediately, but was given pause by the road-beaten face mirroring in the river's surface.

My hair was greasier and longer than ever. A scruffy beard covered my jaw, my cheekbones protruded like overhangs, and my eyes seemed recessed deeper into the sockets.

I looked ten years older and twenty pounds scrawnier and every bit like something that had crawled out of the desert in search of water.

Behind me, ten wagons circled a previously cleared-out campsite. We were the only white people for miles, if not days, but signs of westbound passage were everywhere: trash heaps, ashpits, dung piles, and wagon tracks.

Violet unhitched her borrowed oxen and led them down to the river. While the bulls trotted into the shallows and dropped their snouts for a drink, she squatted along the bank, studied her reflection in the water, then bent forward and dunked her head for a wash.

I was watching her, and wondering if she might decide to bathe the rest of her body, and whether or not it was appropriate to stay and watch.

She rose from the water a second later, took her water-logged dreadlocks into her hands, twisted to ring the water out, and looked upriver in my general direction.

Our eyes connected briefly. A vague smile seemed to warm her face.

I sent a quivering smile back, and was tempted to wave—but like a frightened deer, Violet suddenly perked up and jumped to her feet. Her eyes snapped away and her smile collapsed to a fearful glare. Something was moving in the bushes behind her.

It was Boggs, moving so fast and wild that there was no avoiding him. The big ugly pilgrim pounced without warning, thrashed his hands out, and grabbed a handful of Violet's buttocks.

"Big ol' black booty!" he howled. "Lemme' squeeze it!"

Violet yelped and tried to jump out of his grasp, but lost her balance in the rocky shallows and went plunging into the river with a wild splash. She quickly recovered, however, and went dashing across the river and up the far shore.

Boggs squealed with laughter. "Look at her go! Wet and wild!"

Violet paused at the crest of the far shore and looked back, dripping wet and breathing heavily, her gown soaked to transparency and pressed tight to her frame.

Holy Jesus, I thought. I'd never seen anything so vulnerable and defenseless. Her eyes trembled with outrage, and I was outraged for her, but seeing her in that soaking-wet gown…her thighs bulging against the wet cotton fabric, and her breast…like two ripe plums in a wet sling.

All that, plus the sheer audacity of Boggs's doggedness, had me frozen stupid in place along the riverbank. All I could do was watch.

As though feeling the lewd stares upon her, Violet raised her hands to cover up.

"Don't cover up," Boggs shouted from the opposite bank. "C'mon. Give us a good show!" He entered the water with a heavy splash and began stomping his way across the river with a wild gleam in his eyes, pursuing her like some horny cave-dweller possessed by his primitive instincts.

Violet didn't wait for him. She turned and jumped into a patch of swamp grass, disappearing from sight. Boggs tripped and stumbled in the middle of the river. "Come back here!" he screeched.

No response. Violet was gone, but in her place stood the Wagon Master. *"Goddamnit Boggs! Leave her alone!"*

His voice boomed across the river, a heavy rising tone that echoed from shore to shore and out over the wagon circle, loud enough for every ear in camp to overhear.

Boggs slowed his advance and spread his hands out in a public display of innocence. "Ah, we're just foolin' around, Boss," he said with a childish pout. "No big deal."

Irwin stepped to the edge of the water and pulled the pistol from his belt and held it at his side. A huge Colt Paterson five-shooter. "Now listen here," he shouted. "No woman in this party will be seized against her will. Regardless of colour."

Boggs stiffened upright. The childlike dumbness snapped from his eyes. "You would shoot me over a darkie?" he said. His right hand rose over the handle of the sidearm holstered on his hip, the river's murky current pushing against his knees, foaming white in his wake.

People were starting to gather along the shoreline, and I feared their presence would only compound the situation into violence, bearing in mind the alpha male's instinct to prove himself before the pack.

Irwin's eyes were squinted sharply on Boggs. "Pull that pistol, and you're a dead man," he coldly said.

Boggs gripped his fingers around the handle of his big horse pistol, but then he seemed to think better of it and carefully surrendered his hands outward to make peace. "Okay, boss," he said, looking more or less at Irwin. "There's no need for pullin' pistols. Just havin' a little fun—but hell, I suppose I crossed the line." He nodded, looking down at the water. "You've marked your territory loud and clear, Boss. The sweet blackberry pie is off limits."

He turned with a sulk and started lumbering back towards the wagon circle.

Now that the threat was neutralized, I went dashing across the river to find Violet, splashing past Boggs as he lurched in the opposite direction.

I found Violet crouched low in a hollow of swamp grass. She watched my approach with her arms hugged across her wet chest. Her eyes glared with mistrust, as though uncertain of my motive or whose side I was on—which was understandable, seeing that I had done nothing to stop Boggs's assault on her.

In regret of my previous actions, I removed my duster and held it out, gesturing that I wanted to cover her with it and nothing more. "I won't hurt you," I said gently.

She looked away, saying nothing, but allowed me to wrap the duster over her shoulders. I wanted to say something comforting to ease the tension, but I couldn't stop thinking about Boggs and his bullying prowess. "That shit-eating pig," I hissed, clenching my teeth and punching my hands together. "Hopefully, he passes out face down on a wasp nest tonight, gets himself stung a thousand times over. Karma does exist, right?"

Violet shook her head. "I'm drivin' the man's ox," she said in a quiet, gloomy voice. "Perhaps I'm the one who was out of line."

She stood up and walked across the river. I followed along behind her. When we reached the edge of camp, she thanked me and returned my duster. But I wasn't sure how to respond. The fact that she was so young and harmless and attractive looking, yet subjected to such ill standards was bothering me. Black or not, nobody should ever feel inferior, or in debt, to a half-wit brute like Boggs. Violet was the prime article amongst us, and I wanted to tell her how exceptional she really was, but then she looked dead at me, and I fell apart under her sparkling green eyes. I just stood there lingering, looking rather foolish and feeling unsure of myself: my skinny arms, my beady eyes, my filthy clothes, my belligerent white skin. Then came the overwhelming impulse to run away, and awkwardly I did just that, saying, "See you later," then jogging off back towards my wagon, leaving her standing there, twisting and ringing the water out of her dreadlocks.

* * *

The lone Injun amongst our numbers was an English-speaking Bannock named Takoda. He was a wild-looking, hide-wearing, long-haired native son of the west, who had joined our party in Missouri for what he claimed was a return to his 'homeland' somewhere west of the Rocky Mountains.

And that was all we knew about him. He had a very unsocial demeanor and spoke to nobody except Irwin. He looked at us a certain way, a bitter look that I'd seen before on the faces of other natives who knew enough about the white man and his 'civilized' world to harbor a great discontent for it. Takoda also had this unnerving habit of wandering away from camp without notifying anyone, then returning hours or even days later, again without bothering to report. This made the other travelers generally wary of his reasons for sticking with our party—but he stuck with us nonetheless, for everyone knew that a solitary traveler was easy pickings for the roaming bands of savages said to stalk the western territories.

That evening, Takoda returned to camp with a gutted antelope hung slack over his shoulders. The rest of us were sitting around the campfire eating half-spoiled lumps of salt pork rations. He set up a spit using tree limbs and hung the carcass over the flames, then crouched fireside to watch the roast. The smell of charring meat filled the night air, and hungry eyes began looking Takoda's way—mine included. I started thinking about the last time I tasted fresh meat…months at least…but then Violet came circling around the campfire in her damp gown, and my thoughts turned to her.

I watched her find a space apart from the others, then squat near the flames to dry her gown. She carried a dingy little burlap sack under her arm like a purse, that, presumably, contained her personal effects.

I shifted my line of sight between her and my dinner plate and trying not to seem so obvious about my interest in her activities. She reached inside her sack and removed a frayed strip of yellow cloth, then tied it around her forehead like a scarf to pull the wet hair back from her eyes. This sudden change of hairstyle brought her face wholly into the firelight. Her soft, ebony features glowed handsomely, but there was a somber look in her eyes that made it impossible to decipher what she was thinking. She didn't look upset about the incident earlier, but she didn't look happy about it either. Unsatisfied with the way her gown was drying, she leaned closer to the fire and dropped the sack behind her, which hit the earth with a heavy thud. Whatever else was stashed inside the sack was as solid as a rock.

That's when it dawned on me: She had no spare clothing, nothing to wear but the wet gown on her back.

That's it! I thought. I should lend her some dry clothes to wear.

Why hadn't I thought of this sooner?

Without wasting another second, I dropped my plate of pork and hustled away from the campfire.

My clothes were housed in a large wooden cedar chest that rode in the back of my schooner. I was briefly mortified by the musky reek that lingered up when I opened the lid, for none of my clothes had been properly washed in months, and everything was unfolded and lazily tossed in a heap, with some of my brother's dirty clothes mixed in. I rifled through the heap in search of the least foul-smelling garments, settling upon a long-sleeve wool tunic of Irwin's, a tunic he hadn't worn since I made a joke about how girlish it looked. It was pink in color, snug to the torso, and long like a dress. Such a queer-looking fit that I wondered what possessed him to purchase it in the first place. Had some salesmen fed him a flattering lie? Was there not a mirror in his shop?

Next, I picked out a pair of socks with the least number of holes, along with a halfway-clean pair of navy-colored cotton pants, then folded the outfit neatly over my forearm and quickly returned to the campfire.

Violet was sitting on her knees in the same spot. A light steam was rising from her gown. Without second guessing myself, I walked right up to her and presented the gift of dry clothes.

"Here," I said with an eager smile. "Put this on."

She looked up and blinked with confusion. "Oh," she quietly replied. "Thank you. You're too kind."

I sat down beside her and watched her unfold the clothes and scrutinize them. The navy pants were frayed along the bottom hem but sized fittingly enough for her curvy little frame, and the tunic had that peculiar pink color that women seem drawn to. "It will look great on you," I said, gushing with optimism.

But Violet looked uncertain. "I've never worn pants before," she said. "Won't the men find it inappropriate? I'd rather not offend anyone."

"Don't worry," I said. "Some men may find it unladylike, yes, but wearing a dress just seems so inappropriate for roughin' it across the wild country. Don't you agree?"

She nodded slowly, holding up the pants and staring at them. "They do look comfortable," she said.

Meanwhile, my brother Irwin was hovering around the far reaches of the firelight, making his regular rounds. As he passed behind us, I reached out and grabbed the back of his elbow for a quick word. "Brother, could you ask Takoda if he plans on sharing that meat?"

Irwin sighed heavily, like a man under pressure to satisfy this very same request from other travelers. He looked down at the clothes in Violet's lap. "Is that my tunic?" he snapped.

"You don't need it." I quickly replied. "Unless you're trying to look like a woman in front of the men."

Irwin smacked his lips open to say something in dispute, but paused, distractedly turned her eyes over Violet's sack.

"Is that a pistol in that sack?" he asked.

Violet seemed to stiffen. "Umm, yes. Sir." she replied.

Now studying the sack myself, I saw what Irwin saw: the imprint of a gun barrel poking through the thin burlap.

"Well, let's have a look at it," insisted Irwin.

Without any fuss, Violet reached into the sack and removed a Colt Walker six-shooter with a glossy blue-black finish and an ivory-plated handle. One impressively expensive and dangerous sidearm.

My brother and I shared a startled glance.

"Jesus," muttered Irwin, squatting between us to get a closer look. "Where did you get that thing?" A thoroughly buffaloed look developed in his eyes. He'd never seen a Colt Walker in the flesh and blood, and neither had I, for that matter.

"It belonged to my former master," she said, holding the lethal weapon loosely in her hand. "It was a parting gift. Masta' said it would come in handy when the rations ran out…said that we could shoot animals with it."

"Have you fired it?" asked Irwin.

"Yes, once. We got awfully hungry on the road across the Great Prairie…

and one day, I seen this rabbit hopping along the trail ruts, so I cocked the hammer and aligned the sights and squeezed the trigger, then *Boom*."

Irwin's eyes narrowed. "Who taught you how to shoot?" he asked.

Before she could open her mouth to answer, I chimed in with a question that I felt was more appropriate. "Did you kill the rabbit?"

Violet's eyes flashed between us. "I'm not sure," she said. "When the smoke cleared, I looked around, but no sign of the rabbit."

Irwin raised upright, and his eyes turned distant. I could see that something was bothering him, but whether he was bothered by Violet, and thought of a former slave traveling freely across the unorganized territory with a loaded six-shooter in her bag, or troubled by an accumulation of trail-blazing related stresses, I couldn't be certain.

On the opposite side of the fire, Takoda rose to his feet and crossed over the roasting antelope. From a sheath on his hip, he produced a large buck knife and cut a thin strip of meat from the blackened shoulders of the roast. He bit into the strip and stood there chewing for a moment, then looked at Irwin and said: "I will leave the distribution of this meat in your hands, captain."

Irwin nodded the brim of his hat. The other travelers within earshot began shifting about, early drawing upon forks and knives, but they hesitated to serve themselves. All looked to the Wagon Master for his final approval.

But Irwin was slow to accommodate them. His eyes were still distant.

Chapter Three

W e forded the river that afternoon at a point where the water only rose a few inches above the high wheels. On the far side of the river, we drove upon a wooden post with a single piece of paper tacked to it. Another message from our invisible guide, the infamous Gaylord Hightower:

To all emigrants on the road to California:

Cheering news! Thousands of American settlers have poured into California this season—with hundreds more arriving daily via the great overland wagon route. The American presence in California now vastly outnumbers the Mexican natives, and war is imminent between the United States and Mexico.

I can guarantee a swift victory, for the American emigrant has the heart of a lion and the support of the world"s foremost military. Americans are a sophisticated and organized people, while Mexicans are a barbaric race of Indigenous half-breeds no brighter than black slaves and completely incapable of developing a civilized, lawful nation and defending its borders. Take my word for it, my trail-blazing comrades! The glorious lands of California will soon be ours!

However, until California is officially captured and controlled by the United States, I shall advise that all American travelers, especially those White and Christian, congregate into large wagon parties against the danger of Mexican attacks.

Also, for those settlers lagging behind, I have recently discovered a new route to Gayville—a shortcut and one that will eradicate two or three hundred miles of hard travel. Simply follow the southern turn-off ahead and watch for my messages. The new road is abundant with grass and water, and mostly level, save for the high pass through the Wasatch Mountains, where the rock grade must be taken with caution, although not time-consuming enough to negate the overall advantage.

And be advised, you may cross paths with strange indigenous creatures that wander this region in full nudity, but these heathens pose no threat and should be ignored entirely.

Good Luck and safe travels to all,

Gaylord Hightower

My brother tore the message from the post and read it slowly, pausing and looking up between each paragraph, not smiling over the 'cheering news.' Behind him, the wagons sat idle in the blazing sun, the animals moaning and trembling in place, kicking their hooves into the sandy dirt.

For the second time in many weeks, Irwin was faced with the same dilemma: stay the regular road to California or take a chance on Hightower's latest shortcut.

Choice of route was a matter of life or death in the West. A pilgrim's main objective was to reach California's Central Valley before the onset of winter. One wrong turn, one major delay could throw off the timing of our approach and consequently have us driving up snowy mountains in the midst of winter, which was practically suicide.

While Irwin pondered the message, Boggs stepped behind him and curiously tilted his eyes over his shoulder. "What's it say, Boss?" he snorted.

Irwin ignored him and continued brooding over the message as more men gathered around, waiting on the news.

Boggs began circling about, stomping and huffing impatiently. "I bet it"s another letter from that bastard Hightower," he grumbled. "Probably more bullshit about Gayville and how goddamn gay it is."

Irwin looked annoyed. He held the message outright before Boggs's eyes. "Go ahead, Boggs, read it yourself," he demanded.

But Boggs refused. He shook his head like a stubborn mule and retreated back a step. "Just tell me what it says," he groaned. "I ain't in a readin' mood."

I was beginning to suspect that Boggs was illiterate, but Irwin moved on from the matter and handed the message over to old Milt Crabtree, whose elderly statesmen-like presence amongst the younger men seemed to beckon so. Milt fixed a wiry pair of spectacles onto the bridge of his sun-bronzed nose and glared down at the note. He read a few lines aloud for Boggs's sake, then raised his magnified eyeballs to Irwin. "Well, Captain…" he said. "What are your intentions?"

Irwin mulled over the question with a distant gaze. "I intend to take the new route," he said. "Hell, with summer being halfway over, we'd be fools not to take the shortest route possible."

Milt nodded, removed his spectacles, and replaced them in the pocket of his dusty overcoat. "Very well," he said. "I'm in agreement."

Irwin glanced at the other men in the crowd. "Then we're all in agreement to take the new shortcut?"

Nobody disagreed. A revolution was happening in California and the McEwan Party was lagging a thousand miles behind it. Plus, our provisions were running low, and the salt pork we consumed had the effect of a powerful laxative. Our journey was becoming a wild race against time and the passing seasons, so accordingly, my brother was resigned by logic to take the shortest, fastest route available, even if it detoured off the traditional course. There was simply no time to second guess the changes in route. Summer was almost over and it was absolutely imperative that we cross the Sierra Nevada Mountains ahead of winter—this I can't stress enough—for page fifty-two of Hightower's book says this, '*Along California's eastern border rises the mighty Sierra Nevada. Miles and miles in height, these mountains stand among the clouds like a great wall to the heavens. It is the most stunning and colossal of all the mountain ranges in the west. California-bound travelers should be mindful of winter's effect on high elevation, for every winter the High Sierra and its middle forest region receives snow in glorious abundance. Travelers would be wise to keep a strict schedule and cross these mountains well ahead of the winter months.*'

So what other choice did we have? But to take Hightower at his word and embark on his latest shortcut. He was, after all, the expert. He literally wrote the book on overland travel and was kind enough to leave these messages to follow…and I suppose it was useless to argue against this.

* * *

That evening, we camped at the mouth of the canyon that would pass us through the Wasatch Mountains. Heavy clouds rolled in, and a rainstorm hit just after sundown, stifling any hope for a campfire. After a cold dinner of beans and cornmeal, I sought my wagon bed for immediate sleep.

But sleep would not come easy. I found myself tossing and turning in restless limbo for many hours. Lightning flashed the canvas overhead, the wind kicked and howled, and the rain poured and pattered…but the real problem was that I couldn't stop thinking about things…and by things, I mean her.

She was weathering the storm just a stone's throw away, under the tatty sheet pitched over her wagon. I knew this because I'd watched her climb inside. There was some chatter between her and her two sisters, but they talked in voices that stayed below the howl of the wind, too soft for my inquisitive hearing. Her wagon squeaked with bodies shifting to get comfortable, and that was it, nothing but wind, thunder, and pattering rain, and groaning animals.

Truth be told, I had an eye on Violet's movements ever since the wagons first circled that night, captivated by some school-boy attraction to follow that beautiful brown body wherever it went. I was tempted to climb out of my wagon and say good night to her, but the longer I watched, the more my confidence dwindled, and by bedtime, I was feeling way too awkward to show my face.

But I was fascinated by her. A pure grace of eloquence was seated upon those plump brown lips of hers. She was intelligent, crafty, venturesome, and yes indeed, I was becoming more attracted to her by the day. Yet her most intriguing quality was something that couldn't be seen with the naked eye. For underneath those dazzling looks, there seemed to linger something dark and powerfully, the agony of some tortured past perhaps, now forever conflicting with her present situation. It was reflected in her sharp and calculated movements, her typically serious expression, and the way she tended to avoid the small talk around the campfire.

She carried herself down the dusty road as though running from something. Of course, it was easy to assume that her strange attitude stemmed from her former life of enslavement, and the fallout of that brutal experience had left her guarded and self-alienated.

And the more I thought about that, the more I felt this invisible obstacle in the way of making a romantic connection with her, a giant wall of sorts, and one that separated us down the unequal paths of black and white. A wall that would have to be contested and torn down for love to have any chance.

* * *

I awoke the next morning to a hand slapping the side of my face. "Let's get movin'," grunted Irwin. "Christ, you afternoon farmer you, the day's half gone."

I sat up in bed and stayed that way for several moments, rubbing the sleep from my eyes and listening to the routine commotion outside: that of men breaking down camp and hitching up animals. The storm was long gone, and the breeze was calm again. The sun was several hours high, and indeed, the daily grind was awaiting my half-assed attendance.

But first, coffee.

Violet caught my attention right away as I climbed down from the tailgate. She was standing beside her oxen, bullwhip in hand, toes tapping impatiently against the sandy earth— a young fit body full of stored-up energy waiting to be released upon the wild.

Her gray maids' gown must have dried, because she was wearing it again, not the pants and pink tunic that I had loaned her.

I found two empty tin cups and topped them both off, one for me, one for her.

I approached her gingerly, the two steaming hot cups balancing in my hand. She saw me coming out of the corner of her eye and turned to face me, pushing her ropy dreadlocks behind her shoulders, exposing her cute face to a strong dose of morning sunlight. I reached out with a steaming cup in my left hand, subtly offering it, while keeping the other cup for myself. "Coffee?" I said, trying to fix her with a casual smile, hoping to hide the fact that I'd been thinking about her all last night, and first thing this morning.

"Thank you, Peanuts," she pleasantly said, her green eyes glowing and gracefully connecting with mine.

I laughed, feeling embarrassed. "My real name is Peter," I said.

"I know," she said. "But Peanuts sounds cute to me." She took the steaming cup and lifted it to her lips.

"Careful, it's hot!" I warned, lashing my hands out to stop her.

She paused with the cup right below her chin, then slowly puckered her lips and gently blew the steam from the brim. A gust of warm wind whipped through camp, catching the loose fabric of her gown, pressing it tight to her body.

I shuttered inwardly. "You look lovely this morning," I said.

She glanced down at herself and smiled rigidly. "Thanks," she said. "I returned the pants and pink tunic to your brother earlier this morning."

"But they were a gift," I said. "You can keep them."

She shrugged and said, "Well, to be perfectly honest with you, I felt like a boy in those pants."

I couldn't help my eyes from passing over those child-bearing hips of hers. Her skinny waist. Hardened thighs pushing against the wind. She was all woman, no doubt about that. "I doubt anyone would confuse you for a boy," I said, staring rather blatantly at her body, lapsing in composure and probably sounding like a huge pervert. In realizing this, I looked away, and moved quickly to change the subject. "So, ready for another hot day of trailblazing?"

Violet cocked her head sideways and eyed me curiously. "I've been ready since sunrise," she said. "But some people like to take their sweet time." She sipped her coffee with a frisky smirk, a graceful little gesture of attitude.

"I was up late last night thinking about a woman," I said. "I have fallen hopelessly in love. That's why I'm getting a late start, you see?"

"That's sweet," she replied. "But sleep is important, you mustn't let a woman distract you from it."

"That's easy for you to say," I said. "When you're the cause of my distraction."

Violet glared at me, looking surprised.

I could hardly believe how boldly I was speaking to her. It just poured right out of me. I suppose desire can make a man say crazy things...or say things that you instantly regret, because Violet just glared, then looked away and sipped her coffee.

Good God, I thought, Why did I say that?! My heart started racing. I had flown my flag, but my wooing words just hung stupidly in the air—but then the wind suddenly shifted and blew up the sleeves of Violet's gown, exposing her bare forearms to the sunlight. I noticed a series of dark-colored scars ringing around her wrist. It was distracting and I blatantly stared down at them. There was something seriously wrong about it.

The troubled look on my face must have alarmed Violet. She pulled her sleeves down to cover the scars.

"It's from the shackles," she said, rather coldly.

"What?" I said, looking confusedly at her sleeves.

"I was chained and forced to march down a long road," she said, no longer smiling. " A trip that ended at an auction house. That's when I was sold off to Master Beasley. It was a long time ago."

I lowered my cup, feeling a sudden need to distance myself from my evil white counterparts. "Hey listen," I said. "I'm what they call a *Yankee*, meaning I hale from up *North,* where slavery is illegal...for the most part...and Yankees are mostly good and God-fearing people...mostly..."

I paused, suddenly picturing all the xenophobic, black-hating miscreants that I grew up with back in Boston. My words began to fumble with uncertainty when I continued. "Well...We're nothing like those screwheads down *South...*is what I'm trying to say. Them people are all sick and retarded from centuries of strict inbreeding."

Violet quietly sipped her coffee. I rambled on, working myself into a bitter frenzy. "I mean it. Them Southern Whites are a bunch of illiterate, sister-humping scumbags. I'm serious, Violet. They're simply too stupid and greedy to understand that slavery is *wrong*. And please understand that I am not the type…that my livelihood is not driven by some dingbat inbred determination to get rich by any means…I mean, Good Lord! The South is full of Inbred White Screwheads…I stand by those words no matter the company I speak them too…And I'll tell ya' another thing…I have long agreed with the writings of William Lloyd Garrison and his notion that the American Constitution is pro-slavery and thus unjusti*fiably*—"

I cut myself off mid-spiel because Violet was no longer paying attention. Her head had tilted sideways and her eyes were squinted on something in the distance.

"Peter!" she said, sounding alarmed. "Look behind you."

I turned and followed her line of sight towards the golden foothills beyond. A lone, stark-naked Injun was running downhill towards our camp and waving his hands wildly through the air to get our attention.

"Hello!" The Injun called out. "Hello! Hello!"

The rigid blue peaks of the Wasatch Mountains hovered in the high distance behind the advancing Indian, giving the impression that he had spotted our camp from high up, and came rushing downhill to tell us something. I looked around to see if anyone else was aware of this developing situation and saw my brother conferencing with four or five other men beside the burnt-out campfire, all of them armed and on high alert.

"Hello, America!" "Hello, America!" "Step up!" "Step up!" shouted the Injun, now less than a hundred yards from camp.

I snatched Violet by the back of the arm and pulled her toward the conferencing men. "Let's get involved," I said in all haste.

We hurried across the campground and entered the conference amid a heated debate. Our party had no set procedure for dealing with wild natives. We were a gang of roughnecks and fortune-seekers, and thereby the initial instinct was to charge pistols and rifles to protect life and property, women and children.

We had no sense of obligation to those noble missionaries that first explored the West, no righteous call of duty to deliver the Word of God to the heathens. No. Never us. We were hopelessly American and armed to the teeth, and we viewed anyone of an outside tribe as a potential threat to the advancement of our conquest. We had traveled all this way for land and riches, not to teach cave dwellers how to love Jesus.

"To hell with that savage," Boggs shouted over the crowd. "Remember the Johnson Party? They made friends with some redskins along the way—and what happened? I'll tell ya! They got their throats cut while they slept." He paused to hawk and spit, then added, "Ain't no such thing as an honest Injun."

The crowd stirred anxiously. Terrified murmurs and the clockwork sound of charging rifles filled the air. But the Wagon Master was his usual stern, astute self.

Irwin stood tall at the head of the huddle, his eyes concentrated long range on the incoming native. "I hear you, Boggs," he calmly said. "But in the spirit of friendly beginnings, I say we give 'em something to eat. Then we'll be on our way."

"What do you think, Takoda?"

Every set of eyes turned on our resident native, who was standing low-key behind the crowd with his rifle slung behind his shoulder. His eyes were scanning over the hillsides, as if looking for others who might be watching us.

"Give him a biscuit and a handful of beans," he shortly advised.

"Wait a minute!" Boggs exploded, throwing his huge arms in protest and causing everyone to retract a step. "Feed one of them bastards, and we'll have the whole stinkin' tribe after our rations!"

Everyone was moved except Irwin. His stance was firm; eyes peeled long range. In his mind, he was calculating the adverse effects of being friendly with the wild natives of a lawless territory. And while Boggs's tongue was crueler than usual, there was good reason for such excessive xenophobia: for every California-bound wagon train had been warned about the squalid tribes of this region. Page twenty-one of Hightower's book mentions the following: *Diggers is the general name used for the whole lot of naked humankind that wander the Great American Desert with no horses. The occasional Digger will watch in fascination from a hillside as the wagon trains roll on by, but they seem to lack the social behavior of the eastern tribes and shun away like wild animals when approached.* That was put lightly when compared to the warnings issued by the mountain men during our stop at Fort Laramie: *'Diggers, desert coons, whatever you want to call em'—nothing but a bunch of tricksters and thieves,'* I recall one exceptionally bearded and dirty mountain-man saying it gruffly. *"And beware, them bastards carry bows with poison-tipped arrows, and they'll shoot at passing wagon trains for no good reason but to amuse themselves. The more enterprising Digger will put on a friendly act as a means to get close, then steal your supplies while you sleep. Goddamn savages. they should all be exterminated."*

And now the filthy, neanderthal-looking Boggs was echoing the sentiment. "I say we kill the savage, scalp 'em, and hang 'em from a tree." He said this in all sincerity, staring at the approaching native with a glint of murderous rage in his crusty eyes, Leaving little doubt that he would, for all practical purposes, slaughter and hang the poor red devil. "That's what them wise ol' mountain men would do!"

Irwin raised his hand to stop Boggs's words. "That's enough," he said sharply. "I'll handle this my way."

Irwin stuck his thumb and forefinger between his lips and blew out a loud whistle to signal the newcomer his way.

Boggs cursed something unintelligible under his breath, then turned away and lumbered away, abandoning his interest in the matter.

A delegation of armed and bearded white men held congress with the wild native at the edge of camp. I joined out of curiosity. I wanted to see the native up close, eager to communicate openly with people of this strange new world, to share knowledge, to broaden horizons, or, simply to make friends. I extended a pleasant greeting through a gentle, open-armed gesture. "Hello," I said.

"Hello," the native replied with a bright-eyed smile. He was naked save for a loin cloth. He looked middle-aged in the face, but otherwise appeared very childlike with his short, stocky body and curious eyes. His hair was long and black and caked in filth, and three blue condor feathers protruded from the back of his head like a bird's tail. A primitive tattoo of a blue sun circled his neck.

"How are you?" I asked him.

"Hello, America," he eagerly replied.

I pointed to myself. "Yes, American, hello, nice to meet you. And what is your name?"

"Step up, America," he said.

"Your name is Step-up?"

He nodded. "Step-up! Hello. America!"

"Okay, Step-up. I'm Peter. Do you live here, in the mountains?"

"Step up!" he said, nodding, bright-eyed, oddly friendly. "Hello! America!"

I heard giggles behind me. Things weren't going well.

The only pilgrim not giggling was Irwin. "Words he learned from the shouts of passing wagon trains," he said. "Seems to be the extent of his English. Now C'mon. Stop wasting time. Give him the food, and let's get moving."

The delegation disbanded, and the little native man took his parting gift of a biscuit and a fistful of beans, and plopped down on a rock, and crossed his legs. As the wagon train uncircled and turned up the mountain pass, he sat there watching, grinning, chewing on his food.

Once the train had passed him by, the little man hopped to his feet and casually strolled behind Milt Crabtree's oversized Conestoga. And like a lost puppy, he followed us for the rest of the day, oddly smiling and keeping a safe distance of about twenty or thirty yards from our rear.

That evening, we camped alongside a trickling mountain stream that ran through the base of the pass.

On a nearby hillside, in the dark distance, a tiny fire could be seen, where we all suspected that strange, naked wanderer had also made camp.

* * *

There was no sign of the heathen the next morning. We continued driving deeper into the mountains on a path of little breadth and refinement, meandering through an alpine jungle of Douglas furs and white aspens and thickets of service berries. We towed the bulky wagons up steps of rock at a snail's pace, and crossed and recrossed the stream several times as the passage narrowed further between steep mountain ridges, stone gray in color.

We made only four miles that day, before camping that night beside the stream.

The next day, we only made two miles, too often forced to clear brush and make road with picks and shovels.

The day after that, we made no forward progress at all, halted by a thick undergrowth of brush and trees along a narrow gap of mountain.

The general mood in camp grew tense over our lack of headway. Our first major delay had occurred, as the trail had reduced to a mere footpath through the mountains. There were no more high-wheel markings to follow. No places where brush had been previously cleared to make road. No evidence that Hightower's new shortcut had been previously traversed by wagons of any kind. It appeared that Hightower had only explored the pass on horseback, or worse yet, had judged from some absurd distance away that the pass was feasible without actually crossing through it himself, and thus dooming our party to cut madly into the brush and make our own road through the mountains.

Every able body was ordered to take up a tool for road work, even the women and children, even the ex-slaves.

I have a vivid recollection of the pretty ex-slave Violet hacking away at the mountain jungle with an ax. A soaking wet sweatband tied around her forehead. Her gown drenched in sweat and stuck to her body like a wet rag. The air humid and rife with the smell of chopped wood. Hot sunlight beaming through the trees… Ah, yes, and with a tense look of concentration in her eyes, she assumed a powerful stance, thrusting her weight into each swing, hacking into the furs and aspens, some thirty-five feet tall with trunks as thick as beer barrels. And did I say that her body was soaked in sweat? And hardened and busty from the exertion of her muscles? Jesus Sweating Christ…there was something extraordinarily erotic about that…A busty, sweaty brown body glistening in the sunlight.

I couldn't help but watch her throughout our time laboring in the bush. I took an excessive number of breaks where the view was best, to drink water or casually pretend to pick at blisters on my hands, or I'd stand and walk close by, pretending to inspect the treeline, but watching out of the corner of my eyes, watching her bend over to dig out stumps. Watching her…and stewing with lust.

She was the girl of a lumberjack's dream.

* * *

Amidst the hot struggle through the mountain brush, a single covered wagon rolled up from the east, trudging along the same god-awful 'short-cut.' Its solitary driver was a tall, lanky white man wearing a wiry pair of spectacles, who brazenly jumped from the wagon to initiate an introduction of himself. "The name's Eddy Daulton," he cheerfully said, removing the hat from his thinly-shaped head. "I'm headin' west to Californiay with my wife and our five-year-old son. Hoping to get into the ranchin' business out that way."

The battering sounds of wood chopping died down as our party collectively crawled out of the brush to greet the man. A hard-sweating Irwin staked his shovel into the earth and leaned against the handle.

"You some kind of daredevil? Driving up here all by your lonesome," he gruffly said.

Eddie Daulton smiled, amused by the question.

A blonde-haired German Shepherd trotted towards us and barked at Irwin.

Daulton smacked the dog on the nose to quiet it. "With old yeller on the lookout, there's nothing to worry about," he said with a friendly chuckle. "But striking out on my own wasn't always the plan. I'd come across the Great Prairie in a large wagon party, but fell out of formation when my son became terribly ill." He paused and glanced back at his wagon. The boy mentioned was standing in the bow, blinking innocently. "We held up at Fort Laramie until the little buggers" health returned, then pushed on alone—just me, wife, boy, and dog, following them notes left by Gaylord Hightower."

Daulton looked straight ahead at the thicket of brush blocking the pass. "I didn't expect to be taken up the high road to hell," he said, the mirth in his tone lapsing temporarily. "I swear, if I ever catch up with that pompous-ass Hightower, I might be inclined to deck 'em upside his silly head."

I agreed wholeheartedly. Daulton's remarks instantly elevated him as a man of substance in my eyes.

"I like him," I said.

Irwin wore his usual stern expression. He turned his head and spat. "Well, the bush ain't gonna' clear itself, feller" he said. "Grab a tool and give us a hand."

Daulton wasted no time in fetching an ax from his wagon. I approached him and introduced myself, saying that the rude man in charge was my older brother Irwin, who portrays that of hardass captain, but who has a heart of gold under all that rough exterior. Daulton said he knew the type, said that he had a bossy older brother as well. "They think they know it all," he said. "But aren't they just another nut off the family tree?"

I thought it was a witty thing to say and I couldn't help but laugh. For the remainder of the day, I cut brush alongside Daulton. I enjoyed his fresh repartee immensely. He was dressed in the common clothing of a man going about an ordinary day: a white cotton shirt, brown pants, and a brown bowler hat that made him look foreign and out of his element in the bush...not unlike the rest of us. "I was once a priest at a Roman Catholic church in Pennsylvania," he said. "But I was excommunicated after impregnating a young lady out of wedlock." He nodded at his wagon, now parked in line with our wagons, where his wife and little boy hid under the canvas from the sun.

Daulton put it eloquently that he had fallen on hard times after getting booted from the church; times of begging and stealing, of surviving winters with no heat, summers with no shoes. Then he said he came across Hightower's book, which changed his life forever, convincing him to gamble on the western boom. He got excited when he talked about all the potential and opportunities in California, but was realistic about the dangers and risks. "Of course, gambling is condemned by the church," he said. "I've never turned a card or rolled the dice...but if there's one thing the journey west has shown me, it's that the natural existence of man is a gamble in itself." We were taking turns hacking down a thick aspen, and he paused to wipe the sweat from his eyes. "I hate to say things like this," he continued. "But this semi-circle of men hacking through the bush is scarcely different than a semi-circle of men at a poker table." He smiled nervously, then thrusted his ax into the aspen with a grunt.

Daulton was right, in his own peculiar way. The whole thing was a big rolling of the dice. Indeed, we were just another band of wild boys betting our bottom dollar and believing that we were finally beating the odds this time, that this trip was worth risking our lives. I agreed with everything Daulton had said, but my own vision of the *desperate pioneer* was slightly more romantic than his. I saw a legion of drifters and dreamers who finally had a good reason to abandon the shanty towns of the eastern states. We were the poor offspring of European migrants, sharecroppers, servants, fugitives and religious freedom-seekers who had missed out on the first wave of colonization along the east coast, and the second wave of colonization in the midwest. We were the brave seekers of new beginnings, moving *west* again, invading the virgin lands where the natives still roamed, searching for that deserving rightful share of the American Dream.

No doubt, this trip was the single biggest risk or 'gamble' (as Daulton had put it) any of us had ever undertaken. A wager against starvation. A wager against being hanged by Mexicans or scalped by savages. A wager to finally win a stake of land and riches before it was all gone and missed out on again.

* * *

The Crabtree brothers fell to drinking booze while they labored with the roadmaking, and by sundown, the brothers were babbling drunk and stretched out around the campfire, having emptied an entire vat and now working on a second. The Crabtree family was Scot-Irish and drinking was not an uncommon sight with them. Calvin Crabtree, the eldest brother, had figured out a way to distill whiskey inside of his wagon using an iron still and all the necessary ingredients. The finished product was utterly toxic, and many pilgrims vomited almost instantly, while others were quick to develop a tolerance and liking.

I became quite fond of Crabtree's trail brew myself and thereby found myself lingering around the campfire that night, for the purpose of snaring a nightcap.

I would raise my cup in a toast to another wasted day clearing brush in the mountain forest, and to our new friend Eddy Daulton, the ex-priest from Pennsylvania. Daulton raised his cup and clanked it against mine, having already snagged some trail brew before my arrival, and fast making friends with everyone, being the charming feller that he turned out to be.

** * **

The next morning, we set off on a road that took three days to construct. My schooner stayed in the lead, followed by the ex-slave's wagon, then the ex-priest's wagon, with Boggs and my brother's men in the middle, and the Crabtree family bringing up the rear.

We made six or seven miles that day and finally crested the pass by mid-afternoon. But going down the mountain turned out to be just as treacherous as going up it. The path was steeply graded and hugged tight the backside of the mountain. The wagons banged and slammed, and the oxen skidded in the gravel. Had a single ox slipped off the trail, it would have sent the entire wagon team cartwheeling down the mountainside in a fading scream of shattering wood and broken bones.

But we all made it one piece, and the next day saw us leveling upon the valley of the Great Salt Lake. We set off across an arid plain just south of the lake, driving at a reasonable pace along a sandy road. Then the path entered a salt flat where no foliage grew at all. Nothing but a flat plain, rippling in the afternoon heat.

We lashed every bit of speed out of the oxen to cross the flat before the water kegs went empty, and several oxen died from exhaustion before the drive was through. Albeit, we covered more distance on this single day than the previous ten days combined.

At sundown, we finally prevailed onto less-hospital terrain, having reached a desert oasis known as Twenty Wells.

Chapter Four

Twenty Wells was named for a series of cold-water pools naturally sculpted in a basin of solid orange bedrock. There was a good level campground situated between the pools, and a ring of tall pines walled the basin from the harsh desert beyond.

We circled the wagons and gathered around the pools like tourists on vacation. Some pools were large enough to swim laps inside, others were small as bathtubs, all filled to the brim with water as cold and clear as melted ice. My only complaint about the location, if I had to have one, was that none of the pools had bottoms. We cast a sounding line down several pools, but never did reach a single bottom. Nothing but endless darkness down there. Twenty pools with no bottoms.

As the sun went down and the stars came alive, a huge pyramid of timber went up, dousing the campsite in orange flickering light.

Calvin Crabtree, eldest of the Crabtree brothers, stood before the flames and made this announcement: A dinner of roasted beef would be made available to all pilgrims, free of charge.

The announcement was received with a few lively hoots and hell-yeahs. Then, two large slabs of skinned carcass went over the campfire, salvaged from an ox that had died earlier in the day.

I decided to take a bath and freshen up before dinner. I didn't want anyone to see my ever-scrawny figure, so I chose the pool furthest away from the campfire, then stripped down to my underwear, but hesitated to jump in. My pool was oval-shaped and about the size of a water tank. The water was clear-blue around the rim, but black and eerie looking in the middle where the bottom fell into oblivion. I could hear happy laughter, looked over and observed the giddy faces of my fellow travelers as they jumped and splashed in the pools nearby. Then I said to hell with it, and eased into the water, holding tight to the stone edge, slowly acclimating before gaining the confidence to push off and doggy paddle across the surface.

The cool water had quite a calming effect, and for a while, I just floated freely on my back like a lazy sea otter. Eventually, I dove under and allowed my body to sink down the cold-dark shaft. I spun in a circle several times, before shooting back up to the surface and swimming back to the pool's edge.

Looking out across the other pools, I had a straightforward view of our camp. Entire trees were being fed to the campfire and the flames were soaring higher than the canvas hoods circled around it. In the flickering orange light, I saw several half-naked white keisters, and people lounging around the fire, eating hot roasted beef and passing around the glassy profile of a vat of trail brew, laughing and chattering loudly like winos at a backyard cookout.

It turned into one of those nights when the whiskey passed freely, and nobody turned it down, because drinking by the campfire felt like a time-honored tradition of western travel, and one that was much bigger than ourselves. Perhaps I should mention here, that I was already buzzing before my swim, having used my turn on the passing vat to fill my canteen for my own stashing. I was feeling good and drunk by the time I left the pool. The beef was served steaming hot and blackened to a crisp. Someone dusted off a violin, and a lively tune wailed out, and we sang and danced like a bunch of drunken sailors.

* * *

The music played on until midnight. Things finally died down as men began passing out around the fire or falling back to the seclusion of tents. My brother mumbled something about 'keeping an eye on things,' then staggered off into the darkness to crash, leaving me to wallow fireside with the rest of the night's dedicated drinkers: the Crabtree brothers, the old-timer Jasper, the Irishman Charles Bryant, my cousin Wilbur, and Takoda, whose native grimace remained unchanged despite several cups of the giddy juice, and the ex-priest Eddy Daulton, who humored us with randy stories of his days in the lord's service.

The ex-priest was comedy gold when drunk. Everything he said made us laugh. He was the life of the party, standing there before the bonfire, swaying back and forth in a haggard cord coat with a cup of trail brew fixed in his hand. "Pecker-fondlers!" he cried. "The hardest thing about being a priest…is knowin' some of your comrades-in-the-lords-service are a bunch of pecker-fondlers."

"Let me tell you a story about that sneaky old bastard, Father Morris."

"Now, Father Morris didn't come outright with his intentions for little boys. No, that ol' fart thought he was being clever about it. He wrote letters that confessed his love, then slipped these letters into the shirt pockets of the altar boys during choir practice."

"Oh, but old Father Morris never accounted for the fact that half of Pennsylvania can't read, and them boys needed their Ma's and Pa's to read them letters aloud for 'em."

Daulton paused, jerked, and vomited into the fire.

We all laughed at him.

He laughed at himself, continued his story with vomit drooling off his chin.

"So, one day, a bunch of them Ma's and Pa's got together, and they beat ol' Father Morris something scandalous. They lassoed him by the ankles and dragged him round' town behind the meanest horse they could find!"

Daulton laughed and staggered sideways, holding his cup out, refusing to allow a single drop of trail brew to spill from it. The fire roared and snapped behind him. The glassy surface of the pools glimmered orange, and above the pines, a full moon hovered amongst the stars.

"Hey, Daulton, lead us in prayer!" someone drunkenly called out.

"Alright, just this once" he said, straightening up and bowing his head. "Ladies and Gents, let us pray."

For the sake of it, I found myself bowing my head, closing my eyes, and interlocking my fingers as if sat upon the earthly pew of some midnight fireside church service.

Daulton's words came roaring above the flames. *'Our Father, which art in heaven, hallowed be thy name. Thy kingdom come. Thy will be done on earth as it is in heaven. Give us this day our daily bread, with a side of rotten salt pork that'll surely give me the squirtin'-shits later on."*

A few men chuckled, shaking their bowed heads.

"And forgive us, Lord, for trespassing upon the lands of naked savages and half-wit Mexicans."

"Oh, and lord, please forgive me for squirtin' out liquid shit all over this heavenly desert you've guided me, too."

More chuckles. More bowed head shaking.

"Oh, and lord Jesus, please forgive me once more...for I confess that I've messed my trousers every dog'on day for the last month. My wife can't stand me anymore. She says I stink like the devil....says my innards need cleansing...wants me to become a vegetarian."

"Oh, Lord, please have mercy! Give me the strength to eat nothing but vegetables!"

In the end, someone shouted amen. We raised our heads and chuckled at one another, clapping our hands and slapping each other on the shoulders. All of us, save for one man.

"To hell with all that prayin'," snapped a mean-drunk voice from the darkness.

Boggs punctually appeared in the outer reaches of the firelight, stark naked and dripping wet. He came lumbering towards the fire, his slick potbelly bouncing, his big rangy arms swinging at his side like an ape. He crossed closely behind Daulton, eyeing him darkly as he passed, then stopped before the fire with his fat-naked backside facing the rest of us.

It was the hairiest full moon I ever saw, and I covered my eyes. Someone snickered drunkenly, but I bit my tongue to keep from laughing.

Boggs plopped down and pointed his meaty little toes towards the campfire. "Whoever's got that hooch," he loudly croaked. "Bring it to me."

Nobody moved. The public whiskey vat was tipped completely empty, resting sideways in the dirt between the Crabtree brothers.

"Goddamnit," snarled Boggs. He tilted his head back and glanced around the campfire with a menacing gleam in his eyes. "Priest," he said. "Gimme' your cup."

Daulton held his cup against his chest. "But my good sir, I am no longer a priest," he replied. "I was excommunicated. I live as a layperson now."

"Shut your ass!" shouted Boggs. "I don't give a hoot and hell what you are. I said gimme' your cup."

Boggs slowly rotated on his big keister, reached his big naked arm out, and opened his fingers claw-like.

An annoyed expression came over Daulton's face. He looked down at his cup and stirred it in his hand. "Try asking me again," he said, rather stubbornly. "But this time, do it respectfully. I am not a pushover."

For a moment there, Boggs did nothing but sit and stare at Daulton. Then he rose sharply to his feet, lunged and snatched Daulton by the neck, and threw him to the earth in one violent thrust. The cup flew from Daulton's hand, hit the ground, clanked and cartwheeled across camp, coming to an empty rest against the high wheel of a wagon.

Every bystander froze stupid with shock. A dark stain traced the cup's flight. Boggs looked at the stain and snarled, then shot a mean glare over the stunned faces of the audience.

Mine must have been the weakest-looking face.

"Pee-nuts!" he croaked. "What's in that canteen?"

My heart jumped. "Whiskey," I quickly answered, afraid to lie to him.

"Give it here," he demanded.

I sprang to my feet and hustled to retrieve Daulton's empty cup. I refilled it with a quick splash from my canteen, then offered the cup to Boggs, hoping this would distract him from confiscating the entire contents of my canteen.

Boggs glared down at the cup and snarled. Then he snatched the cup from my hand and walked back towards the fire.

I sat back down, thinking about how much I hated that bastard. The others started moaning their goodnights, slowly standing and retreating to bed, and eventually I found myself alone with Eddy Daulton, who simply nodded off next to the fire in the same spot where Boggs had thrown him. I strolled back to my wagon and finished the evening with the usual routine: removing my boots and hanging them above the wagon bow to air out the sweat-rancid insoles, then spreading my bedroll across the wooden bottom of the wagon, between the gear and food barrels.

Then I stretched out. But sleep didn't come automatically, and for a long time, I just laid there staring up at the canvas hood, and feeling the spinning sensation of whiskey on the brain. Then I heard a soft tapping sound of footsteps, which was nothing startling or unusual, as men often awake in the middle of the night to go searching for a bush to piss on.

I took a gander through the bow anyways, curious to see who was creeping around.

Surprisingly, it saw Violet, prancing gingerly along the edge of the pools. And though I couldn't see her face, the curvy silhouette that her body made against the moonlight instantly gave her away. She was the only woman amongst our numbers with a body like that.

She stopped beside an oval-shaped pool, and with her backside turned to my line of sight, she started undressing herself. She pulled her arms through her sleeves and took her top completely down…unaware that I was watching her from under the dark shade of the wagon canvas, about twenty feet away.

Sweet brown knockers! I could hardly believe what was happening. Her half-naked body took center stage under the moon's pale spotlight. A sight so vivid, so surreal, so sensual, that I wondered if I was having some sort of vision caused by improperly brewed whiskey.

Or maybe I was just dreaming.

Yes, that makes sense, it's only a dream. Nothing this extraordinary could be real. To test this theory, I turned away from the tailgate, stooped low behind the pork barrels, and slapped myself in the face.

The sting of the slap lingered painfully real across my cheekbone. Nothing seemed to change. No, this was no dream, and when I tilted my head up, Violet was still undressing—now pushing her gown over the soft hump of her buttocks. Once the gown cleared her rump, it dropped all the way down and crumbled into a tiny heap.

Oh Jesus Good Lord in Heaven! It was like watching the unveiling of an African Goddess.

She took a step away from the gown, extended her leg over the pool, and tested the water with her toe.

I couldn't be certain, but I thought I saw a cold shiver quake those magnificent thighs. Then she squatted down and quietly waded in, vanishing underwater, leaving nothing but a subtle ripple on the dark surface.

I glanced around the pool, the campfire, to see if anyone was watching.

Nothing but crickets and snores, and excited pounding of my heart.

Then Violet emerged along the edge of the pool. Facing my direction this time, she seemed to rise from the water in slow motion, her dreadlocks slicked behind her, water dripping off her naked body. It was so lost in this utterly wonderful moment, that I barely noticed her eyes, they were gazing towards my wagon.

Holy Smokes! Was she looking at me?! I froze up with my heart racing in panic, wondering if I should reveal myself…go down there and tell her how bad I want it…then make sweet love to her along the edge of the pool.

Yeah right. That only happens in fantasies. In reality, if I stepped out of the shadows, she'd probably freak out, scream to high heaven, quickly cover herself up. My very presence would be a total outrage. She'd see my sweaty palms, the glaring protrusion in trousers, and she'd know that I had watched her bathe in the nude.

Pervert, she would cry.

PERVERT!!

But either way, she seemed content to be alone. So I withdrew further under the shadow of the bow—breathing slowly, sweaty palms and a head full of fantasies.

Violet stared at my wagon for another minute or so, then snatched her gown back on and quietly darted away.

Chapter Five

*The Great Basin: Elevated above the sea level between 4 & 5000 ft: a desert surrounded by lofty mountains. Thinly inhabited by savage tribes, which no traveler has seen or described. **

*As illustrated on a large blank space of an 1845 topographical map of Mexican Territory (A region that would ultimately span nearly all of Nevada, and most of Utah.)

The road took a downhill course away from Twenty Wells and gradually leveled upon a long stretch of desert plain. The sky was cloudless, the sun was scorching, and a white glare rippled off the desert floor that brought my eyes to a permanent squint. Combine that with the drained-empty feeling that stalks behind a randy night of boozing, and the drive became an extra toilsome one. By high noon, I was seeing huge blind spots and was forced to give it up. I had Wilbur take over the driving duties, then climbed into the wagon bed to eat lunch in the shade of the canvas.

I ate a small piece of charred beef leftover from last night's cookout, with a handful of pine nuts and a cup of lukewarm water. The meager meal was hardly minded though, for my thoughts were stuck on the sultry memories of last night.

Then I remembered how Violet had stared in the direction of where I was hiding, before snatching her clothes back on. And the more I thought about that, the more nervous it made me.

You drunken idiot.

Did she catch you looking?

Does she know?!

And if she knows, what does she think of me now? A pervert? A scrawny little white boy *who likes to watch.*

If so, then she's got me all wrong.

I left the wagon right after lunch, feeling this deep urge to confront Violet and mention something about last night in order to set the record straight about my character. I had the notion to tell her straight up that I wasn't a pervert, perhaps say something like this: *'Hey, Violet. Listen. I watched you bathe last night, but I'm no pervert. No. I'm really a sweet guy, full of good intentions...and besides, I was drunk and just minding my own business when you came along and started stripping out of your clothes...so I couldn't help it. I'm really sorry...sorry for catchin' your midnight showing of nudity...but hey, Violet, listen, ah, well...to be perfectly honest...it was the most amazing thing I ever saw. Ever. What I mean to say is...is that I really, really enjoyed the show...and I love you. Want to get married?"*

Or don't mention last night at all, and avoid the struggle of having to explain myself. Maybe just strike up a casual conversation about any random subject matter…talk about the weather perhaps, the ever-rising heat…and if the conversation concludes without the subject of last night coming up, it meant that I was in the clear. She didn't see me. I'm no pervert.

Right?

Sounded like a fine plan to me. I jumped from the tailgate and skipped to the side of the road with my eyes fixed back east, waiting for the black wagon team to approach.

You could hear them coming a mile away. Wobbling wheels, loud squeaking axles, the wooden frame creaking and sagging from the stress of Violet's siblings lying inside.

Violet was walking out in front as usual, single-handedly driving the oxen and looking ever more desirable in the light of day, clothed in all. Last night, she was the strip-teasing chocolate goddess of my wildest dreams, but today, she was back to being an absolute trailblazer, coming over the rugged landscape like some unstoppable moving force, free and beautiful and fully in control of her own destiny.

And she was coming my way, this raving black beauty too real for the world.

And there went my confidence, collapsing like a house of cards. My nerves seized and I froze up under the blazing sun, looking and feeling like a drifting hobo. My face was unwashed, my shirt was plastered in sweat, pants chalked white with dust, boots looking like a hundred-thousand miles had been walked in them, a hat with a frayed brim and a lopsided crown. A poor skinny white boy who used to catch rats for a living, who then turned out to be a creepy little pervert who likes to watch.

My plan was suddenly full of flaws. I should have at least cleaned my face or dawned a fresh outfit first.

I had a nervous meltdown right there on the side of the road. I looked back at my wagon, desperately wanting to catch up with it, but before I could flee, Violet brought her hand up and waved at me.

It was too late to disengage. I meekly waved back and began trotting alongside her, grinning like a fool and trying to think of something witty or charming to start off with, but nothing too overbearing.

Her twinkling green eyes were fixed on me, waiting for it.

"Hey, there!" I blurted, loud enough to be heard over the wagon clatter.

"Hay's for horses," she said with a cute smile, her face shining with sweat, her dreadlocks tied into a ponytail that whisked in the dusty hot air.

"You're in a chipper mood today," I said.

"Yeah," she said. "I got some good sleep last night. I took a nice relaxing bath in one of those pools, and after that, I was out cold."

I groaned inwardly. I could picture it perfectly from memory; her standing there by the pool, wet, naked and doused in moonlight, no towel covering her stunning lady parts. Then I tried not to picture it, for the sake of maintaining my composure. Change the subject, I thought. Say something about the weather.

"Man, it's hotter than a Dutch oven," I said with a gasp, wiping a surge of nervous sweat from my forehead. "I wish we could go back to Twenty Wells.

I sure could go for a swim right now."

I couldn't focus. My mind kept circling back to last night. Pool. Naked. Wet. Moonlight.

"Me too," she agreed. "I'd love to strip out of this sweaty gown and dip my hot body into that cold water."

Lord Almighty, I thought. What is happening here?! Was she messing with me? Or was she being serious?

"I…umm…"

I didn't know what to say. But my eyes couldn't look away. I couldn't help but look down and stare through the neckline of her gown, right at those two sweaty brown balls of flesh, banging around under a thin layer of gray fabric. "Ummm…well…hopefully there's a pool at the next campsite," I heard myself say.

She arched her chin up and wiped the sweat from her neck with her hand. "That'd be nice," she said. "Maybe we could go swimin' together."

I felt my teeth mash into my bottom lip. Sweat gushed from my every pour. We were walking side by side. But Violet was definitely leading me on. I raised my eyes from her breast to discover that she was looking at me. Still smiling. Still walking. I smiled back and kept walking.

Suddenly, she let out a strange-sounding moan. She doubled over and covered her mouth with her hand, her eyes welling up with tears.

I was confused by her. "What's wrong?"

"I'm sorry," she muttered through her hands. "But my lips are horribly chapped. The harder I smile, the more it hurts."

It hurt to smile. That was all. I cataloged the irony of the moment in my mind for amusement later on, then pushed forward.

As a proper gentlemen should, I moved quickly to ease her suffering, which steered my brain in the direction of the grease bucket dangling under the rear axle of her wagon. The axle grease was made from boiled animal fat, which also made a decent skin ointment.

"Wait right there," I told her, then stepped to her wagon and reached my hand into the bucket underneath. I scraped a dark smudge of grease onto the end of my finger, then turned back to Violet. "Rub this on your lips," I suggested, showing her the smudge.

"Rub that on my lips?" she said, studying the gooey muck on the end of my finger with an uncertain look.

I assured her it would work. "Do you want me to rub it on?" I said, raising my finger closer to her lips.

She cringed, but slowly came around. "Okay," she said. "Slap it on me."

We both stopped dead in our tracks and stood face to face. Violet closed her eyes and puckered her brown lips as if kissing the air, and I smeared the grease across her top and bottom lip.

Her dry lip skin felt like sandpaper against my fingertips, but quite frankly, I'd take any excuse to kiss her right then and there.

Violet didn't take well to the grease, however. She jerked her head aside and spat. "Good Gawd!" she cried, gagging and spitting and jerking around. "It really honestly tastes like dogshit."

I laughed and brought my greasy finger up to my own lips and applied the muck. "It's not that bad," I said, grinning with my thin-graded pink lips—lips that were nowhere near as plump as hers, or as chapped.

"Why do white people have thinner lips than blacks?" wondered Violet.

"To match our flat keisters." I smartly replied.

We shared a laugh at that, but our laughter was cut short by a sudden high-pitched scream. We both froze and shot our heads back towards the rear of the column, where the scream had resounded from, and watched helplessly as a covered wagon went skidding off the trail, pulled by a pair of oxen gone mad.

Somebody shouted out, *"Runaway wagon!"* And several drivers sprang into action and gave chase.

Violet instinctively jumped towards her wagon and leaned on the yoke, rubbing her oxen between the horns before to keep them calm. I turned away and rushed towards the rear.

What I saw next would haunt me for the rest of my life. In the dusty wake of the runaway wagon, a man lay face down in the ruts. His left leg was broken and bent unnaturally. A pool of red blood slowly spreading into the sand around him.

I stood over the man, watching his limbs twitch. No idea what to do.

Boggs approached, lifted his foot, and kicked the man to roll him face up.

Half of the man's face was crushed into a paddy of blood, bones, and teeth. One of his eyeballs dangled like an egg on a red string. I staggered back, mortified. My skin flushed hot. Mouth watered. Bile surged into my throat. I turned away and spewed onto the trail ruts.

Boggs started laughing at me.

Irwin came rushing up behind us.

"How the hell did this happen!?" he shouted incredulously, kneeling down and jabbing his fingers into the man's bloody neck, feeling for a pulse that was obviously no longer present, for one look at the half-flattened skull told of instantaneous death.

More pilgrims came racing up in a turmoil of whimpering and cringing disgust.

"Who is it?!" someone cried out.

"It's Henry Beck," said Irwin solemnly.

* * *

A shallow grave was dug only a few yards from the trail. There was no time to build a coffin, but we did the dead man some justice by placing a wooden plank over the corpse to keep the coyotes from digging him up and gnawing him to pieces. The funeral was brief and attended by only half our members, while the other half stood with the oxen.

I joined the lamented crowd standing over the grave and quietly held my hat in my hands while Irwin said a few words in passing. Here's what can be said about the departed: Henry Beck was a middle-aged white man of German descent, no wife, no children. Irwin called him an 'old friend', but I hardly knew the man and my immediate feelings over his death were scrambled and not necessarily grief-stricken, more shocked and disgusted than anything else.

The grave was marked by a tiny cross made of two sticks lashed together with a strip of hide—which also marked the first loss we'd suffered since the start of this journey, breaking a line of safe fortune that had stretched all the way back to Boston.

Nevertheless, as soon as the funeral was over, the drivers were ordered to return to duty, the animals were whipped back up to speed, and the lowly desert valley rumbled with our slow progress once again.

* * *

We clattered on across an empty desert for another four or five miles before the road descended a slope and zig-zagged through an oasis of tall willow trees that shaded the course of a tiny spring. We crossed the spring and were angling back towards the open desert when the discovery of a message post brought the train to a halt. A single piece of pale-yellow paper was tacked to the post.

I was the first of our party to confront the message post and examine it, while cousin Wilbur held the oxen in place. Right away, I recognized Gaylord Hightower's regal penmanship scrolled across the paper.

To all emigrants on the road to California,

If you are reading this, then bravo to you and your party's success. You have bested The Great Prairie and braved it into the heart of The Great Western Desert, and are now that much closer to the heavenly lands of California!

However, there's troubling news to report. I must warn you of—'

That was all it said. The paper was torn. The bottom half of the message was lost.

By Jesus! What was Hightower warning us of?! Had we driven into hostile territory? Were the natives on a warpath? Was the Mexican Army waiting around the next bend to ambush us?!

In a fit of distress, I plucked the message from the tack and waved it over my head, screaming to high heaven.

Irwin came racing up on his horse and reigned hard before me. I gave him the terrible news right away: "It's from Hightower! He's trying to warn us of something, but the message has been tampered with—what he's warning us of, *it doesn't say!*" I shot my eyes towards the message post and frantically looked behind and around it, searching for anything resembling a scrap of paper. "Maybe somebody meddled with it," I anxiously suggested.

Irwin dismounted in a flash and snatched the half-note from my hand. He studied it front to back, then his head snapped up and his eyes squinted over the desert. "Maybe the wind tore it," he said in a voice much steadier than mine, for Irwin had a knack for being calm and resourceful in situations where everyone else was flipping cow chips. He pointed towards a field of sagebrush downwind from the post. "Start looking over there," he commanded, then turned abruptly to wave down the approaching wagons. "Spread out into the bushes!" he shouted, gesturing wildly and waving the half-piece of yellow paper in the air. "We *must* find the other half of this message!!"

Word of the broken message passed quickly down the line, and within minutes, every man, woman, child, ex-priest, and ex-slave was scouring the desert in the stifling heat, searching for a scrap of paper, or what seemed like a needle in a dry-prickly haystack.

Of all people, it was Boggs who found the missing half. He came vaulting out of the scrub brush like a man with a fire in his breeches, holding up the other half of yellow paper and looking downright satisfied with himself.

"What would you do without me, Boss?" he proudly snorted, handing the paper to Irwin with a slight bow, like a fat bellboy expecting a tip.

"Sleep better at night," grunted Irwin in his usual stern tone. He snatched the paper from Boggs and matched the two fragments together.

"What's it say, Boss?" said Boggs. "More donkey shit from Hightower? He wants us to take the scenic tour? Drive in circles 'round this goddamn desert until our hides are tanner than leather?"

Irwin ignored him and read the message quietly to himself. When he was finished, he looked up and asked, "You didn't read it?"

"Read what?"

"The piece of message you found; you didn't read it first, before handing it over?"

Boggs tilted sideways and spat a long nasty wad of brown juice. "That's what I got you for," he snapped. "Now tell me what it says."

Irwin looked down at the two pieces of paper. "Well," he said. "Hightower's warning us of a candy shop up yonder."

"A candy shop?!"

"Yeah, a candy shop. Hightower says they sell the best damn peach ice cream he's ever tasted. He recommends we stop in and try a scoop."

Boggs looked confused. "Peach ice cream?" He turned his eyes west and glared over the tree-less, sand-colored, heat-rippled landscape, as if to confirm the unlikeness of a candy shop operating out there.

"Goddamnit!" he snarled. "Ain't no damn candy shop 'round here."

Irwin folded his arms across his chest. "You sure about that, Boggs?"

Boggs shook his head like a flustered buffalo. "Okay, boss, now you're really startin' to piss me off. I'm serious. Tell me what the goddamn message says."

Irwin tightened his jaw. He took a step closer to Boggs, squared his shoulders, and took a sort of 'try me' stance, showing no sign of being intimidated. "You know what, Boggs?" he said. "A man who can't read a map might have a hard time reaching California on his own."

Boggs seemed to consider Irwin's threat. He changed his tune quickly, withdrew a step, and turned his eyes down to avoid Irwin's piercing glare.

"Look at me, Goddamnit," commanded Irwin. "And speak to me with proper respect, before I crack your brain-less head open and let all the hot air out."

Boggs slowly looked up and smiled nervously. "OK, Boss," he muttered. "I understand. You gotta' maintain order. Ain't nobody reachin' California alive unless The Captain keeps order."

"That's right, Boggs," snapped Irwin. He stared Boggs down for another tough second, before finally lowering his eyes to read the two pieces of paper aloud.

'—I must warn you of an additional dry drive that awaits beyond the next ridge. I had not anticipated this when I set off in this direction in search of alternate routes to Gayville, and I apologize for this minor setback and the temporary hardship it may cause. Pilgrims should drive in all haste to cross this waterless stretch before water reserves are entirely exhausted. I further advise that all wagon trains break here, beside the spring, to allow the oxen time to feed and build strength in advance of the dry drive. Follow the spring north for a hundred yards and you'll find a meadow suitable for grazing.

I must stress again that water and food should be strictly conserved from here on out. And no natives or Spanish speakers should be trusted.

See you in California,
Gaylord Hightower

Chapter Six

We broke off the trail unusually early and made camp in accordance with Hightower's advice. The animals were driven to a nearby meadow to graze, and the wagons were circled along a sandy bank beside the spring. A campfire went up as soon as the wagon brakes were locked. An ox that had died earlier in the day was hung over the flames.

Wanting to relax and be alone with my thoughts, I wandered upstream until I found a small sand beach of my own and sat along the water's edge.

Several hours of daylight remained. The sky was perfectly blue. Beige-colored mountains loomed to the east and west.

I sat there awhile, just staring at things, taking in this strange desert world around me. The surrounding cottonwood trees made good shade from the blasting sun. I removed my boots and dipped my trodden feet into the spring. The soft sound of trickling water set my mind at ease, and I rested my back against the warm sand, closed my eyes, and took what the Spanish call a 'siesta.'

I came awake to an uproar of voices. An argument broke out around the campfire. Dozens of pilgrims were suddenly pushing and pulling and shouting over one another. I sat up and brushed the sand from my shirt, slowly realizing that the brunt of the argument was aimed at the Wagon Master, who was standing tough but alone on the opposite side of the flames. His loyalty to Hightower's changes in route was being called into question.

"Shortcut my ass!" somebody shouted. "That Hightower is full of hogwash! I think he's *trying* to get us all killed!"

"My oxen won't survive another dry drive." shouted another. "And what about water supply? What about the rations?"

"Yeah, just what the hell are we supposed to do, *Irwin!?*"

Tempers flared like an angry town hall meeting. Weary travelers sporting long dusty beards were bitching and groaning and pointing fingers. Insults were fiercely tossed about. Someone suggested that Irwin and Hightower were queer together.

At that point, I stood up and pushed my boots on in all haste, hoping I could reach Irwin before he broke somebody's jaw.

But Irwin genuinely tried to be civil. He gave his men an ear, let them voice their concerns, and took the abuse with his arms folded across his chest; his jaw clenched, teeth mashed, his usual expression more or less.

'Now everybody shut the hell up and listen!" Calvin Crabtree, the stocky, thin-haired whiskey distiller, stepped forward from the mob and spun around to face it. He produced a map from the inner folds of his duster and held it into the sunlight to illustrate an alternative route through the desert—but this sent a wave of negative rumbling through the mob, and somebody shouted, "To hell with your stupid map, you drunken fool! It wouldn't lead us to a bucket to piss in."

This insult came from Crabtree's own brother Daniel, and the two brothers began a sideshow of huffing and cursing at one another, while the old man Milt Crabtree, easily the wealthiest and most influential man amongst us, stood silently in the background with a sullen look in his eyes.

We were all showing signs of wear and tear, and the solidarity of our party was cracking under the pressure of passing time and changing seasons and our desperate run against it. The calendar was well into September at this point, summer was almost over, food rations were nearly depleted, and our oxen were in bad shape.

There were plenty of reasons to worry. But the Wagon Master had heard enough of the whining and bitching. He suddenly pushed his way into the mob, seized Calvin Crabtree by the collar of his coat, and yanked him back. "Keep your goddamn heads!" he shouted. "All this bickering and carrying on for what?! Over an extra dry drive?!"

Now, the way Irwin saw it, a little hardship was expected on the emigrant trail no matter the route taken, and to see grown men whining about it made him so angry that he yanked Crabtree's collar perhaps a little harder than he likely intended, and Crabtree went flying into the crowd like a bowling ball, knocking people out of his way. "It's nothing we can't handle," Irwin fumed. "To disregard Hightower's guidance now would send us wandering into the complete unknown with weak animals and rations nearly exhausted. Only a desperate fool would consider such a thing."

Crabtree staggered back to his feet and snatched his hat from the dirt, glaring at Irwin with rage in his eyes.

Irwin watched him. Calvin raised his left hand over the butt of his revolver.

Old Milt placed a hand on Calvin's shoulder. "Tuck it away, son," he said, then gave Irwin a nod to continue with his speech.

Irwin took a calming breath, turned a burning stare over the mob circled around him, then continued in a lower but equally exacting voice. "I'm not forcing anybody to stay course," he said. "If you feel better off taking another route…and drivin' up some unproven trail, then by all means, go your own way…you have my blessing."

He paused, let his words hang in the dusty air, then coldly said, "You's gonna' need all the blessings in the world."

A tense silence followed. Irwin seemed to wait for someone to challenge him. When nobody spoke up, he made a definitive decision on the matter. "I'm sticking with Hightower's route. And if you aim to survive this, I suggest you follow."

Irwin turned his back on the mob and walked away. I chose not to follow him, and lingered around the campfire instead to overhear what men might say behind his back. Several pilgrims continued to grumble displeasure over the additional dry drive, and Calvin Crabtree was boiling mad about Irwin shoving him down. But nothing came of it.

Irwin paced around the outside of our wagon for a time, brooding intensely and cursing under his breath, before climbing through the tailgate and disappearing underneath the wagon canvas.

Moments later, he re-emerged with his big 'Brown Bess' musket rifle.

A dreaded feeling came over me right then. Worried that he might shoot somebody, I left the campfire and went sprinting after him. When I caught up, he was jamming the ramrod down the forty-inch barrel to set a charge.

"What are you doing?!" I said breathlessly. "What's the matter with you?!"

He glared at me, grimacing, nothing friendly about him. He slammed the ramrod down twice more with a vengeful clench in his jaw, then swung the big musket behind his shoulder. "I'm going hunting," he said, rather calmly, but with a clear edge in his voice. "I need to shoot something." He turned and started for the desert wilderness beyond the spring, saying nothing more.

He was bottling up his emotions, saving his rage for the trigger and the slaughtering of some poor animal, and I wanted to slap him in the face to snap him out of it. Because the cold truth of the matter was this: Irwin was just as concerned over Hightower's route blunders as anyone. The difference was that Irwin hid his fears well inside that hardened outer shell of his, and thereby allowing himself to become the scapegoat for everything going wrong in our travels.

And let me say this about my brother: although the motives of a gold miner may seem selfish and greedy, Irwin hardly possessed either of these traits, nor did he deserve to be cornered and jeered and forced to explain himself by a party of hair-brained fortune-seekers that certainly would have suffered greater losses without him.

And perhaps all I really wanted to do was hug him, tell him things would be okay. But I didn't. I just watched him walk away from me. Because things were not okay. Because I was just as weary of Hightower's guidance.

After the whole mess between Irwin and the mob had passed, I decided to do some laundry. I came to this decision based on these three factors: 1) We made camp earlier than usual. 2) Irwin went hunting without me and left me standing around with nothing to do. And 3) I had no clean clothes, and the dirty laundry heap inside my cedar chest reeked like rotten death.

I carried the dirty laundry down to the spring and soaked the whole heap in the current, rancid underwear and all. After that, I wrung out each garment and laid them across a smooth shelf of rock to dry. The whole job only took about fifteen minutes and left me in a cleanly sort of mood, so I returned to the wagon to clean and organize the inside of the cedar chest.

Minus the dirty laundry heap, here's what remained inside the chest: two tattered wool blankets to guard against the cold weather we expected in the mountains, a tobacco pipe hewed from a corncob, and a stack of books that included my diary; a small little book with a red leather cover that I'd given up writing in months ago. Stashed between the blankets were a handful of percussion caps and a small three-barreled pistol known as a 'pepperbox' for its uncanny resemblance to a household pepper shaker. Here was everything I possessed in this world, and it took only a minute to tidy it all up.

The pepperbox made a permanent home inside the cedar chest because it was far too dangerous to carry on my hip. It was hammerless and had a hair trigger, and any one of its three barrels tended to go off at any moment. It had ignited twice without provocation, and the second time all three barrels exploded at once and blew a canon-sized hole in the sidewall of our wagon, since shored up with scrap wood.

When the pepperbox did fire properly, it was horribly inaccurate and thus no good for hunting. I once took aim at a tree trunk for target practice but ended up killing a poor squirrel in a bush about twenty feet to the left. I had purchased the unruly pistol down in Boston's waterfront market the day before departing for California, feeling obligated to arm myself against the merciless savages of the wild territories, the subject of which strained nearly every conversation regarding Western travel.

I remember the salesman who sold the pistol to me, the shit-eating grin on his face when he made me for an easy mark.

"Headin West, are ye?" he said, lurking behind the countertop of his rickety booth.

I was.

"Oh, I've got the perfect gun for ye."

The salesman had mean-looking dark eyes, oily black hair slicked behind his ears.

"Come have a look-see, feller." He leaned his elbow against the countertop, looked around to see if anyone else was listening, then pulled the pepperbox from underneath the countertop and placed it between us. "This here is state of the art," he said. "A gunslinger's dream and a savage's worst nightmare."

He even had the audacity to look me dead in the eyes and say this: "She's a straight shooter and a quick reload in a pinch." Everything he said was horseshit. Nothing about the pepperbox was state of the art. And I have since developed a strong dislike for people like him: charlatans and hustlers who sit behind rickety countertops and peddle cheap, worthless crap to the trusting public.

Anyways, tidying the wagon and washing my clothes took all but twenty minutes combined. With the entire afternoon still at my disposal, my attention fell to my stash of books. *The Legend of Sleepy Hollow*, *Paradise Lost*, and *The Rime of The Ancient Mariner* were among my collection, but it was *The Life and Strange Surprising Adventures of Robinson Crusoe* by Daniel Defoe that seemed to call out to me. I had been thinking a lot about that book, and how its tale of misadventure was quite relative to our current predicament. I took up the book and sat back against the tailgate to ponder it. The black leather cover was frayed, and the paper text was creased and yellowed with age. I'd probably read the thing twenty times over, yet I never ceased to be sucked in by Defoe's epic intro about the foolhardy desires of young men to venture from the comforts of home in search of fame and fortune.

"Robinson Crusoe's father begged him to stay home," I said, speaking aloud to an imaginary version of Violet sitting next to me.

She was leaning against my shoulder, her pretty green eyes glowing with curiosity over the story.

I went on reading aloud, bearing in mind the unlikeliness of her being literate…Then I started thinking: why not teach Violet how to read? I closed the book, sat upright, and gazed up at the canvas hood. My head filled with this wonderful fantasy where I saw myself pacing over Violet and barking out instructions, being her dashing mentor while she enthusiastically jotted down notes, attentive and busy, being my gorgeous pupil. And with these fantasies on the brain, I spent the next hour converting *Robinson Crusoe* into a sort of textbook, this by highlighting words in the text with a lead stick pencil, words that seemed easy to teach, such as bird, boat, ocean, and fish.

I made notes in the margins and drew several sketches on the blank pages. Once the conversion was complete, I snapped the book shut and climbed out of the wagon to go find Violet.

High hopes were burning inside of me like a small fire, but finding Violet wasn't so easy. The search took me around camp several times. I checked the inside of her wagon twice, jumped the spring twice, circled the campfire three times, and canvassed a grove of willow trees.

I finally found her sitting alone atop a rocky knoll that overlooked the meadow where our animals grazed. She was looking west, watching the sun drop behind the mountains.

As if startled from a hypnotic trance, her eyes snapped alert and pursued the sound of my approaching footsteps.

"Hey, Violet," I said, feeling the butterflies flapping around inside my gut, but moving way too fast to allow my nerves to overtake me. "I'm here to teach you how to read," I said.

She glared at me. Her cute face tensed into a grimace. "What?" she said.

I squatted beside her, pushed the book into her lap, and quickly flipped through the pages to show her the pictures I'd penciled in. "Check it out," I said, pointing enthusiastically to a sketch. "Your first assignment…as my student…is to match the pictures with the words."

Violet looked confused. "You're gonna' teach me how to read?" she said, rather lamely.

I smiled nervously. "I'm no English Professor, but what the hell? Let's do it."

She glanced down at the book, a flat-undecided sort of glance, then she looked over her shoulder in the direction of camp.

"Okay," she said, slowly warming up to the idea. "Let's do it."

I clapped my hands like the eager whippersnapper that I was, then flipped the book to page fifty-eight to show her the drawing I was most proud of: a rough depiction of a black man being chased through a palm-leafed jungle by a white man. There was a caption above the white man's head, like in a comic book, and I read the caption aloud to her. "'Friday! Please don't leave me!'" it said.

Violet studied the drawing for a moment, then pulled back. "Is Friday the name of the black man?"

"Yes." I nodded.

"Why is he running from that white man?"

I shrugged. "Well, the book is about a white slaver named Robinson Crusoe—and Friday is his slave, and together they are lonesome castaways on a deserted island because Robinson's slave ship crashed and sank in the middle of a great ocean...but ah...never mind all that malarkey about slaves and shipwrecks...my apologies...maybe I should have chosen a less-controversial book, but no worries, the point is, I want *you* to keep this book and study the pictures and words and the individual characters of each word, which are called *letters*...and altogether called the ABCs or the Alphabet...or the English Alphabet rather...but it's Latin based...I think."

Violet closed her eyes. "Can I tell you a secret, Pee-nuts?"

"Yes," I said, perking upright. "You can tell me anything."

"I knows the Alphabet already."

She said this in a low, sheepish tone that was almost a whisper, then looked at me with a grin that can only be described as the shrewdest, most elegant grin that's ever graced the free world. She pointed to the caption and slowly read the letters aloud, "F- R—I—D- A -Y." Then she put the letters together inside her head and slowly attempted to sound them out. "Fah-er-eye-dee-ahh-eyyy."

"Yes!" I nodded zealously. "Friday! You got it."

She giggled, looking pleased with her own smart thinking, then flipped to the next picture and went on deciphering the caption. Her head fell comfortably against my shoulder, her dreadlocks dangled between us, and her body settled against mine with her legs folded Indian style, the open book in her lap.

I really had every intention of being a good teacher, but feeling the warm softness of her skin through the thin fabric of my duster had a profound effect on my concentration. I was hardly prepared for the romantic harmony of the moment: alone with the girl of my dreams and a spectacular sunset on the horizon, the rugged beauty of the mountains, a pink sky full of fading light and energy, a desert landscape full of wonderment and bizarre life.

Someone around the campfire started playing a fiddle. Its slow whine drifted up to us, giving the evening a pleasant vibe.

With pretty green eyes, Violet continued spelling out words from the book. "I-S-L-A-N-D," she said, then looked at me, beaming with enthusiasm, wanting to know what word she spelled.

I was watching her lips, but I could barely focus on what she was saying. "Island," I slowly answered.

"Island," she repeated with a thoughtful nod, then returned her eyes to the pages and swept her finger over the next word. "O-C-E-A-N," she spelled, and again, looked up with those glittering green eyes, waiting for my instruction.

My mind was drifting deeper into the fog of lust, however. My eyes sank low and locked onto her lips. I slid my left hand across the small of her back, clutched her waist, and pulled her close. The voice inside my head told me to kiss her. "Ocean," I said quickly, then plunged forward to push my lips against hers.

Of course, everything went wrong from there. Violet snapped her head away, dodging my lips, and her hands lashed out and pushed against my chest. "What are you doing!?" she yelped, leaning back and glaring at me with trembling-wide eyes.

I grew timid and backed off. "I'm sorry," I said in a panic. "I thought the moment was right."

"Oh," she said, reaching up to wipe the trace of slobber I'd left upon her cheek. "I thought we were just reading." She looked down at the book and slowly resettled beside me, but not as comfortably as before.

I felt like a reject. I closed my eyes and shook my head. "Sorry," I repeated. I wanted to shake off the shame and move on, but in the back of my mind was this notion that Violet's cold-shoulder rejection had nothing to do with my looks or my scrawny figure or my lack of hygiene, but everything to do with her former life of enslavement. I wondered, was her ability to love damaged? Was she so unaccustomed to ordinary human affection that she instinctively rejected all advances? Was it because I was white?

I didn't dare to engage her on this topic. Instead, I desperately moved to recapture the vibrant energy we had moments ago. "Yes, let's get back to the book," I nervously blurted, readjusting. "Ocean," I said. "You had just read the word ocean…"

Violet stared down at the book in her lap for a long, uncomfortable moment before speaking again. "The ocean," she quietly said. "That's where slave ships go to get blacks."

I looked down at my hands and thought twice about what she said. "Africa," I said, correcting her. "The ocean is an enormous body of water—the other side of which is the continent of Africa. That's where blacks come from."

Violet nodded and her eyes went distant, her smile long vanished. "Africa," she thoughtfully said. "That's where white people go to kidnap blacks, lock em' in chains, and drag em' across the ocean on slave ships."

"Yeah…" I said drearily. "That's basically it."

"What happens to Robinson Crusoe and Friday?" she asked. "Do they make it off the island?"

"Well," I muttered. "The two of them are stranded, alone, on that desert island for something like twenty years. Robinson teaches Friday his language, and the two of them become the best of friends… almost lovers, in a way… like an old married couple…until they're finally discovered by pirates and returned to England."

Violet thought on that for a moment, saying nothing. An agitated look gradually came over her face, until she looked downright disappointed.

"What's wrong?" I asked.

"Nothing's wrong," she muttered, frowning and shaking her head.

"Talk to me," I said pressingly. I wanted to put my arm around her in a comforting way, but our energy was so strained at that point, echoed in her rigid body language and miserable expression, that I was afraid to touch her. A short silence passed, before Violet turned to me and said, in a rather harsh tone, "Back on the plantation, reading and writing and keeping books only made trouble. Hell, just sayin' something smart got ya' sent to the licking post to be whipped with a cowskin."

She looked indifferently down at the book, shook her head, and looked away. "I'd rather just be ignorant," she said. "Things are better off that way."

It was shocking to hear her speak this way, with such malice and bitterness, and I wasn't sure how things got to this point, or what to make of it, except to take it as a clear indication that she was still ailing from her previous life as a slave.

We both stared miserably at the book in her lap, Violet looking tortured by some awful memory, me trying desperately to think of something positive to say.

And for a long, frozen moment, we sat this way, like two separate species from two different worlds that were never meant to understand each other.

Then, an unexpected call for help snapped us both from our glum musings: *"Peter! I need your help."*

It was my brother Irwin, just returned from his hunt. He was standing at the edge of the meadow and frantically waving both hands to get my attention.

"I just killed some kind of horned mountain goat," he called out. *"The corpse is about a half-mile upstream. Come help me drag it back to camp."*

I sighed with annoyance and slowly rose to my feet. *"I'm coming!"* I shouted back.

As I turned to leave, I felt a tug on my pant leg and looked down to find Violet staring up at me. "I'm sorry about my mean attitude," she said. "I'm not used to talking freely with white folks. Sometimes, I forget we're not on the plantation anymore."

I nodded and turned my eyes over the surrounding desert. "We're far from the plantation," I said bluntly. "Nobody's gonna' lick you for learning how to read. Not here. Not on Irwin's watch. Now take that book and study them words and letters."

Violet half-smiled and looked west, where the distant mountains were swallowing the last traces of sunlight. "I'll study," she said, cradling the book against her breast. "See you later, Peter."

I doffed the tip of my hat to her, then jogged away.

* * *

The Wagon Master had the wagons rolling by sunrise. We followed a faint trail that gradually passed us through a range of barren, brown-colored hills of volcanic rock. The view from the top of the pass was utterly gut-wrenching: a full-scale panorama of a barren salt flat stretching for miles and miles on end.

Hightower's additional dry drive.

The wagons went on streaking across the flat in a torrent of shining white dust and lashing bullwhips. As the sun fell away, we found ourselves still in the midst of the flat, and thus we pushed on through the night, lashing every bit of speed out of the animals. At dawn, we found ourselves halfway between the hills previously descended and the mountains we were striving towards, so we continued on without sleep, sunbaked and feebly postured, all of us coated in white dust like bodies exhumed from a morgue. And into the darkness for the second night in a row we went, the flat ground sparkling like a frozen lake in the darkness, the moon swelling to twice its size above the flat, the stars coming alive more numerous and mesmerizing than I'd ever seen before.

On the dawn of the third day, we drove upon a green oasis of a willow thicket shading the course of a spring. The white sand ended where the willows sprang up, and the road meandered onward through the trees, leading us to a shallow stream of fresh water and a previously cleared campsite nestled in the shade.

Boggs was the first to reach the campsite, having arrogantly ridden ahead on horseback while the rest of us struggled to haul in the wagons. We found him passed out, butt-naked, in a pool of brown water next to the spring.

As soon as the wagons were circled and parked, I stumbled down to the stream and cupped handfuls of water down my piehole until I felt sick. I ended up passing out next to the spring like a bloated dog.

* * *

I awoke to an uproar caused by the two natives that had wandered uninvited into our camp. I sat up with a miserable groan and brushed the ants out of my hair. Men were awakening all around me, grumbling and rising from the sand. The spring was only a few feet away, and the two natives were standing on the far side of it, making signs for food with their hands. Both were naked and weaponless, middle-aged males with long, dirty hair and childish physiques and eyes as wild as the desert beyond.

There was no cause for alarm, but nobody awoke in a charitable mood either, as paltry as our rations were, and somebody shouted, *'Get lost!'* and somebody else tossed a rock, and the two Indians eventually left our camp empty-handed.

Though the spring was meager in flow, it was determined to be the headwaters of the Humboldt River, the crooked course of which we aimed to follow for the next several hundred miles until the final desert crossing, the so-called Forty Mile Desert. At no point would the river be anything more than a trickle of swampy water, but it saved us from wandering thirsty and aimlessly through the desert. We were still several weeks away from the California border, by all estimations, but the river made us feel positive about our progress, and the overall mood of the party returned to that of hope and determination for the time being.

Chapter Seven

*'All those who went with me to California, as well as all other foreigners,
who are residing there, are extremely delighted with the country; and
determined to remain there, and make California the future home for
themselves, but also, of all their friends, and relatives, upon whom,
they can possibly prevail, to exchange the sterile hills, bleak mountains,
chilling winds, and piercing cold of their native lands, for the deep, rich
and productive soil, and uniform, mild and delightful country, will form
the subject of several successive chapters, which it is believed, willfully
show, that the casual allusions, heretofore made to this country, are, by
no means, mere, gratuitous exaggerations.'****

—Gaylord Hightower, *The Pilgrims' Guide to the West, pg. 2*

***Copied verbatim: Hastings, Lansford *The Emigrants Guide to
California and Oregon*, Apple Books, 1994 (reprint of the 1845
edition)

I was filling a bucket in the shallows of the river, when a naked black man suddenly approached me from behind. It was one of Violet's younger brothers, his name Donavon, and he was dripping wet from a bath and wearing nothing but a grin full of bright white teeth. His dark skin glistened in the golden beams of sunlight that slanted down through the tree canopy hanging over the river. His napped hair had absorbed the murky water like a sponge, and soaked bundles of it sagged down his neck. Taking me by complete surprise, he began speaking to me in a backwater vernacular that, in order to understand, I really had to set my ear to.

"Needs a hand wit them pales?" he said, standing knee deep in green water and holding his arms out in a friendly gesture, a move that accentuated the Mandingo-sized manhood dangling between his legs, that, quite forcibly, drew my eyes like a big creeping snake.

"No, it's no trouble," I mumbled, trying not to look at him.

At the risk of sounding queer, I must admit that this young black man's well-endowment had me feeling somewhat self-conscious, but the notion quickly passed once he stepped ashore and crossed over the measly pile of rags he called clothes and began replacing these rags around his lanky body. As he bent slightly to retrieve his tattered shirt, a trace of sunlight beamed over a series of hideous scars streaking across his back. At first, I thought the poor fella had been clawed by a bear or chewed up by a vicious dog, but then I thought better of it. Scars like that on a former slave? The only animal capable of such viciousness was old Johnny Cracker with a snake whip.

"My sister is *so* beautiful," he said, rather unexpectedly. "Man, white men always fallin' in love wit her."

I slowly climbed out of the water and set the bucket aside, suddenly curious about him. "Who exactly?" I wondered. "What white men?"

"Shet," he whistled. "How 'bout every dog-on peckerwood that's ever held her papers." He grinned at me and whistled again. "Shet, man. This ol' peckerwood cotton farmer named Steadman *had* her first, and I mean *had her*, until we's got sold off to the Beasley plantation."

I stared at him, confused. "Had her?" I whispered, more to myself than to him, struggling to pin down the meaning of the phrase.

"You know what I mean," he said, grinning peculiarly. "Had her doing the dirty work 'round the manner. Fluffin' the pillows. Polishin' the knobs." He laughed, then lowered himself to sit on a rock, drew up a brown-colored strip of old hide and wrapped it tightly around his foot…his shoes.

I sat down beside him, suddenly feeling queasy.

"You okay, man?" he said with a chuckle. "You lookin' awfully white."

"I'm okay," I said, blinking my eyes and shaking my head. "Let me ask you this: When Violet arrived on the Beasley plantation, did the new master *have her* as well?" I asked this, knowing the answer would most definitely be Yes, but something inside me wanted to hear Donavon confirm it.

"Man," he whistled. "Shet. Both Massa' Beasley *and* son. They took a whole lotta pleasure outta her."

I felt sick to my stomach. It wasn't the answer I expected. It was a nasty thing to hear, and right away, I regretted my interest in the matter. "Jesus," I muttered. "Master *and* son, that's horrible."

Donavon shrugged. "It's horrible, alright,'" he said as he started wrapping another ragged strip around his other foot. "She's had to lay with a whole lotta' white men—and somehow drove 'em all *crazy*."

"Crazy?" I repeated, glaring at him. "What do you mean crazy? What happened!?"

He paused to pull up his tatty britches and belted them with a frayed piece of rope.

"Well, now," he said thoughtfully. "That peckerwood cotton farmer Steadman, her first Massa', well, he done kilt his wife."

"Killed his wife!?" I blurted.

"Yes, sir." He nodded. "Kilt her dead. But they hung a half-bright jimmy named Jerry for it."

"Wait a minute," I said. "You're telling me that Violet was the reason this Steadman fella murdered his wife?!"

Donavon shrugged. "I's can't tell it for certain," he said. "But Violet was laid up in Massa's bed the night of the killin'…then, bout' a month later, Steadman sold every last slave he owned, sold his farm as well. Said he was sick and tired of blacks. Said he was gon' back to Ink-land."

"And what about Master Beasley?" I asked. 'What craziness became of him?"

Donovan smiled brightly. "Sheeet." he chuckled. "Man. So one day, clear outta' the blue heavens, Massa Beasley decided to set us free…gave us that ol' farm wagon and a couple sacks of cornmeal, tells us to drive west… He tells us, *'Don't stop til' yous' found California…'* And that was that. No more bein' a slave. How's that for crazy?"

I agreed that it sounded crazy. I'd never met anyone named Beasley, but suddenly I was picturing the man as though I'd known him for years—a tall, stout, middle-aged white man with suavely graying hair—a sort of southern dilettante who spoke with a charming molasses-like drawl and took privilege with Violet wantonly…until he suddenly became overwrought by some midlife meltdown or moral reckoning…and guilt-tripped into releasing Violet and her siblings from bondage.

So many questions were spinning around my head at that point, but what I really wanted to know was this: was Violet some kind of comfort girl? But before I could ask this question, Donavon suddenly stood up, fully dressed in his rags now, and declared that he was returning to camp. I nodded my head distractedly and watched him pick his way through the bushes.

I stayed by the riverbank for another hour or so, watching the sunset over the barrens and racking my brain to make sense of the crazy story I just heard. Just how crazy was it? That a slaver would abruptly set his slaves free? Young and valuable slaves at that, slaves of breeding age and in the full prime of their laboring ability.

And the more I thought about it, the less sense it made. In a nation founded purely on the pursuit of wealth, what kind of man would forfeit such a valued asset for nothing? I tried thinking of another example; another time in history when a white man so willingly relented a position of power, but when nothing came to mind, I found myself recalling those suspicious notions raised by the Wagon Master when we first crossed paths with Violet and her undocumented sibling clan.

But what difference did it really make? Whether she was free or a runaway, a rape victim or a willing tramp…the bottom line was that she was a stone-cold fox and her scandalous past only made me fantasize about her more. And thinking about all those rich white men taking privilege with her, it only served to arouse my own erotic cravings. I could almost feel the insane lust that gripped her former master, the kind of lust the drives a man to murder his wife, and it excited my blood. I wanted to watch the wife die and see the slaver hang while the plantation fields burnt to the ground. I wanted to make savage love to Violet atop the warm sand by the river, or in the bushes behind the wagon circle. I wanted whatever I could get from her. I wanted to own her in the lewdest of ways like the slavers had before me.

And this notion pressed on my heart something wicked. I went for a swim in the swampy river to shake it off.

* * *

It was long after dark when I returned to camp. The campfire was still burning strong, but the pilgrims around it were mostly laid out, snoozing under the cover of lowered hats.

Calvin Crabtree and the ex-priest Eddy Daulton were still awake, lazily passing a dented tin cup back and forth. I was tempted to join them for a nightcap, but then I noticed Boggs lurking in the half-darkness nearby. He was sitting alone and sharpening a stick with his knife, occasionally peering up and glaring around the campfire like a dumb child with no friends.

Other than that, all was calm. The chirping of the crickets made the loudest sound, underscored by baritone croaks of the bullfrogs in the nearby river.

It was one of those tiresome nights when the party collectively turned in early for a good night's rest.

But not me. I was too energized to sleep. I went for a casual stroll around the outer perimeter of the wagon circle, hoping this would tire me out.

It was a fine night for a walk. The night sky was clear, the moon was full, a cool breeze blew off the desert, and the canvas hoods were glowing orange with firelight, guiding me like a ring of giant lamps in the lonely midnight hour. I thought about a number of things as I strolled, but mostly thought about You Know Who.

Then I had this strange feeling—ike the kind of feeling you get when walking alone at night, and it feels like someone's following you…which drew my attention to a dark meadow just beyond the wagon circle, where, to my surprise, I spotted Violet.

She was the lone feature in the meadow, sitting in the grass with her head bowed as if engaged in prayer.

I wasn't sure if she had spotted me or not, so I ducked into the darkness behind a wagon and stayed there for a while, watching to see what she would do.

It occurred to me that a right-minded man might save himself the guaranteed trouble of pursuing a woman with such a promiscuous history, that I should walk away, move on, and find a more stable woman to lust after. A woman more naturally suited for a man like me. An easy-going white woman with a plain old pancake body.

But it was too late for all that. The laws of attraction had already skewed my better judgment. She was extremely beautiful, and color be damned, for that sweet ebony body was what made her so eye filling. I admitted to myself that I was a fool for love, or just a fool period, and considered the possibility that I was under the influence of some black magic spell. Then I stood up and started across the meadow, heading straight for her with my heart pounding a mile a minute.

Her head lifted to the sound of my footsteps, and she turned to face me. The first thing I noticed was the open book in her lap, *The Life and Strange Surprising Adventures of Robinson Crusoe.* Then I noticed the tears. They were falling down her cheeks in wet streaks, and her eyes were flooded and twinkling with a mix of water and moonlight, the sight of which gave me pause. "Why are you crying?" I asked, forgetting all about the clever greeting I had rehearsed inside my head.

She closed the book in her lap. "It's nothing," she quietly answered.

Nothing, my ass, I thought. I grew hot and spun around in a circle, glaring around the meadow for a face to blame. "Who did this to you?!" I said, balling my hands into fists. "I'll knock his teeth out!"

Violet smiled and wiped the tears from her eyes. "Nobody did anything," she quietly said. "It's just that...I don't like reading my book beside the campfire, because I feel like people are judging me, so I came out here to read. But I can't see a darn thing. Even with the full moon, it's still too dark."

"I have a lantern," I said in a flash, and before another word could pass between us, I was dashing back to the wagon circle to fetch some reading light.

Hurried by a powerful desire to please her, I detached the glass lantern from the front end of my wagon (what we called the headlight), popped a match, and lit the thing as bright as a torch. Then, I swiftly returned to the meadow.

Violet watched my approach with an eager smile this time, no suggestion of tears on her cheeks. The book in her lap was open to the pages again, and I sat in the grass beside her, placing the lantern before us. "Ready for some reading lessons?" I asked.

She perked upright, posturing her voluptuous chest against the glassy light. "Ready," she said with a willing nod.

We ended up sitting together for several hours. Reading, talking, laughing, and gazing at the stars, while the moon swung overhead and a cool night wind blew off the desert, gusting and hissing through the dry bunchgrass at our feet. Nobody bothered us. I taught Violet how to properly grip a pencil, and she practiced writing in the margins of the book. She was an eager study, and I gave her my undivided attention throughout, keeping my hands and lips on a tight leash this time.

Sometime around midnight, the wind became too strong to bear comfortably, and we said our goodnights and fell to our separate wagons.

It had turned out to be a wonderful evening, and I was feeling good about things as I climbed into bed. I could hear the Wagon Master snoring from his tent nearby. He was sleeping soundly, and it was all thanks to that swampy little desert river trickling along the edge of camp. There was plenty of water to drink and enough grass to restore the health of the oxen, plus the river's rich ecosystem, in contrast to the surrounding desert, offered a variety of small game to shoot: pheasants, grouses, quails, jackrabbits, and squirrels. We made chowder out of frog legs and turtle meat—and it all combined to improve morale and give the Wagon Master a night of well-deserved sleep.

But the peaceful times never seemed to last very long on the western trail, and sure enough, as I laid my head to rest, an unfriendly rustling of voices around the campfire caught my attention. I sat up in bed and listened.

"You Whore! I'll break your jaw!" someone shouted.

"Touch me, and I'll slice your goddamn head off!"

An argument was growing louder and nastier, and it was a troubling thing to overhear. But with Irwin out cold, I took it upon myself to check things out.

It came as no surprise to find Boggs at the center of the fracas. He was crouched in a defensive posture beside the campfire with a stunned expression struck across his face as if he'd just been slapped. His hat was missing, and strangely, his shirt was missing, too.

Calvin Crabtree was taking an aggressive stance opposite Boggs with a green-tinted glass bottle in one hand and a sharp little dagger-blade in the other. Crabtree was a whole head shorter than Boggs, but heavy shoulders and muscular legs gave him a squatty but formidable build. And like Boggs, Crabtree had a mean streak in him. Both men drank excessively and tended to throw bitchy tantrums, and now their mean drunken worlds were colliding.

The ex-priest Daulton was there too, lying on the ground between Boggs and Crabtree, leaning upright on one elbow and holding his side with his hand, his specs removed, his eyes full of confusion.

Calvin Crabtree swung his dagger through the smoky night air, then pointed the blade at Boggs's face. *"Back off!!"* he screeched, his drunken-mean eyes mirroring the firelight like two hot coals jammed into his skull. *"I mean it!"* he hissed. *"I'll cut your berries clean off!"*

Boggs grinned, looking unafraid of the whiskey man's blade. "C'mon feller," he grunted. "You got all the makings to brew up another batch—and another batch after that. Why get yourself killed over one measly bottle?"

Crabtree leaned forward and swung the blade so wildly that it spun him in a circle. *"You walrus!"* he growled. *"Killing you would be a favor to the world."*

Boggs raised his left hand to the walnut handle of the double-barreled horse pistol on his hip. "It'd be self-defense," he said calmly, but with a menacing edge in his voice. "The priest as my witness."

Still lying on the ground and holding his side, Daulton rolled his head loosely from side to side, first looking at Boggs, then at Crabtree, his eyes blood-shot and unfocused. "My good Gentleman," he said with a slur. "I say we let bygones be bygones." He smiled drunkenly and scooted his butt slowly across the dirt, trying to clear himself of the space between Boggs and Crabtree. "I think we all could use another drink," he said. "Yes, that will bring peace and harmony to this party. Let's each have a drink and be merry."

Then Daulton glanced at the hand that was holding his side. "I'm bleeding," he said. "Yes. I deserve a drink for this…"

At that point, I was pretty certain that the ex-priest had been stabbed.

Meanwhile, Boggs was shifting his beady eyes over the flickering orange reaches of the firelight, as if checking for witnesses before committing some heinous act. His thumb was on the hammer of his pistol.

I watched all this from behind the trunk of a cottonwood. I wanted no part of their quarrel but was curious to see how things would play out. I suppose a dark part of me wanted to see Boggs and Crabtree kill each other, because, in my heart, I knew the world was a better place without those two drunken fools. But I kept that to myself and stayed hidden.

Crabtree seemed to realize that nobody was around to stop Boggs from shooting him. A look of genuine alarm came over his sloven-drunk face. "I quit," he grumbled, holding his arms out to make peace and letting the blade slip from his hand. "Hell, what's the point," he said. "We might all be killed tomorrow by savages or Mexicans." He shrugged and raised the bottle to his lips. "Might as well drink it up."

But Boggs wasn't satisfied. He lunged like an ape and snatched the bottle away from Crabtree, then raised his barrel-sized leg and kicked him square in the chest. Crabtree went hurling backwards into the darkness, rolling like a dead sack down to the river's edge.

Boggs stayed by the fire and took a few quick swills, then slowly lumbered off into the darkness with the bottle in hand.

Once the coast was clear, I circled around the campfire and kneeled beside the ex-priest.

"How bad are you cut?"

Daulton raised his hand and studied the blood on it. "Ah, just a flesh wound," he said. "No need to worry, old boy, that Crabtree fella stabs like a woman."

"What did you do to deserve it?"

Daulton looked at me and smiled. "While Crabtree was taking a piss, I snatched his bottle and started chugging it." He chuckled and looked towards the darkness where Crabtree had rolled away. "I would've chugged the whole thing, had that bastard not stabbed me."

I shook my head, picked up a stick, and threw it into the fire. My impression of Daulton had changed drastically since the day we first met, and not for the better. I was starting to see him for who he really was, or what's becoming of him along the turbulent journey west: a man less distressed with life when drunk. When sober, he was a nervous wreck because he knew very little about pioneering, and he feared for the safety of his wife and young son. Life on the trail wasn't as easy or agreeable as he originally envisioned, so he hankered for booze, and hankered for it publicly.

I felt genuinely concerned over his downward trend, and I must have shown it through the expression on my face, for Daulton patted me on the knee and said, "It's okay. I have an addictive personality. Today it's the giddy sauce, but tomorrow I might be hooked on something else entirely, like drinking coffee or eating bugs or tugging on my pecker." He grinned stupidly, then lurched sideways at the discovery of his spectacles lying on the ground beside him. He blew the dirt from the lenses and replaced them crookedly upon the bridge of his nose. "Ah, I can see again," he said, looking bewildered at the campfire as if seeing it for the very first time.

I couldn't help but laugh at him. I offered him a sip from my canteen, and we talked a little while longer. Despite Daulton's drinking problem, I enjoyed his company, as queer as it often was, and I felt the makings of a lifelong friendship developing between us.

"For a long time, I was addicted to the church," he explained. "And that's how I became a priest. But nowadays, I prefer to be addicted to anything else. The worst addictions are not those that draw us into obvious sin, like drinking and whoring and gambling, but those that offer us great evils masking as greater goods."

"What do you mean by that?" I asked him.

"What do I mean?" he repeated, turning his eyes down and taking a moment to compose a thoughtful answer. "Well," he said. "It's easy to believe in something, or someone, when they're telling you exactly what you want to hear."

I took the canteen from him and screwed the top on tight. "I think the whiskey is turning your brain to mush," I said frankly.

"I know," he agreed. "But don't waste your breath on fools, for they will despise the wisest advice." ***(Proverbs 23:9)

Chapter Eight

'After six or seven days of following its fading course across the barrens, the Humboldt River will eventually die a desert's death and completely run dry, while the empty riverbed extends into a salt depression roughly forty miles long, that once crossed will deliver emigrants to the Truckee River, which flows down directly from the Sierra Nevada Mountains that divide Alta California from America Territory. The Forty Mile Desert is the final desert crossing of the journey, and quite possibly the most strenuous portion thereof. Man and beast alike should be well fed, watered, and rested before its undertaking.'
—Gaylord Hightower, *The Pilgrims' Guide to the West, pg. 54*

The Forty-Mile Desert was about as welcoming as the devil's backyard. A white salt flat with no end in sight, parted by a scarce road that was pot-marked by the decaying corpses of draft animals, black and reeking and covered in buzzing flies and twitching maggots. Here and there, an abandoned wagon wilted in the shimmering heat, ominous signs that previous travelers had taken to foot in desperation.

Five straight months of traveling through the wilderness had left our animals in bad shape, wagons in desperate need of repair, and men on the verge of madness. And now this. A forty-mile dry drive from one extremity of desert to the next, with the summer heat at its peak. The timing was just godawful. In a place that kills the weak, we were starting out already half-beaten and ill-equipped.

But we drove on. We had no choice.

Roughly ten miles into the desert crossing, we came upon the dubious relief of Boiling Springs. Here, several hot pools simmered and bubbled along the desert floor with water that was hot enough to kill a man instantly.

Desperately thirsty oxen charged the boiling water and plunged their snouts, only to scold themselves. One particularly stupid beast dove outright into the pool on a suicide trip.

We stopped long enough to watch that ox thrash around in the boiling water, dying its hideous death, then we re-filled the kegs and drove on into the sunset, marching directly westward on a wide-open road of sand and bones.

Irwin led the way as usual, walking his horse instead of riding it. I followed behind him, doing my best to steer the dead-tired oxen. Not a single word passed between us all night. We let the great constellations overhead do the talking for us instead: Taurus, Scorpius, Cygnus the Northern Cross, and the Big and Little Dipper, all blinking in a navy sky like guiding beacons on an inverted road map that kept us from wondering completely lost across the empty midnight plain.

Dawn revealed a distant mountain range spanning the entire western skyline. At last, the Sierra Nevada Mountains were no longer a destination visualized inside our weary minds, but a developing picture before our jaded eyes.

And an utterly colossal one. Hightower's lofty description was no mere exaggeration. Terraced ranges, stone gray in color, soared above the clouds and stretched north to south as far as the eyes could see. No way around it. No avoiding the climb. California, it seemed, was protected by a great wall that only the strong could overcome.

A trace of snow crowned the tallest peak, the sight of which heightened our fears and vindicated my brother's unsympathetic command to drive on without rest, even as more animals dropped and men stumbled to avoid the carcasses.

By nightfall of the second day, the water kegs went empty, and the formation began to break apart. Wagon teams became unevenly spread across the midnight plain. Old Milt Crabtree's Grand Conestoga became stuck in a sinkhole and had to be abandoned, Boggs's horse went hysterical and had to be put down, and the oxen pulling the ex-slave's wagon dropped dead. With no oxen to spare, the ex-slaves went on without a wagon, holding their meager possessions in their hands as they rushed across the dark desert.

They looked like people escaping a fire, and I felt bad…but I had my own problems. Aside from the vertigo from lack of sleep, and the leg pains, hunger pains, thirst pains, and general pain throughout, the weaker of our two oxen had dropped, and Irwin decided to yoke his horse Ringo beside the lone surviving oxen. The big quarter horse and the sickly ox made an odd and turbulent pairing, like an ornery young woman attached to an ugly old man. Ringo bitched and bucked and pulled the wagon erratically, and I was forced to lash him several times. I hated to do it—whereas some people, like Boggs, genuinely seemed to derive pleasure from whipping animals.

* * *

I woke in a spasming panic. Freezing-cold water was racing over the sidewalls and flooding the wagon bed. Holy Moses in Hell! Water everywhere! Pouring over my lap, rushing through my crotch! I was starting to float away, and screamed for help, HELP! Then I jumped from the bow of the sinking wagon, landing in a clear rushing bronco of a river.

As I swam towards shore, I felt my feet touching bottom. The river was only waist deep.

I took a calming breath, gathered my wits, looked around, and slowly realized that Ringo had picked up the scent of water while I was knocked out in the wagon bed, then went storming across the rest of the desert, and plunged into the river.

Stupid horse. I walked out of the river and into a large campsite edged by groves of green forest and lush meadows. The wagons were circling for the night and men were driving the animals into the meadows for grazing. The Sierra Nevada loomed large and picturesque across the western sky, her foothills just a day's ride away.

According to Hightower's book, this was the Mexican border. The desert was through, and the California dream was just a hundred miles or so from becoming reality. Our progress was undeniable. We were Trailblazers! And the land of Milk and Honey would soon be ours.

But the presence of a small cemetery along the northern edge of camp put a damper on the mood. The cemetery was dedicated to previous travelers who didn't make it over the mountains. I counted twelve graves in total. Seven marked by wooden crosses, four marked by piles of rock, and one marked by a vertically planted oxbow.

A large willow tree hung over the cemetery, its dark weeping canopy a fitting backdrop.

A clutter of paper messages was tacked into its bark like ads on a signpost. Naturally, I took a gander. Some of the messages were hand-written obituaries of those buried below, some were letters written to loved ones back east, and some were rather alarming warnings to fellow travelers, like this one: *"Beware, the rattlesnakes of this region are the largest I have ever seen. Saw one yesterday about 12 or 15 ft long, and as thick as a log. This is no fabrication."*

Another message told of a skirmish between pilgrims and Mexicans, and gave fair warning not to trust anyone who wasn't 'White American', this dated August '46, two months ago.

The final message I read, tacked at the very bottom of the tree, was hardly coherent. Something feverishly scribbled about large grizzly bears stalking down from the mountains to steal away life and rations.

And that was it. There was no good news tacked on the cemetery tree, and no word from Hightower. No doubt there had been some unexpected challenges for travelers here, in this region, and now it was our turn to pass through.

How wonderful, I thought, suddenly convinced that my head would soon be ripped off by a giant poisonous snake or a monster grizzly bear.

But then a massive blaze was built in the center pit. Steaks went over the open flames, and a vat of trail brew made its rounds. We toasted to the hard-fought battle in the desert, and to the fallen, and gorged until our bellies were bloated, and by sundown, I was simply too drunk and exhausted to be concerned over snakes, or bears, or which tribe's ancestral land we rested upon.

* * *

For his breakfast, the whiskey man Calvin Crabtree plucked a salmon from the river. Noble samples of pan-fried, orange-colored meat were passed around the campfire. I tried a piece…and was blown away by its scrumptiousness. It tasted entirely apart from any fish I had ever known. Subtle in texture yet explosive in flavor. Oily yet refreshing.

My first taste of California, and it was as rich and fabulous as anything described in Hightower's book.

I could feel my mood improving. The morning air was cool and crisp, and the mountains glowed spectacularly in the early sunlight. Huge fish jumped in the river rapids, and as I walked around camp, refreshed from a good night's sleep, I felt an emotional flicker of what truly felt like hopefulness. And for a moment there, I wallowed in it. There was no telling what treasure awaited on the other side of the mountains, and I was as excited as ever to find out.

While the animals were given extra time to graze and gather strength for the home stretch, I prepared a hook and line, determined to catch my own salmon.

On my way down to the river, I spotted Violet standing underneath the willow tree that hung over the cemetery. It was my first time seeing her alone in many days, and while I was anxious to talk with her and rekindle my loving interest, I couldn't help but stand back a moment and watch her bless the day with her beauty. With her back turned to me, she bent over to read one of the messages tacked to the tree, and I watched her rump bulge against the seams of her gown.

I bit my bottom lip. It was one of those stimulating visual aids that yearning lovers like myself tend to take full advantage of, and store in the memory bank for a lonesome night. Then Violet stood straight, and I watched her eyes widen and glare towards a patch of forest upriver.

She took a step backwards, as if sensing trouble.

I followed her line of sight to the forest. Dark shapes were moving between the trees, and a snapping, rustling sound caught my ear—the sound of something moving closer towards our camp.

A dreadful feeling came over me.

Violet took another step back.

Here it comes, I thought, the terrible things we'd been warned about.

I watched the dark shapes emerge from the tree line along the edge of the cemetery. One by one, a posse of wild-looking men banded together in plain sight. They came armed to the teeth: bows, war clubs, battle axes, machetes, swords, pistols, rifles and muskets of all different types and eras. The misfit weaponry of a gang of pirates.

A small, dark-skinned man stepped in front of the posse. "Hola," he called out to her, waving his hand. "Buenos dias, senorita." He wore a straw hat with a bowl-shaped brim that was so ridiculously large that it shadowed not only the man's face, but everything within three feet of him. I knew this type of hat was called a sombrero, but I'd never seen one so big and silly-looking. His clothes were black, his suit jacket black, and a silky red sash wrapped his midriff, housing two flintlock pistols and a brace of knives.

I raced up to Violet's side and snatched her by the back of the arm. I had a bad feeling about things, and I wanted to flee immediately. "C'mon! Let's go get Irwin," I said in all haste. As I pushed her away, I glanced back and saw the little sombrero man watching me, having raised his head to draw the brim shadow from his face. He had a pencil-thin mustache, stretched extra thin by a broad grin. "Mi hablo con el Capitán, por favor?" he shouted after us.

I had no idea what he was talking about, and I didn't respond. I just kept going, pushing Violet away.

"Who are they!?" she asked, looking fearfully over her shoulder.

"Hell if I know," I said, pulling her into an all-out speed walk towards the safety of the wagon circle. I genuinely had no clue who those guys were, or what they wanted, but they looked dangerous.

I guided Violet through the outer ring of wagons, and angled towards the campfire, where a group of concerned-looking pilgrims was gathering. The Wagon Master stood tall at the center of the huddle, trying to manage the crisis. I naturally gravitated to his side, my habit when the dung was about to fly.

"I don't like the look of those guys!" I eagerly reported.

Entering the huddle at the same time, Boggs agreed with my report. "I agree with Pee-nuts," he snorted. "Looks like a gang of horse thieves. They probably think we're easy pickins'. I say we give em' a show of our guns, then tell em' to piss off." He panted heavily and slapped his big greasy fingers against the handle of his big horse pistol.

The Wagon Master pulled his pistol and checked the charge, then quickly re-holstered it. "You know what, Boggs?" he said. "You might be right. Them fellas look suspect. I want you to watch my back on this one."

Then Irwin looked Boggs dead in the eye and said, "But don't draw your pistol unless I've drawn mine, *understood?*"

Boggs nodded that he understood. "If they ain't White and Christian, don't trust 'em, ain't that right. Boss?"

It was the first time Boggs and Irwin saw eye to eye on any subject matter, and it gave me an unnerving feeling. "I'm gonna' go get the pepperbox," I exclaimed, before turning and starting for my wagon to fetch my volatile little pistol.

Irwin and Boggs walked stride for stride beyond the wagon circle to meet the posse. The rest of us followed behind like the curious onlookers of a gang showdown. With the pepperbox loaded and tucked in the pocket of my duster, I fell into the crowd behind Irwin. Part of me wanted to be out front and included, but as always, I felt more secure under my big brother's tall shadow, watching his back.

The little dark-skinned man with the huge sombrero spread his arms apart in a gesture of welcome. "El Capitan?" he cordially enquired, raising his chin, drawing back his brim shadow, intensely friendly eyes.

"I'm the Captain, alright," grunted Irwin, taking his typical authoritative, unfriendly tone. He stood firm before the posse, eyes sharp under the brim of his hat, hands ready to draw in a flash.

Boggs stood at Irwin's side, huffing and trembling like a big hairy monster let out of the cage.

The rest of us were frozen behind them.

"Welcome to Mexico," graciously said the little sombrero man, performing a slight bow like a hostess, and fluidly switching from Spanish to English with a heavy Mexican tongue. He spluttered through an introduction of himself. "My name is Hector Gomez. The Departamento of Las Californias has assigned me to this district. I am a border agent, here on official capacity." He looked over our party and flashed a mirthful grin. His mouth was full of silver-capped teeth that glittered in the sunlight. Gold and silver rings decorated all ten of his fingers. Nothing about him looked official, but then he opened his coat and pointed to a small silver badge pinned to the left breast of his black undershirt. "Official," he said with a dignified nod, tapping his gold-ringed finger against the silver badge. "You wish to enter Las Californias, No?"

Irwin squinted his eyes. "That's right," he gruffly replied.

"You must pay first," said Gomez with a subtle clap of his hands. "Nobody passes without payment."

"Horse crap!" interrupted Boggs, suddenly agitated and leaning into Irwin's ear. "They tryin' to jack us, boss! *Highway robbery!*"

Irwin sharply lifted a hand to Boggs's mouth to silence him. "Let me handle this!" he snapped.

Boggs sagged and smacked his fist together. "Don't give these yahoos nothin,'" he muttered.

Gomez looked both amused and annoyed by the bickering. Stroking his thin mustache, he said, "It would be wise to pay."

Gomez then raised a hand and snapped his fingers in a cavalier way—a que that summoned a primitive-looking man with a blue-painted face and a head full of dirt-caked dreadlocks, who came forward with a spear held high with some sort of bloody mass staked on the end of it, that, from a distance, looked like a severed human head.

Suddenly there were murmurs and whimpers being uttered all around me.

The expressions on the faces of my fellow travelers began collapsing with terror, as we all came to realize that the bloody mass on the spear was, in fact, a severed human head.

Gomez took the spear from the blue-faced Indian and turned it in his hand, so that the dry-swollen eyes of the human head glared blindly in our direction.

The crowd collectively gasped in outrage. Some looked away, while others stared in disturbed fascination at the slack-dead face of a young white man, looking no older than twenty-five or thirty, drooping blue eyes and neatly cropped blonde hair caked in dry blood.

"This man…he says that California will soon belong to America. He refuse to pay," said Gomez, in a voice entirely devoid of compassion.

"Do you recognize this man?" he said, nodding the severed head towards my brother.

Irwin and Boggs looked perplexed at one another.

"No," answered Irwin. "I've never met a man without arms or legs."

Gomez smiled. "I understand this man was a famous writer of books in your country," he said. "Gaylord Hightower *was* his name."

A low murmur of dreaded confusion came over the crowd. Since none of us had ever met Hightower in person, this claim could not readily be confirmed.

Plus, the rotten-gray deadhead on a stick was nothing like the dazzling, sparkly-eyed world-renowned writer I had pictured inside my head.

Irwin raised his chin. "That ain't Hightower," he said, naively.

"No?" Gomez rotated the spear, so that the deadhead swiveled around to face him. He stroked his thin mustache and looked with slight uncertainty into the drooping dead eyes, then he shrugged and raised his hand to make another snapping gesture with his fingers, summoning another posse member forward.

The new goon came with a self-assured stroll and pirate-like attire, a muzzle-loader slung casually behind his shoulder. He carried a leather-bound book in his hand, that he passed over to Gomez.

Before taking the book, Gomez staked the severed head into the ground, as if planting a flag. The head swung back and forth for a moment like a cattail in the wind.

Gomez took the book and flipped through the first few pages, then began reading aloud.

"I woke up this morning feeling as smart, strong, and capable as ever! I thought to myself: if California aims to join the United States, then it shall need a governor, and no man on earth is better suited for the job, then a shooting star like myself..."

The first few lines delivered a self-loving style one would expect from the famous writer/adventurer, which left little doubt in my mind that Gomez was reading from the personal diary of Gaylord Hightower.

And by the weary expression on his face, the Wagon Master seemed to grasp the gruesome truth as well.

"What do you want?" demanded Irwin.

Gomez grinned like a raccoon. His metallic teeth flashed in the sunlight. "My men will inspect your wagons, and take whatever they please," he said decisively.

Boggs drew his pistol and leveled the sights on Gomez's face. "The hell you will," he growled.

Gomez stiffened, and his grin collapsed. His eyes crossed down the barrel. His hands crossed over the handles of the pistols tucked against his belly. Behind him, his posse drew their weapons, suddenly sharp-eyed and alert like a pack of wolves.

Me, the crowd, we all cringed up.

"You no captain?" said Gomez, carefully nodding his chin at Irwin and looking strangely unafraid, as if he was used to guns being pointed in his face.

Irwin placed his right hand near the handle of his five-shooter. "I'm in charge alright," he told him. "And you bastards ain't jackin' whatever you please."

Gomez nodded. "Okay, my friend. I give you time to think it over. We come back manana...at sunrise." He took a slow, retreating step back, then half-turned on his heels, and waved his arm upriver, in the direction from which he came. "Vamonos!" he called out to his men. "Manana."

And just like that, the Mexicans left as unexpectedly as they arrived.

* * *

Night fell over the wagon circle. A chilly wind blew down from the mountains as a million glowing stars faded in. The moon rose in the baleful shape of a sickle.

A few of the men settled around the campfire to drink trail brew quietly, while others turned into wind-battered tents to sleep.

But I doubt anyone slept soundly following the visit from those Mexican thugs. I certainly couldn't sleep. For a while, I just sat on the tailgate of my wagon, watching over our camp and brooding gravely about the murderous schemes and threats of violence from that 'Border Agent' Gomez.

His crooked act had left such an impression that I had all the faith in the world that he would return with his posse in the morning to see their plundering act through. It was madness! Corruption! Lawlessness! What gave him the right to take advantage of poor, innocent travelers like this?! That dirty little Mexican crook!

It was a cold night with a brisk wind, but I was sweating all over and restless, and the more I thought about Gomez—his silver teeth, his pencil-thin mustache, his stupid-looking sombrero, the hotter my skin felt.

I was boiling mad, but nobody was more pissed off than the Wagon Master.

"To hell with those Mexicans," Irwin simply said to me.

He leaned into the wagon, grabbed his shovel, then turned away and walked off into the darkness until he reached the edge of the cemetery and the exact location where he and Gomez exchanged words earlier.

And there he stood in complete silence with the shovel barred across his shoulders. He stayed like that for several moments, an embattled figure doused in faint moonlight, staring off into the night. Then he lowered his shovel to the earth, and there he began to dig.

He dug hard and deep, thrusting the steel shovelhead into the earth with a highly stressed concentration that bordered on violence. When he was satisfied with the depth of his hole, he tossed the shovel aside and took up the severed head of Gaylord Hightower by its blood-crusted hair. He pulled the stick out of Hightower's throat and dropped the head into the hole, then started shoveling dirt back overtop.

The ex-priest Daulton walked up and removed his hat in mourning. He started mumbling through something that sounded like a eulogy, but he was drunk, and hardly anything he said made any sense.

More men walked up and removed their hats.

I had never witnessed anything so forlorn, so absurd: a funeral held in the dead of night with only a severed head to be buried.

I wasn't sure what to make of it, and for this reason, I stayed put on the tailgate of my wagon.

That's not to say that Gaylord Hightower wasn't in my heart. Although I hated him for leading us down this wretched path, he didn't deserve to die the way he did at the hands of those filthy Mexican pirates.

Once the hole was filled, Irwin packed the loose dirt with his boot until the ground was level, then turned to the men standing solemnly over the grave and said this: "Tomorrow, when Gomez returns, I will present him with a peace offering of two hundred dollars...plus thirteen pieces of gold and silver jewelry, and two vats of whiskey."

The two hundred dollars was the sum of a collection taken up in the crown of his hat a few hours earlier.

"What if Gomez isn't satisfied?" someone said. "What then?"

Irwin staked the shovel into the dirt with an angry thrust. "Goddamn it," he hissed. "We're still drivin' into California...regardless of whether that shit-eating Mexican accepts the peace offering or not."

Chapter Nine

The sun was several hours high when Gomez finally appeared. He and his posse materialized out of the tree line along the edge of the cemetery as they had the day before, looking like a gang of train robbers, more or less.

Irwin donned his hat and rose to his feet. Boggs stood large and tough at his side. The settlement money and jewels were stuffed into a burlap sack, the neck of which was twisted tightly around Irwin's fist like a knuckle bandage.

Gomez, wearing his big sombrero, his silky red sash, and its threatening lot of pistols and knives, halted his men and briefly studied our camp. His goons spread out evenly to the left and right of him, holding their rifles, swords, war clubs, battle axes, and machetes.

Our camp was momentarily silenced by the sight of them. I could hear my pulse pounding in my ear as I climbed down from the wagon, cautiously moving towards the cemetery with the rest of the party.

Gomez stepped face to face with Irwin and doffed the large brim of his sombrero. "Buenos dias, my friend," he said in a mirthful tone, like a man who didn't lose a wink of sleep over the crooked life he leads. "It's a beautiful morning, no?"

The sun was cresting over the trees, the river was roaring, and the mountains were magnificent in the golden light. But Irwin was in no mood for small talk. He held out the money sack and spoke straight to the point. "The contents of this here sack settles our debt and guarantees our safe passage into California."

The steely look in his eyes was as definitive as his words. If Irwin was afraid, he didn't show it.

Gomez caressed his thin mustache, then snatched the sack from Irwin's hand. He jingled the contents with a swinish, silver-toothed grin. "For me?" he said in a queerly elated voice. "My friend, you are too kind."

Gomez reached inside the sack, came away with a gold pocket watch, and held it up to the sunlight to study it. An American-made Pilkin timepiece with a gold-plated case that flipped open with the push of a tiny gold button.

Gomez grinned a sleazy, crooked grin.

By now, the entire party was aware that the deal was going down, and everyone had congregated close together behind Irwin like one large grieving family. I stood in the middle, the ex-slaves to the left of me, the Crabtree family to my right.

Milt Crabtree, the senior patriarch, watched with a somber expression as the family heirlooms teetered in Gomez's vile hands.

Gomez dropped the pocket watch back into the sack, then passed the sack to the blue-faced Indian lieutenant at his side. He pointed at the two whiskey vats and uttered something in Spanish, prompting two of his men to carry the vats away.

Then Gomez held a finger to the wind.

"And one more thing, my friend."

"What?" said Irwin, his face grim.

Gomez turned his eyes to the three black women standing together in the rear of the crowd. He lifted his hand and pointed at Daphne, Rose, and Violet.

"The three negro women belong to me now," he said.

Irwin shook his head. "No," he said flatly. "Them blacks are as free as the wind blows. They ain't going nowhere against their will."

Gomez tilted his head sideways, looking puzzled. "You are white American, no?"

Irwin nodded rigidly.

Gomez wagged a finger in the air. "Okay, gringo. I tell you a story now. Once upon a time, I had a Gringo-American friend named Johnny Walker.

He was a terrible friend, that Johnny was, a real crooked son-of-a-bitch and a rotten gambler. But he was a hell of a thief. I tell you, that gringo bastard loved to steal…even more than me."

"Anyways, Johnny Walker says he was from a place called *Ten-nah-see*…Yes, I think I'm saying it right…*Ten-nah-see*…and he talked about *Ten-nah-see* all the time. He say that blacks work the fields like cattle in Ten-nah-see… he say that in America, the black is…how do you say?…*dis-pose-a-ble*. He say the negro means *nothing* to the gringo."

Irwin sucked his teeth. "I don't give a hoot in hell what Johnny Walker from Tennessee says. Them blacks behind me ain't slaves. They free people of color, *goddamnit*."

Gomez ignored him. His eyes were small and distant in recollection, his finger still twirling in the air.

"…And let me tell you another thing, my friend. I caught that *pinche cabron* Johnny Walker sleeping with my second wife. And that's the end of Johnny Walker's story. He was the handsomest gringo I ever shot. Blonde hair like a palomino and eyes bluer than the *ocean-*"

Boggs impatiently cut in. "C'mon boss, I'm tired of hearing this bean-eater's mouth. Let's give him what he wants and get on. We're talking about a couple of worthless darkies here, who cares what happens to 'em."

"Shut your goddamn mouth, Boggs," Irwin hissed.

"It's okay, my friend," chimed Gomez. "You give me the negro *chicas* now. I treat them fair and you pass into California. No problema. Okay, my friend?"

Irwin took a moment to consider his reply. A short, uncomfortable silence followed. A cool gust of wind whipped through camp, beating against the canvas hoods. Irwin peered over his shoulder at the crowd of innocent travelers behind him. He looked directly at Violet. She helplessly stared back, the breeze fluttering through her dreadlocks and batting her ragged gown.

Irwin never looked in my direction, but something in his manner said that he was thinking of me. As for my own train of thought, I was considering the pepperbox. My hand was jammed inside my pocket; my sweaty fingers gripped around the handle. Feeling both eager and afraid, I visualized myself pulling the pistol and blasting away, then racing over to Violet's side, grabbing her tight and whisking her away, protecting her from being gang raped by criminal savages.

But the situation was too tense for sudden movements, and I remained rigid in place amongst the stunned crowd, holding my breath and waiting to see if my brother would trade the woman that I loved, for the authorization to pass into California.

"No," finally said Irwin, turning back to face Gomez. "You can't have her."

Gomez shrugged. "Ah, silly gringo," he said. "You gringos are all the same. You think you're so righteous….think you are so… how do you say?… *sup-per-rior*." He nodded at his own quick thinking. "Yes, sup-per-rior. That's you, my friend."

"Ah, but you forget one thing, my friend, that is this: California is still part of Mexico… *and you*, my friend, have no privilege here."

"Trespassers!" he shouted at the crowd. "Every one of you pig-faced Gringos!"

Gomez paused, took a breath to recompose himself, then turned back to Irwin.

"Sure, year after year, the gringos come to Californias in greater numbers—and soon they will drive me out or kill me—do what gringos have done since Hernán Cortés…"

"Ah, but not today, my friend."

"No me jodas, amigo!"

"I'm still in charge here."

He squinted grimly. "Now you give me that negro *puta*— or you turn around and go home." Then he pointed directly at Violet, or so it appeared that way in my shit-scared eyes.

But Irwin would have none of it. "Goddamnit. I said NO. You can't have her."

He leaned forward and spoke impatiently, his face beat red, his temper visibly slipping.

"Now, I already gave you every cent and every piece of jewelry we have," he said. "Take the sack and *go*."

Gomez's eyes darkened. "No chicas—No deal!" he screamed, making a quick chopping motion with his hand. "No passage to California, my friend."

Gomez pulled his pistol, held it at his side. His posse drew up their weapons.

Irwin scanned his eyes over the posse, but held pat and meshed his teeth, trying to hold back an explosion of anger, or considering the consequences of such an explosion.

But Irwin was merely a man. He exploded anyways.

"Now you listen here, you little Mexican prick! I've had about enough of your slippery shit. We're driving west through the mountains with or without your consent." There was a volatile, fuming edge in Irwin's voice—a seething, boiling-point level of irritation that I'd never heard from him before. "Try to stop me, and I'll roll the high wheels right over you. Crush your head like a pinata!"

Then, in one fell swoop, Irwin turned abruptly on his heels and started back towards the wagon circle.

As he stormed away, he grabbed Boggs by the sleeve of his coat and pushed him along. *"C'mon, Let's go!"* he ordered in all haste. *"Break down the camp, hitch up the oxen."* He shooed the crowd back with a hurried wave of the hand. *"Shows over! Move along. Get these goddamn wagons back on the road."*

Gomez called after him. "Wait a minute, my friend!" he shouted. "Before you go, there is something I must show you."

Gomez raised his hand and snapped his fingers.

The blue-faced Indian came forward holding a spear with a bloody head staked on the end.

Gomez grinned wildly.

His metal teeth sparkled.

"Maybe you recognize this man," he called out.

The blue-faced Indian took center stage and drove the stake into the earth. The severed head now faced the dreaded pilgrim audience like a new cast member of some playact in Hell. It was the bloody slack face of Takoda, the lone Indian amongst our ranks. His eyes were like rotten eggs drooping out of the sockets. His jaw was slack, mouth stuck open, sort of giving his face an expression of outrage, similar to the expressions on the faces of the crowd.

"This man, he tries sneaking into Mexico without paying," said Gomez.

A terrible silence followed where nobody seemed to know what to do or say.

Irwin took a long look at the severed head of Takoda. A dangerously foreboding expression came over his face. The expression of a man pushed too far.

A few heart-pounding seconds passed, then Irwin simply pulled his pistol, cocked the hammer, and shot Gomez in the chest.

BOOM! The unexpected blast shocked everybody in place, but only for a split second. A battle erupted, and more explosions rang out. Every man with a gun scrambled to shoot or flee. Rifle balls screamed in every direction. Boggs drew up his pistol and let loose like a madman, firing at anything that moved. The Crabtree brothers raised a formation of rifles and blasted hot slugs at anybody that looked halfway Mexican, and in the matter of a few wild seconds, many posse members were cut down as they rushed to escape, while the others scattered into the tree line or disappeared upriver.

I yanked the pepperbox from my coat pocket, but the shootout was over by the time I cocked the hammer and rotated the barrel, and I never fired a single shot.

Lowering my gun and squinting through the gun smoke, I counted six dead or dying Mexicans sprawled out on the ground, including 'Border Agent' Gomez.

* * *

Incredibly, nobody fighting on our side was harmed during the shootout. The ex-slaves were safe, Crabtree was grateful to have his jewels returned, and Boggs was delighted to pluck the gold and silver rings from Gomez's dead-stiff fingers.

But I lost track of Irwin. He was last seen walking down towards the river. Meanwhile, the wagons were ready to roll. All I had to do was release the brake and drive off. But I hesitated to do this without our captain.

I left the brake engaged and went down to the river to see what was troubling him. I found him sitting alone on a rocky beach near the water's edge. He was just gazing out over the water, strangely unguarded, a still and quiet figure beside a roaring river.

I paused on a high bank above the beach and watched for a moment to see what he would do. Which turned out to be nothing. The timing of it was odd, considering the pressing need to flee the scene of the crime.

I realized then that something was terribly wrong with my brother. I rushed down to the beach to talk to him. The beach pebbles made a loud crunching sound under my feet as I approached him, but Irwin was unmoved by it.

"Irwin?" I said as I crossed before him. "Are you okay?"

His eyes slowly raised to meet mine. His face was white and grim. His right hand was clutching the lower part of his chest, his left hand wedged down in the beach pebbles to keep himself propped upright. By the dreaded look in his eyes, he was clearly hurt, but he didn't want to alarm anyone, so he came down to the river to suffer in private and figure out what to do next.

"Are you shot?" I asked.

"I'm shot," he shortly answered.

"Well…let's have a look at it."

He stared blankly for a moment, straining to breathe, then he carefully removed his duster, wincing as he pulled his arms through the sleeves. The entire left side of his white undershirt was soaked in dark red blood.

"Christ almighty," I gasped. "You're bleeding everywhere!"

Irwin peeled his bloody undershirt away. There was a small puncture wound just below his left nipple, and with each breath he took, a bright new squirt of blood ejected from the wound and dripped in a crooked red streams down his abdomen.

He looked down at the wound and plugged it with his finger.

"It's not a leaky canoe!" I snapped. "You need a doctor."

Irwin winced his eyes shut, mashed his teeth. "Then run into town and get me one!" he groaned.

"What town?" I said in all earnestness, looking up and down the river.

Irwin opened his eyes and stared at me, a cold look that made me feel stupid about the asinine way I was acting. "I can feel the bullet inside me," he said, wincing his eyes shut again. "I need you to pull it out."

"What?" I said incredulously.

"Listen to me," he said. "Go to the wagon. Grab my vanity kit. Make sure there's scissors inside of it. And fetch me a clean pair of clothes…"

I understood what the scissors were for. Irwin wanted me to jab the scissors into his wound, feel out the bullet, and pluck it free from his body. I went along with his instructions, trying to act brave, or not so yellow-bellied about his bleeding and dying.

"And get some trail brew," he uttered.

I left the beach in a frenzied panic.

As I rummaged through the wagon bed, Violet approached the tailgate and watched me with a concerned expression. "Peter?!" she said. "Is everything okay?"

I wanted to grab her and tell her that Irwin had been shot, but I didn't, because I didn't want to cause further distress, or, more importantly, further delay. The most important thing right now, I felt, was that the wagons drive away from this location immediately, before the Mexicans regroup and return to exact revenge. "Take Ringo by the reigns!" I yelled back at her. "Get this party moving up the trail. I'll catch up. Don't worry. Just get movin'!"

I slung the leather strap of my whiskey canteen over my shoulder, jumped over the tailgate, and sprinted back down to the river.

A cloud of woodsmoke was hanging over the beach. Irwin had made a small fire and was kneeling over it, snapping twigs to feed into the flames. Blood was dripping from his fingers.

"Place the razor and scissors into the fire," he instructed, his voice trembling, straining to maintain its authority.

I laid the vanity kit down on the beach pebbles. Its leather-bound cover opened like a book, the grooming instruments sheathed in leather pouches on the inside: a comb, a small mirror, a shaving blade, and a pair of scissors made of steel.

I placed the sharp end of the scissors into the fire and waited until the steel was glowing red like a branding iron.

Thinking about what transpired next still makes me squeamish. The whole thing was a nightmare. A nerve-wracking shitstorm of cursing and intensive labor. Picture something similar to childbirth. But with a bullet instead of a baby.

"Get this damn thing out of me already!"

"Hold still, Goddamnit! I can't latch onto the bullet unless you hold the fuck still!!!"

I made several stabs at it, trying my darndest to concentrate through the cursing and the gushing blood, while Irwin made animal-like tortured sounds in dramatic fashion. I could feel the mad beating of his heart through the scissors as I stabbed and dug around his insides. After the fourth or fifth stab at it, I felt something foreign lodged between the bones in his upper ribcage. I latched onto the foreign body and plucked it free. A squirt of his hot blood followed, splattering across my face.

A tiny black ball, shiny and wet with blood, dropped to the beach.

Picture a bloody pearl spit from the mouth of an angry clam.

Irwin fell flat on his back, huffing and kicking divots into the beach with his heels, fighting to get control over the pain. *"Gimme the whiskey,"* he grasped.

I uncapped the canteen in a hurry and passed it to him.

He snatched it. Poured a huge gulp of whiskey into his mouth in one mad swoop. Coughed and spit it down his chin, then poured another splash over the wound.

"Now close me up," he said, gasping, breathless, looking at me with tears in his eyes.

I waited for him to calm down, then I removed the red-hot razor blade from the flames, pressed it against the wound, and fried his blood to a black crust, while Irwin squealed like a stuck pig.

After that, I stood up and walked over to the water's edge. I was trembling as I washed the blood from my hands.

When I turned back to check on Irwin, he was slumped forward on his knees, looking down at the beach pebbles and shifting through them with his hand. He found the bullet, raised it to eye level; a small black ball of lead, fired from the musket of some Mexican scumbag.

He grunted and tossed the bullet into the river. It hit the water with a soft plunk and sunk like a stone.

Chapter Ten

Irwin slept in the wagon bed for the entire drive. Once we were parked and the brake was set, I walked to the rear and leaned into the bow to check on him.

In the dim shade of the canvas, his ghostly white face prodded from the end of a buffalo blanket like a dead man in a casket, eyes sealed shut, body laid stiff. And for a heart-pounding second there, I thought he was actually dead, which threw me into a panic. I grabbed his foot and shook it madly. "Irwin! IRWIN! Wake up!"

His eye snapped open and darted about with the bewildered glare of a man uncertain of where he was, or how he got there. Then came a groan, a slow lift of the head, a trembling hand reaching for his canteen.

He guzzled the last drink of water, then hurled the empty canteen against the tailgate. It clanked and bounced off the sidewall and settled at his feet.

"Why are we stopped?" he grumbled in a weak, raspy voice, his bloodshot eyes adjusting on me.

"The sun is almost down, and there's a good, level campsite," I said. "There's plenty of tinder thanks to all the pine trees about…and another one of Crabtree's oxen just died, so they'll be fixin' beef steaks with wild onions and pine nuts."

While I updated him on the current state of affairs, I reached over the tailgate for the empty canteen and began refilling it from my own.

We'd driven deeper into the mountains. The front ranges of the Sierra Nevada now surrounded us on all sides, while the Truckee River cascaded into a canyon of its own making, its banks becoming near vertical cliffs that dropped along the southern edge of our current encampment.

"Goddamnit," grumbled Irwin. "Who's calling the shots?"

"Boggs is in the lead," I said, lamely.

"Christ," he muttered. "And those rotten Mexicans, any sign of 'em?"

"No, do you think they're following us?"

Irwin laid his head back against the pillow and shut his eyes. He opened his mouth to speak, but broke into a violent cough instead.

I replaced the canteen at his side, refilled to the brim. "Go back to sleep," I encouraged him. "I'll bring you some steak when it's ready. We got everything under control."

"The hell you do," he croaked between wheezes.

He coughed again, covered his face with his blanket, and said nothing more, eventually slipping into a wounded slumber for the remainder of the night.

* * *

On the next afternoon, we topped the rise over the initial range of summits and ascended into a mountain valley where the most magnificently blue lake awaited.

I stirred with a mix of intrigue and horror. Intrigued because the wagon path ran beside a sandy beach that edged a shallow lagoon with water that was crystal clear down to the sandy bottom. Horrified because the grand pinnacle of the Sierra Nevada mirrored in the lake's surface, and the mountains were white with snow, and the western pass lay above the snowline.

Boggs veered off the trail, rolled his wagon right over the beach, and parked in the sand. The Crabtree Brothers followed and parked beside him. The wagons were parked parallel to one another; no effort had been made to circle them.

I followed them down to the beach, set the brakes, and walked to the rear to update Irwin on the situation. "The lake, the pines, the mountains, it's as pretty as a painting," I said in awe.

I was about to tell him how the mountain pass beyond appeared to be blanketed in snow, but then I heard footsteps approaching and felt a large hand grip around my shoulder. It was Boggs, huffing and puffing like a spent horse.

"Step aside, *Pee-nuts!*" he growled, pushing me aside and leaning his bushy head through the bow to examine Irwin.

"You look as bad as the oxen, boss," he said, removing his hat and looking somewhat mournful. "Hell, all the more reason for stopping here for a while. Rest and let wounds heal…and do some fishin'."

He paused and waited for Irwin to respond.

But Irwin said nothing. His eyes were closed, head rested on the pillow, face white and clammy with fever.

As asinine as he sounded, Boggs was right. Irwin looked bad. And he smelled bad. And he wasn't eating.

But I could tell that Irwin was listening, call it brotherly intuition…but he didn't reply because everything Boggs had said was stupid, because only a fool would make camp at this high of elevation with old man winter on the doorstep.

But it didn't sound that stupid to me, or not as stupid as it should have sounded, in retrospect. Because I was weary of traveling and ready to throw in the towel. And in that moment, it made no difference to me, whether we stayed by the lake or went straight for the snowy pass. I just wanted to do what was best for Irwin's health.

So, deplorably, I entertained Boggs and his notion to 'rest and let wounds heal'.

"What's a while?" I asked him.

Boggs shrugged his husky shoulders. "A few days," he said. "We'll wait for rain to wash the snow from the pass."

I stared at him. "Wait for rain?" I repeated, thinking twice about it. "But winter is coming. The weather's only getting worse."

Boggs stiffened, and his face darkened. "Listen here, *Pee-nuts.* I'm stickin' by this here lake for a while, and them Crabtree boys are stickin' too! We're haulin' valuables in our wagons, mining tools and whiskey vats and shit like that, and we need healthy oxen to make the haul over them mountains yonder." He batted his crusty eyes to the west, in the direction of the snowy pass. "Rest and let wounds heal," he said with a grunt. "And do some fishin'."

Just then, the Irishman Charles Bryant approached. Without beating around the bush, he told Boggs that sticking around the lake was a bad idea, said that he was separating from us and pressing on towards the high pass alone.

"You goddamn Irish cocksucker!" shouted Boggs. "You gonna' make an easy meal for a hungry pack of wolves!"

Bryant shook his head, turned to me, and spoke in his scratchy Irish accent, "For the record, I'm glad Irwin shot that low-down Mexican. I woulda' done the same thing. Irwin is a good man, and the world needs more men like him."

I nodded solemnly, feeling like I was standing at my brother's funeral.

Bryant reached out with a small cigarette rolled in a green leaf. "Here, take it," he said.

I took the cigarette from him and twisted it in my hand.

"Take care, friend," he said, in a tone that was glummer than anything. "Irwin's in my prayers."

Calvin Crabtree approached as Bryant turned away.

"This lake is full of fish!" Crabtree gleefully reported, turning and pleading with Bryant as he walked away. "I say we give it a couple of days. Do some fishin'. Give Irwin a chance to heal. Hell, maybe it will rain…and the rain will wash the snow from the pass…"

I shook my head, looking down at the cigarette in my hand. Bryant continued to walk away, saying nothing.

"Forget him," grumbled Boggs. "That Irish whore."

In the wagon bed, Irwin let out a harsh-sounding cough.

"So we're stayin' a few days, boss," said Boggs, glancing back into the wagon bed at Irwin, then glancing at me. "Take it or leave it. I couldn't give two shits bout' you, or your big-lipped cotton-pickin' girlfriend…I only came back here to pay respects to the boss man. Let em' rest in peace in knowin' that his ol' pal Boggs is gonna' be alright without 'em."

"Pay your respects?!" I shouted incredulously. "You ignorant goat! Irwin ain't dead yet."

"Yeah, but look at him…any day now."

"Any day, my ass," I hissed naively. "Irwin's gonna' make it over the mountains, while your fat keister freezes to death by this lake."

Boggs cocked his head to the side, hawked and spat. "Go on then!" he huffed. "You little rat bastard, scurry up that mountain."

Suddenly, I didn't feel like arguing with Boggs anymore. What was the point? He was a half-wit, and he didn't even know it. He couldn't read a map, and he knew nothing about pioneering. All told, he was just another fat, greedy white man gone west to plunder, and following his lead would finish us off for sure.

"Whatever you say, Boggs," I said defeatedly, exhaling and folding my arms across my chest. "You can stay by the lake, but Irwin and I are going straight over the pass."

Boggs glanced at the failing body of his captain, then puffed his chest and said, "I wasn't askin' permission."

And the conversation ended there. Boggs turned away and lumbered back to his wagon, while Calvin Crabtree lingered a moment, staring at Irwin with a sorrowful glint in his eyes.

I picked up a rock and thought about throwing it at the back of Boggs's head, but didn't. I angrily chucked it towards the lake instead. The rock hit the clear-blue water with a subtle plunk. A circular ripple marred the mirror image of the white mountains, but only briefly.

I turned back to the tailgate. Irwin was awake and staring vacantly up at the canvas hood. "Why didn't you say anything to Boggs?" I snapped.

He cleared his throat, spat a bloody wad onto his blanket.

"I'm tired of talking," he said in a faint, phlegm-cracking voice.

I slammed my fist against the tailgate. His wounded tone and lack of fight were getting on my last nerve. I wanted to jump over the tailgate and storm into his bed, snatch him into a good wrestler's underhook, and shove him out of the wagon in a burst of tough love, forcing him to be the boss man again.

But I didn't do that either. I just stammered and squirmed and passively said, "Irwin, you should get up and walk, or at least eat something…or you're going to rot away."

Irwin coughed, cleared the phlegm, spat. "Just let me rot then," he quietly said, sounding too weak to put up a fight. "But let me give you some advice before I go: I would *not* attempt the high pass without Boggs or the Crabtree Brothers…Strength in numbers, remember."

A long, wicked spell of coughing came over him. His body heaved and convulsed under the blanket. When the coughing finally passed, he whimpered from the pain of it, then he was out again.

And that was that. We would make camp on the beach. Rest and let wounds heal. Maybe do some fishing.

* * *

I was sitting on the tailgate, twisting the little green cigarette in my hand and gazing over the lake. A cool breeze whisked through the pines, and an orange sun was tumbling behind the white mountains. A coyote howled at the waxing moon.

I was trying not to think about everything that was going wrong with our journey. Then I thought about whiskey. What better way to forget your troubles?

I drew up the whiskey canteen and went to work. Following my third or fourth drink, I noticed Violet walking along the shoreline nearby. She was lifting rocks in search of crawfish, and she was alone. Her siblings were off in the opposite direction, scavenging a pine grove for food.

Small translucent waves crashed softly at her feet, and a gusting wind blew her dreadlocks back, exposing her chocolate face to a kiss from the crimson sunset.

Despite the depressing circumstances, it was a beautiful place to have a drink. I took another sip and closed my eyes, letting the cool wind rustle through my hair. I could feel the buzz coming on, feel it pushing my worries to a comfortable distance.

Then I felt a hand touch my knee. It was Violet. "How's your brother?"

she asked, standing on her toes to peer inside the wagon.

"Not good," I said, shaking my head sadly. "He hasn't moved or eatin' in days."

Violet's head sank. "I just don't understand this world," she said. "The worst things happen to the best people, while the rotten ones just keep getting away with it."

I nodded my head in agreement. "At least God made whiskey," I said, looking down at the canteen in my hands and feeling sentimental about it. "Care for a drink?"

Violet glanced at the canteen with a pensive sort of look—a look that said she knew the power of whiskey, knew that I was offering something much stronger than water.

"I thought you'd never ask," she said with a smirk.

She took the canteen from me, raised it into the air, and said, *"Here's to Life, Liberty, and the pursuit of Happiness!"* She followed this declaration with a huge gulp that she swallowed down without so much a cringe or a gag.

I was floored by her. "What was that?" I said with a laugh.

Violet shrugged and passed the canteen back to me. "It's your turn to make a toast," she said.

"A toast?" I said, taking the canteen from her and slowly raising it. "Well… okay. Here's to Gayville. I hope it's as gay as they say, and I hope Irwin gets to see it." I followed up with a huge swallow, then gagged, wrenched, and convulsed. I swelled up like a frog choking on a big horsefly. Calvin Crabtree's trail brew was downright rancid, but it sure got you feeling warm and friendly in a hurry.

"You don't seem like a first-timer," I said. "Hell, you drink like a sailor's gal."

Violet giggled, took a seat on the tailgate next to me, and turned her green eyes over the lake. "It's definitely not my first time," she said. "No. My first-time drinkin' hooch was in a hay loft with Billy Beasley."

"Who's Billy Beasley?" I asked.

"Masta' Beasley's son," she said.

"Oh. So, your first drunk was in a hay loft…with the Master's son?"

"Yeah, it made *doing it* more bearable."

"Made doing *what* more bearable?!"

"You know…*doing it.*"

I paused to take a drink and consider the meaning of *doing it* and all its lewd prospects. Then I took a long, slow sip, trembling and gasping as I swallowed.

Violet watched my struggles with a cute little grin, but I couldn't tell if she was amused by the ugly faces I was making, or by something else entirely. Something sexual in nature.

"Violet, can I ask you something?"

"Go ahead."

"You did *that*…I mean *it*…with *both* your former Master and his son?"

"That's a heck of a thing to ask a lady!" she snapped, suddenly agitated, even though I thought it was a perfectly reasonable thing to ask.

"But to answer your question: Yes. I *did* them both. But I had no choice in the matter. Slavery is a tricky business like that."

She took the canteen from me, swallowed another long drink, then spoke with a cooler head. "I suppose you want to know the details," she said.

I stared at my shoes, unsure if I actually wanted to know the details.

"Well, I ain't into given' details," she said. "But I'll say this: my affair with Masta' was a bit-on-the-side sort of thing…a wham-bam thank you, slave…while my affair with Billy was more of a puppy-love, coming-of-age kinda thing."

"See now, Masta' Beasley humped me wherever he damn-well pleased, but Billy only humped me late at night, in the privacy of the hay loft, and it usually took several hours of drinkin' for young Billy to work up the courage. He would talk and talk and talk beforehand…and I mean that boy could talk…he'd talk about his ma and pa, talk about things he'd done in school, talk about going places and seeing things in the world, talk about white people things that I knew nothing about."

"I'd just sit there in the hay, listenin', sippin' from the jar of liquor we'd pass back and forth…until Billy was finally done talkin' and ready to go."

And I sat there listenin' and sippin' likewise, but on the tailgate of a wagon, overlooking a wondrous lake on the edge of the known world. It almost sounded like Violet was taking a step to liberate herself from her promiscuous past, and it felt good to be the guy that she was venting to. I waited until she paused to take a drink, then I asked the biggest question on my mind.

"How old was Billy?"

"Oh, funny you should ask that. One night…say bout' four years ago…Billy told me that we was both eighteen, that we was born just weeks apart. He said that I was born on February three of eighteen-twenty-four. He'd looked it up in Masta's books. I never knew my birthday until that moment."

"I think today is October 21st," I said. "Or maybe it's the 22nd…I don't know anymore. Irwin kept better track of the date than me."

I glanced back at Irwin's blanket-covered body, but I might as well have been staring at the sky, because my mind was somewhere in the clouds, thinking about Violet and all her humping around the plantation.

"Violet, have you any children?"

"No." she quickly answered. "Masta' always covered his parts in lambskin— and I suppose he passed that knowledge to his son."

I suddenly hiccuped, and trail brew came surging out of my nostrils. I coughed and gagged and turned away, wiping my face with my sleeve.

While I struggled to get ahold of myself, Violet grew silent and stared out across the lake. Along the far southern shore, an osprey launched from a tall grove of pines and glided over the lake to hunt for fish. Violet's eyes followed the bird of prey as it banked into a gentle descent and skimmed across the surface of the water. Its wicked talons unfolded, then it struck the water, snatching a big silver-colored fish and rising high above the lake in one elegant swoop.

"Wow, did you see that?!" she cheered.

I did, but I wasn't feeling so cheerful about things.

No, I was feeling whiter than ever. And guilty by association. And I wanted to tear my skin from the bone and wave it in surrender like a bloody white flag, and show her that I'm not like the others, that I'm not part of the evil white conspiracy to control the world.

Or tell her that I want *our* first time to be a mutual agreement…and not a fling in a stinking hay loft.

Or tell her that a lambskin isn't necessary. Let's just go raw. Impregnate her with my half-black baby and make her mine forever.

I didn't say any of that, thank God. But it was hard not to, because I was feeling the trail brew. And my thoughts were on the tip of my tongue. Luckily, Violet spoke first.

"I'm starting to feel it," she said, looking tenderly at me, eyelids at half-mast.

I felt her hand move playfully over the top of my thigh.

"Starting to feel what?" I said, perking upright.

Violet laughed, stole the canteen out of my hand, and swilled another drink.

"I'm feeling the courage to go for a swim," she said, suddenly excited.

She jumped down from the tailgate and bounced on the balls of her feet. She smiled brightly at me, looking like she was ready and willing to try anything. "Let's take one more drink, then go for it," she said, pushing the canteen back into my hands. "I love the water. I practically taught myself how to swim."

I considered her proposition, pictured her soaking wet and stepping in and out of the water. Then I clapped my hands enthusiastically and jumped down from the tailgate. "Let's do it!" I yelped.

Violet took another long swig, then bent forward to untie the rags she called shoes. "Let's get away from the others," she said. "Let's walk along the beach until we find a secluded spot."

Directly in front of us, the Crabtree siblings were fooling around by the water's edge, stripping out of their ragged garments and wading into the surf to wash the filth from their skinny white bodies. Our camp was full of activity that I hadn't noticed. Men were piling tinder for a fire, and Boggs, the ex-priest Daulton, and Calvin Crabtree men were standing around it, passing a vat and chatting loudly.

I agreed that we should go for a walk. And why not? The timing was perfect. The sun was setting, and a mirror image of a brilliant red twilight painted the surface of the lake.

With our bare feet sinking in the cool sand, we went prancing on down the shoreline. We walked side by side for a while, skipping rocks, shooting the breeze, and giggling about all kinds of things, until the beach ended at a natural jetty of huge granite boulders.

I looked at her with a curious grin. "Still want to get in?"

"Yes," she answered with a happy nod.

She pulled her gown over her head and threw it aside. And just like that, she was standing there in her underwear. And by God! There they were. Two luscious balls of brown-nippled breast.

"Should I take off my underwear?" she asked.

I made a thoughtful face, trying not to stare too hard. "I'm probably gonna' remove mine," I said. "To keep them dry."

She nodded, then quickly pulled her underwear down and jumped out of them.

Now in the stunning nude, she turned away and went prancing along the edge of the jetty and waded into the water. I stood there for moment, beside myself, watching the jiggle in her bare rump as she stepped further out. Then I pulled off my shirt and pants and kicked them into a pile. I stepped to the edge of the water, feeling bold, and grinning like the luckiest bastard in the world.

Violet made a yelping sound as she plunged down into the water. "Come on in," she called out, now neck deep and doggie-paddling with her hands. "It feels great!"

I dipped my bare toes into the water. It was actually cold as ice, but the whiskey was pumping hot through my veins. I pulled my underwear down quickly and jumped in before she could get a good look at my emaciated frame and pasty whiteness.

I weaved circles around her like a playful dolphin. She splashed and giggled, then came surging out of the water, threw her hands over my shoulders, and pushed me under.

I grabbed her leg and pulled her down with me. Her warm body clutched against mine as we sank into the cold, clear water.

Then we surfaced, facing one another. Her legs were wrapped around my waist, and our parts were touching. Above the jetty, a black outline of pines stabbed into the last traces of daylight.

It was Violet who kissed me first. Kissed me right on the lips, hard and fast and full of tongue. Then she pushed me away and slowly climbed out of the water. She found a flat slab of boulder and laid upon it. Then she called me over.

I fell on top of her and took a savage grip of her wet naked body. Words can't describe what it's like to make love to Violet, but I'll say this: it's like being lifted to a place that only a beautiful black angel can take you. Absolute Heaven, if I had to call it something.

But for an instant, there, I had this troubling feeling that I was taking advantage of her, like the white slavers of her past. But when I tried to ease up, she clutched me tighter and stared deeply into my eyes with a wild intensity, wanting it badly, refusing to let me go.

I sensed this doomed sort of passion in her lovemaking, as if our worlds would soon come to a burning end, but I didn't linger on the notion very long, for the bodily sensations I felt were nothing short of euphoric, and the warm bursting of my seed blew my mind to mush.

When the deed was done, we just laid there on the jetty for a while, warming each other with our bodies and counting the stars as they came alive.

I remembered the little green cigarette in the pocket of my trousers, and we shared a smoke. Then we made love one more time, before Violet finally got up and pulled her clothes back on. When she was fully dressed, she stood over me and said she wanted to return to camp.

"Do we have to leave?" I said with a pout. I wanted to stay on the jetty forever, because to leave this place meant a return to reality…Irwin's failing health…and our slow descent into chaos and starvation…and I loathed to face it again.

I laid back on the boulder and closed my eyes, satisfied enough with life to die a happy man. "I'd rather just lay here, with you, all night," I said, wistfully.

But Violet was anxious to return to camp. "I need to check on my brothers and sisters," she insisted. "And you should check on Irwin." Her tone was calm but sort of testy. She looked at me with eyes that said this: I gave you what you wanted, now take me home.

Chapter Eleven

A frosty wind was lashing through the bow when I awoke the next morning. I rolled over to check on Irwin. He looked white and stiff enough to be dead.

I tried to shake him awake, but he only coughed and wheezed, refusing to move or open his eyes.

"I'm heading out for coffee," I said.

Nothing. No response.

It was early and the sun had yet to clear the mountain peaks to the east. The air was cold and rife with the crisp smell of pine forest. A thick fog hung over the lake and a thin layer of frosty dew covered everything.

It was the cold and gloomy morning of an oncoming winter, no doubt, but I rose in a warm giddy sort of mood nonetheless. For after three months of chasing Violet down the high road through hell, we had finally tested the waters of our love, and it made the struggle seem all worthwhile.

My hopes for the day were high, and riding the tail of my soaring confidence came this rich little plan to invite Violet on a fishing trip and catch a fat lake salmon for dinner.

We'll make it a date. Just me, my golden-brown ladylove, and the bluest lake ever.

It seemed like a good way to spend some quality time with her and demonstrate my commitment beyond a one-night flyer. Plus, it was a good opportunity to teach her a thing or two about surviving off the land.

In preparation for said fishing date, I set about knotting a hook to a ball of yarn, then dug up a handful of earthworms for bait.

I donned my cleanest clothes: Brown trousers, a white-ish shirt, and a brown vest.

Violet was already awake, sitting upright, watching my approach with squinted eyes. A canvas sheet was spread over the beach beneath her, and three or four tattered wool blankets were thrown together to shield her and her siblings from the cold mist blowing off the lake.

"Morning, Violet" I gaily said, prancing across the sand with an eager grin and a fistful of earthworms wiggling in my left hand.

Violet rose to her feet with a blanket wrapped around her shoulders. She looked about fourteen years old in that moment, her green eyes puffy from sleep, her ropy locks falling every which way. "Good morning," she said with a drowsy yawn. "How's Irwin?"

I looked back at my wagon, its canvas hood looking ever so dingy against the creeping white mist. "Still sleeping," I said. "He coughed throughout the night and cursed everything and everyone, but now Daulton's wife is tending to him, so I'm off to catch a salmon." I nodded towards the lake. "Wanna' come fishing? I could use the company."

The commotion I was causing had set forth the awakening of the other ex-slaves. Daphne rolled over and Donavon slowly lifted his head, blinking confusedly at the daylight. Violet looked down at them, wavering over my invitation. I stayed rooted before her, growing more nervous with every lingering second, the earthworms wiggling out through my fingers.

"Fishing," she said evenly, without eye contact. "Okay. Sounds fun."

I offered my hand to her, but she ignored it and instead followed behind me at her own leisure pace.

We walked along the beach until we came upon a shallow cove and the rocky jetty where we held congress last night.

I stopped and stared glowingly at the exact slab of hard rock where we'd laid.

"A bed of roses," I said. "The scene of my finest hour."

Violet, however, looked tired and said nothing. I figured she was just hungover and shrugged it off.

We sat down together on a flat portion of rock along the water's edge. I hooked the earthworm three times over while it wiggled in agony. "So it don't fall off," I explained.

Violet yawned and nodded meekly.

I tossed the line out and settled in, staring dumbly into the crystal-clear water, waiting for the king salmon to come lurching across the bottom towards my bait.

The jetty looked different in the daylight. The boulders were more jagged, and beyond it, the pointed crowns of the pines faded into the morning fog. The mountains were completely obscured.

Violet sat quietly with her arms wrapped around her knees, hardly looking interested. After a few dull minutes passed, she leaned forward and toyed with her hair in the water's reflection.

At that point, I couldn't stand the silence any longer. I suddenly exploded with raw emotion. "I could sing it from a mountaintop!" I professed. "Last night was amazing!!"

I jumped to my feet and rambled passionately about our "first time" and how it "changes everything". I figuratively gave her the keys to my heart, demonstrating this by actually reaching out with my fingers pinched around an invisible key, then delivering a long flattering tribute to her physical gifts and outright beauty.

I'd never felt so bold. So eagerly in love.

But the bootlicking and the buttery compliments seem to float right past Violet without stopping. She looked unimpressed, sitting there with a sulky expression that said she'd heard it all before and was not surprised by my enthusiasm for her. And as such, my fiery homage was followed by a short, uncomfortable silence.

"I hope you catch a fish soon," she said, so quietly that I barely understood. "I'm starving."

"Patients my Queen," I insisted, trying to sound lively and devoted, although Violet's quietness was beginning to bother me. There was something different about her today; something was certainly off…but I chalked it up to a bad hangover and tried not to linger on the matter. All new relationships have their rough patches, I thought, but love endures all in time.

I tried to focus on fishing. I jerked the line in a tactful fashion and trolled the bait across the surface of the water, hoping these maneuvers would somehow attract a monster fish to my hook.

But it was hard to focus. I could feel her sitting glumly beside me. I thought about planting a kiss on her lips, figuring that might snap her out of her funk, but when I puckered up and leaned into her, she cringed and stiffly curled her lips against her teeth. I ended up kissing her on the cheek instead. A mild, awkward peck of a kiss that she took rigidly, saying nothing.

Feeling buffaloed, I turned my attention back to the fishing line and stared down at the water.

* * *

Violet sat there for another hour or so, watching me fish with a bored look on her face. Not a single fish was caught during this time, and with every empty hook reeled in, her bored look seemed to harden or settle more permanently until she finally stood up and declared that she was walking back to camp. She needed to check on her family, she explained, without eye contact or a smile of any kind.

I said goodbye and watched her skip away.

Then it was just me, an empty hook, and my frustrated thoughts.

Rather fittingly, the day withered cold and grey. A heavy overcast settled over the lake, concealing the mountains, the western pass, and the future horrors that awaited us.

Sometime around high noon, I stood up and moved to the far side of the cove where the water was darker and deeper, figuring a change of scenery might help. I was determined to catch something, because my mind was stuck on this happy little vision where I saw myself bringing the whole party together for what we called a 'fish fry' back in Boston. I saw my fellow travelers filling their empty stomachs with the tasty salmon that I caught, and singing my praises for it, slapping me on the back and commending me on my shrewd fishing skills. And with my newfound hero status, Violet's unpleasant attitude would take a turn. She'd come to stand beautifully at my side and gaze upon me with eyes full of admiration, utterly impressed by my masculinity and woodsmanship. And everyone in attendance would understand that she was *my love...* And after dinner, she'd whisper into my ear: *'Hey Peter, let's go back to the jetty and go for another round.'*

Indeed, I had the golden vision. So there I sat by the water, hooking worms and relentlessly casting my line, and hoping all this time and energy spent might work out in my favor.

Then I heard strange rustling in the bushes behind me. I thought it was Violet, but no. Boggs appeared about ten feet to my left, stomping towards the water's edge without a hat or a shirt. He suddenly jumped off the rocks and plunged into the water, making a huge splash like a cannonball falling from the clouds.

Now standing in knee-high water, he unbuckled his belt, pulled his pants down, and dug into the ratty bush between his legs, fondling for his pecker.

The next thing I heard was the trickling sound of water hitting water.

Boggs was like a pig in the wild, greasy and filthy and free to shit and piss wherever he pleased. He groaned and rolled his bushy head around to look my way. "Pee-nuts!" he snorted over the trickling sound. "Catch anything yet?"

"Nothing," I miserably replied, looking down at my hook, watching it float limp across the clear water like some kind of repellent, and feeling ever more disappointed in the day.

Boggs raised his hand from his pecker and scratched at his face. "Hell, that's 'cause you're doing it all wrong," he said. He pulled his pants up and squinted his eyes down at the pee-stained water, looking very closely, then drew his pistol.

BOOM!

The gunshot echoed sharply across the cove. Birds exploded from the pines in screeching panic. Boggs squinted closer at the water to see if he'd shot anything.

I shook my head. "You brainless monster," I muttered. "You're scaring all the fish away."

Boggs ignored me. He started waving his pistol above the water in a sloppy figure-eight motion. BOOM! He bucked off another ear-splitting round. Water shot up from the surface and sprayed in his eyes. Only a person with dogshit for brains would fish this way, I thought.

"Goddamnit," he grumbled, wiping the water from his face.

"Anything?" I asked, fake smiling.

Boggs watched the water for a moment. His face slowly collapsed into a disappointed snarl, and he holstered his pistol and turned back towards the shore. "You'd better catch something," he hollered. "We're out of fresh meat until another animal dies…or until somebody shoots that useless horse of Irwin's."

* * *

The sky was dim with nightfall by the time I quit. I had withstood twelve hours of boredom to catch one skinny little sunfish about the size of my hand. It was enough to feed a man for the night, but not enough to feed an entire wagon party. In the end, the fat salmon eluded my bait, and the fishing trip was, by and large, a failure.

I returned to camp only to discover more disappointment. As it turned out, I'd been out-fished by the Crabtree Brothers, who had caught four pink-striped salmon, each the size of a man's thigh, plus eight other smaller fish—this by dragging a large net along the bottom of the lake. They had rekindled the campfire and were pan-frying the fish with wild onions and a sprinkle of salt, and the evening morphed into that jolly fish fry that I had fantasized about, only without me as the hero. The man of honor went to Calvin Crabtree instead, who was dressed for the part in a pair of silky black trousers with a clean, blue button-down shirt and black suspender straps.

And he was in a cheery mood. He laughed as he took my little sunfish and added it to the frying pans. "Young man, you come fishing with me tomorrow morning," he said. "I'll teach you a thing or two."

His face was clean-shaven for the first time in months, his thin hair was neatly combed over his balding scalp.

"I'd like that," I lied.

Clearly, he'd taken a bath in the lake to freshen up for the occasion, but his breath still reeked of trail brew.

After our little talk, Crabtree removed a frying pan from the fire and walked around the campfire with it, showboating the huge pink fillet of salmon steaming in its midst. With a slight bow, he presented the fillet to the ex-slaves. Violet reached out with her plate. Crabtree tilted the pan, and the fillet slid down onto her plate in a globule of hot fish grease.

Violet tore off a chunk with her hands, then passed the plate down to her siblings, who each pounced on it like starving children. Beyond them, the mountains were outlined black against a gray night sky. The lake below was dark and silent. The beach glowed in the orange light of the roaring fire.

Crabtree lingered over Violet for a moment, grinning like a volunteer at a soup kitchen. Violet uttered a thank you and flashed a tender-eyed smile, and Crabtree took it as an opening to start a conversation with her.

I couldn't hear exactly what he was saying, but he said something that made her laugh—a happy little laugh that one typically makes after hearing a flattering line.

I gritted my teeth as they spoke, watching with one hawking eye from the opposite side of the fire, hardly minding the plate of hot salmon sitting on my lap.

A most powerful feeling of jealousy came over me. My heel started tapping anxiously into the sand, and baleful thoughts concerning Violet's promiscuous past swirled around my brain, plus the fact that Calvin was the only Crabtree brother without a wife and children.

And the more I thought about that, the more it set my teeth on edge. And sure, I probably looked crazy, sitting there, staring and twitching and mumbling to myself…and not wanting to be seen in this pitiful state, or witness any more of the flirty moves Crabtree was making on Violet, I decided to step away and fall back into the darkness behind the wagons, where I could grumble to myself out of public view, and wonder just who in the hell was Crabtree trying to impress with that comb-over?

With the exception of our wounded captain, the entire party was gathered around the warm light of the campfire to eat fish and drink trail brew. Everyone was eating or talking, laughing or prancing around the beach. Everyone was having a gay old time.

But not me. I viewed this elegant scene from the shadows like an uninvited guest. I felt lonesome and depressed. I'd been out-fished by a drunken fool with a comb-over, and my ebony princess wanted nothing to do with me.

"Trouble in paradise?" said a faint voice.

It was Irwin, still lying stationary in the wagon bed, but cognizant and speaking for the first time in many days. It was a good sign that his health might be improving, but my frumpy mood was burrowed deep, and my sense of humor was spent. "Whatever," I said with a dismissive wave. "She's been acting strange ever since… well, ever since we went swimming last night."

"Take it easy on her," he said in a voice that barely cracked a whisper. "The less you talk, the more you'll get laid," he said. "Trust me."

I stepped closer to the wagon bow to talk to him, but my eyes were peeled at the activity around the campfire. "That makes no sense," I muttered. "What do you know about women anyways? Besides that red-headed whore back in Boston…the one you spent five years financing. What was her name? Margret? Or was it Ginger? Whatever, it doesn't matter because Violet is no whore. She's a lady. A homemaker. The marriage and have-your-children type. Not the type that charges a fee for services."

Irwin started to say something, but his speech was overpowered by a thunderous, phlegm-snapping cough.

"Can you shut up," I hissed at him. "I can't hear what he's saying to her."

In the orange glowing distance, Calvin Crabtree took a step closer to Violet and reached out with a tin cup, offering it to her.

Violet, still holding a smile, reached out and accepted the cup. She gently sipped and handed it back to him. Then he said something and pointed in the direction of his wagon, and she stood, and together they walked away from the fire, and out of my line of sight.

"Where the hell are they going?!" I grumbled, glaring into the darkness where they disappeared.

"Stop all that caterwauling and go over there," said Irwin, straining to hold his cough down. "Before your woman bares another man's child."

"Shut up," I said, highly annoyed.

Impatiently, I waited behind the wagon for Violet's return to the campfire, which took about ten minutes, but felt like an eternity. She was wearing a new shirt when she finally appeared, an oversized lemon-colored button-down that hung loose over top of her gown. She sat in the same spot, beside her siblings, while Calvin Crabtree moseyed over to the opposite side of the fire. He brandished a tobacco pipe, pulled a hot stick from the fire to spark it, then sat on a log with his legs crossed, taking long drags and blowing huge clouds of blue smoke with a satisfied air.

I was done playing games at that point. It was time to man up and take a more direct approach to the matter, I thought. Time to confront Violet head-on, and do it now before another man snakes his way in.

I took a steel grip of myself and vaulted out of the darkness, approaching Violet from behind. I kneeled beside her and spoke right away. "Hey, is everything okay?"

A startled look shot across her face. She glared at me, then rolled her eyes back towards the fire. "I'm fine," she said shortly.

She looked unconcerned about me, or indifferent to my lingering presence, and it made me feel low and unwanted. I started to say something in my defense (or to rescue my pride) but was sidetracked by the gawking stares I felt coming from the fire-glowing faces of her siblings, stares that seemed to be ridiculing my love-sick state. I tilted my head sideways and shot a mean glare back at them. They reacted by altogether looking away from me, all four black faces turning in unison.

But it still felt like they were listening to me. Distressed by this, I spoke softly so nobody but Violet could overhear. "Want to go for a walk with me?" I asked, desperately wanting to get some distance between us and camp, and reclaim the magic we shared the night before.

"We could go swimming again," I said. "Still got a splash of trail brew in my canteen."

There was an awkward pause ahead of Violet's response. She glanced at her siblings and half-yawned, then said that it was too cold to go swimming.

All hope seemed lost after that, but I still had one last desperate heave left in me. "I could set up a tent beside my wagon," I quietly pleaded. "You could stay the night with me…."

Violet's eyes shifted slightly in the direction of my wagon. "Oh, I don't think so," she said. "No. I'd rather sleep with my family."

My desperate heave landed with a dull thud. I felt thoroughly defeated and stood up to leave, but I couldn't accept the rejection without saying something petty as I departed. "That's the ugliest shirt I've ever seen," I muttered, bitterly. "You look like a giant banana."

Violet made no reply to this. Her eyes stayed fixed on the fire as I walked away.

Not another word passed between us that night. And just like that, in less than a day's time, our relationship went from hot glory in the sunshine, to a cold shoulder in the rain. It felt like I'd climbed to the top of the world's most glorious mountain and finally planted my flag, only to go tumbling down the backside, an uncontrollable slide back to loneliness and misery and for reasons that made little or no sense at all.

Her hot and cold behavior was totally baffling. It broke my spirit and kept me awake long into the wee hours that night, trying to find meaning in it.

But at the end of the day, all I could do was accept her sporadic behavior as part of the business of loving an ex-slave with a damaged soul. And I accepted the agony, because I'd tasted the sweet blackberry pie, and I was hooked.

Chapter Twelve

I went to sleep to the sound of rain pattering against the canvas hood overhead but awoke the next morning to the sight of **snow**. A fresh inch of it had accumulated on the ground between the wagons.

Camp stirred with trepidation as men measured their waking, blinking eyes against the snow. Wagons were hitched up in all haste, no debating it, no conferences. Boggs simply pulled out first, followed by the Crabtree Brothers, then the ex-priest, and the ex-slaves walking between the wagons with blankets wrapped around their bodies for warmth.

And back on the emigrant road, we went. Heading for that final drive over the mountains and trudging along ever so slowly on an uprising path through the snowy pines, with the canvas hoods battered by a biting wind and dark, heavy clouds hanging over the western peaks.

My wagon took up the rear. Cousin Wilbur drove the animals while I walked behind the tailgate in my leather snow boots, cocooned against the cold everything i owned: several layers of socks, shirts, and pants, and wearing a gray wool frock coat that I considered my winter coat.

Just beyond the head of the lake, the trail passed an abandoned log cabin centered in a snow-spotted clearing amongst the pines. It was a small, primitive dwelling with no windows and a mere opening for a front door. Nothing unusual about it—but it was the first cabin we'd seen in months, which seemed to warrant a closer look.

Boggs halted his oxen. He drew his pistol and turned his eyes over the cabin, while the other wagons caught up and parked behind him. Calvin Crabtree went forward with his rifle. Boggs and Crabtree briefly conferred, then Crabtree stepped towards the cabin with his rifle shouldered like a lawman raiding an outlaw's hideout, but making a ton of noise as his boots crunched through the snow.

He paused about ten feet from the doorway.

"Anybody in there?" he called out.

No response.

Crabtree hesitated a second, then continued through the doorway without invitation. We all waited in the windy cold to see what would happen. A long moment passed before Crabtree reappeared through the doorway with his rifle slung casually behind his shoulder.

"Ain't nobody…" he said with a shrug.

"Nobody?" snorted Boggs.

"…Nobody."

We drove on. Beyond the cabin, we began a steep-graded ascent into the mouth of a canyon that would pass us through the high Sierras. The snow was three inches deep, then four inches, then five, increasing with each added increment of altitude, while our overall pace decreased to a frigid crawl.

A drift of snow fell from a pine and pummeled our wagon with a heavy thud. I watched to see if Irwin would move or open his eyes, but he only wheezed, and that was it. Then I heard footsteps splashing towards me through the snow. It was Violet. She placed a hand on the tailgate and glanced through the bow to study Irwin. Her other hand was clutched tightly to the tattered wool blanket wrapped around her head and body. She looked like a ragged nun, despite her saucy hellcat ways.

"How's he doing?" she shouted against the wind.

I glared at her, surprised by her initiative to speak to me, a sudden shift from the cold-shoulder treatment.

"He's a corpse heading for a hole in the ground," I said miserably. "I can't escape the thought that he might be dead the next time I check on him."

Violet looked down at her feet and skipped to avoid a puddle of wet snow. The wagon went on slowly, creaking up the snowy trail. "We should have stayed by the lake or returned to the desert," she said. "I think we're making a terrible mistake by climbing higher into these mountains."

I looked at her and sighed. "You're probably right," I shouted back. "But I'm just following Boggs and the Crabtree Brothers like everyone else...and you didn't seem too worried about following Calvin Crabtree around the other night, or eating his fish or wearing his ugly yellow shirt and going off to his wagon *to do God knows what.*"

Violet stared back at me, skipping across slushy ruts to keep up. "We didn't *do* anything," she said. "But sometimes a girl has to be friendly in order to secure herself a meal, something your white ass wouldn't understand."

I matched her steely glare. I was crazy in love with her and it was frustrating—frustrating to not know what I was going to get from her on a day-to-day basis, a frustration that boiled over into my reply. "So that's what it's all about?" I shouted, stomping my boots through the slush. "You just love a man when you're hungry?!"

Violet's eyes narrowed. "I'd rather starve!" she shouted. "Then give my cooch to a white man for a measly bite to eat. I can provide for myself. White men are only good for getting in the way of that."

I was ready to say the most unflattering thing I could think of, when I noticed the dark heavy clouds seemed to be moving down from the high western peaks, and entering the canyon ahead.

"Looks like more snows a-comin'," I said with a fiery snap. "I'd change that tune if I were you...and start lovin' on any white man with food to spare...that's if you aim to survive the winter." It was a terrible thing to say, but I was a powder keg of raw emotion set to explode. "You hear me, woman?" I shouted. "More snows a-comin'! Time to start choosing up!!"

A harsh gust of wind thrashed through Violet's blanket. She looked up to study the stormy skies. "I aim to survive," she said in a lower, withdrawn tone. Her green eyes seemed to capture the storm's intensity with a quivering twinkle, then snap downward as she shuffled her feet sideways to avoid another slush hole in the road.

I half-expected her to continue moving away from me, on account of my hissy fit, but then she caught back up to the tailgate and fixed me with a challenging stare, waiting for me to say something else.

I grew timid and looked away. I loved her too much to continue arguing with her. I took a calming breath and found myself staring down at my leather snow boots, then looking at her feet and the pitiful tangle of rags wrapped around them.

I watched her step in and out of a slush hole.

"I want you to have my boots," I said. "My foot is probably bigger than yours, but you can stuff rags inside the insoles to fill the extra space."

"I don't want your boots," she said, coldly.

I lifted my head and stared her down. "You need my boots, or you'll get frostbite, and your feet will turn black and fall off. I'm from New England. I know a thing or two about snow. And you're from…well…I'm not exactly sure where you or your people hail from…but it's somewhere warm, I suspect…and I doubt you know anything about snow. I'm not trying to get in your way, Violet. I'm merely trying to help."

"My feet are fine. I don't need your boots."

"What did I do wrong? Why don't you want me?"

"You haven't done anything wrong. It's just a bad time to be involved with someone."

"I would marry you."

"What!?"

"I would marry you." I wildly repeated, then pointed to the tallest, snow-covered mountain in view. "If there was a church up on that mountain, I'd carry you up there in my arms and have the minister make you my wife."

Violet rolled her eyes down to the snow at her feet, saying nothing, holding her blanket from the gusting wind.

"Maybe it's a bad time to be in love," I said. "But the heart wants what it wants. I love you…and I'll do anything for you to love me back."

It felt liberating, saying these things.

Violet slowly raised her eyes to look at me. "Anything?" she said with sudden interest. "Okay. Take me hunting."

"Hunting?" I repeated, confused by the request. "You mean, like, hunting for animals?"

She nodded. "Yup. That kind of hunting."

"Umm, sure. Yes. Why not? Let's go hunting."

Violet's face softened, and her eyes turned over the wind-gnashed pines that edged the trail. "We can shoot something," she said. "Something meaty, like a deer. When's the best time to go?"

I looked thoughtfully at the dark, menacing sky. "We'll have to ride the storm out first," I said. "Then we'll go."

She nodded. "You can teach me all about hunting," she said. "Let's go as soon as we can."

"It's a date," I said, smiling warmly against the cold wind. "We'll shoot anything that moves."

The coming storm would see an end to the warm sentiment. The sky turned utterly black, the wind howled violently, and the snow fell in such a dense cascade that everywhere I looked was suddenly white.

I lost sight of Violet. Lost sight of my own wagon. Ran dead smack into the tailgate and fell backwards into a heap of snow.

Looking up from the ground, I saw millions and millions of egg-sized snowballs showering over me.

And the snow piled up so fast that all we could do was make camp on the spot. Men scrambled in the raging whiteout to park wagons and tie up animals. I helped Wilbur set the brakes, then lent a hand in excavating a dugout under the high wheels so that the ex-slaves had a place to hunker down and ride out the storm. Then I nestled up with Irwin in the wagon bed to keep him warm with my body heat. The only thing left to eat was pine nuts and dried apple slices. I tried feeding the apples to Irwin, but he refused to chew and swallow.

Chapter Thirteen

The storm was gone when I awoke the next morning. It was bitterly cold, and for a long time I just laid there in the wagon bed with my ear pressed against the wooden floorboards, listening to the ex-slaves in the dugout below. I could hear them shifting around, snoring and groaning, one tight pile of ragged black bodies trying to keep each other warm.

I peeked my head through the bow to find the wagon buried to the top of the high wheels in snow. Frozen and still was the outside world. White as far as the eyes could see. Pure sparkling white.

The imprint of the trail was no longer visible. No trees, no rocks, no tracks, no traces of man or animal. Nothing but an ocean of snow.

I wrapped myself in my blanket, leapt off the tailgate, landed in waist-high snow with an icy splash. For a long moment I just floundered there, astounded, horrified, shivering, a frosty cloud of steam exhaling with each breath.

The sun came and went behind scattered cloud cover. Behind me, six snowy canvas hoods of six buried wagons loomed in six drifts of snow.

Everything white and buried.

It slowly came to my attention that our herd of animals was thinner in number than the night before. Then I noticed the two soft humps of glittering snow in the middle of camp, where two oxen had laid down to die.

Then it hit me like a frozen snowball: Ringo was missing.

My heart fluttered with panic and my head spun in a circle, eyes searching for any sign of the big brown quarterhorse. A broken piece of leather harness dangled from the wagon sidewall where Ringo had been hitched, but because the storm had erased all tracks from the snow, there was no telling which direction he'd wandered off in.

I now stood in a waist-deep hole that my revolving feet had packed down, sullenly staring over the white hellscape like a man who had just lost his very own soul. I heard the crunching footfalls of men gathering to discuss what to do next. Men that were bitterly cold and half-starved, the dire tension of which coursed through their conversation. They spoke in confused outbursts about food and shelter and looked around for a trail to follow with eyes that were wide and sullen and searching like mine.

Boggs loomed over the gathering crowd with an ax in his hand. The two dead oxen lying under the snow drifts belonged to him and were the last of his animals. He pointed the ax at the snowdrifts with a hungry gleam in his eyes, and babbled something about it being a 'fine morning to cook a hot steak.'

The more stable voice in the crowd belonged to Calvin Crabtree. He announced that he and his brother Brian were setting out on foot to find a way through the pass, leaving the rest of us behind to wait with the wagons and animals, and to watch Boggs butcher a bloody quagmire in the snow.

I added nothing to the group discussion, but returned to the wagon to inform Irwin of the latest development. "We've lost sight of the trail," I said, despairingly. "Oh, and Ringo wandered off. He chewed through his reins last night."

Irwin remained mute and motionless save for his breathing. I stared at him, feeling like I was on the verge of a nervous breakdown. Everything that could go wrong, had gone wrong. Snow everywhere. No trail to follow. No Ringo. No animals save for one sickly ox that was too weak to pull the wagon through the deep snow. No idea what to do about Irwin, or where to go from here, or where the next meal was coming from.

Fuck, I thought. Fuck, fuck, fuck, fuck. Never had things felt so beyond my control, so hopelessly fucked!

I lowered my head against the tailgate and covered my face with my hands. A sob sputtered out of me. Then another. Water flooded into my eyes, and the dam that held it all back broke. I cried into my hands. Then I heard footsteps crunching through the snow, coming closer. I lifted my head, wiped the tears, saw Violet approaching with her Colt Walker ominously gripped in her left hand.

She was wearing both the yellow shirt and the pink tunic overtop of her gown, with pants underneath to maximize warmth. She looked like a cross-dressed ragdoll against the snow-white landscape. "I'm ready for our hunting date," she said, her pretty green eyes sparkling with eagerness and intent.

"Okay," I said, choking back the sobs.

"Great!" she said. "While we're gone, my siblings will look after Irwin, and dig the wagon out of the snow."

I nodded meekly without looking at her, trying to hide my watery-eyed face. "Let me get my pistol," I said and reached into the wagon bed for my little pepperbox pistol.

Irwin's gunbelt lay in a heap between the empty food barrels, and when I saw it, it gave me pause.

"Irwin?" I said. "Can I borrow the Paterson?"

No reply. I took up the gunbelt and strapped it around my waist. The Colt Paterson was an impressive sidearm—big, reliable, and precise, and having it holstered on my hip helped restore some of my confidence.

I took Violet by the hand, and we went on high-stepping downhill towards a grove of pines that stuck out of the snow like Christmas trees. I led her into the grove, assuming that the nesting grounds of the forest was the best place to hunt game.

The grove was dark and dense. The branches formed a solid canopy over our heads, and the forest floor was snowless; nothing got through the canopy save for a few beams of golden daylight that crisscrossed the darkness like tiny little spotlights. A brown carpet of pine straw crunched under our feet as we advanced side-by-side between the sappy trunks. I drew up the Paterson and walked cautiously, my ears trained to the sounds of the forest, my eyes scanning, searching for signs of animals.

Violet, making an attempt to be keen and focused likewise, stepped lightly while holding the Colt Walker upright like an axe. Whenever she heard a suspicious noise, she would point the long barrel in the sound's general direction and squint her eyes down the sights. I kicked a pinecone by mistake and watched in horror as she swung the barrel in my direction.

"Mother of God!" I loudly whispered. "Be careful with that thing. And don't shoot until you have a clean shot. The report of that big pistol will spook every animal in the forest."

Violet nodded her head, acknowledging my wisdom, then refixed her sights ahead. We stalked a little deeper into the woods, before taking a break at the root of a huge evergreen to discuss strategy. I had a grasp on the basic elements of hunting, but wondered if there was a better way to go about this; perhaps lure the animals into a trap using bait, or stage some sort of mating call, rather than stomping through the forest with our guns swinging around like a couple of hillbillies.

But Violet seemed to have other ideas. She placed her pistol down on the root of a tall pine and stepped inside my breathing space.

"My hands are freezing," she said with a frisky shiver. "Can you help me warm them?"

Before I could react, she lunged at me and pushed her hands through the inside of my coat, hugging tight around my bare waist.

Her fingers felt like frozen icicles against my skin. I yelped and tried to leap out of her frigid grasp, but she hugged me tighter, shoving her hands further down the waistline of my trousers.

"Jiminy Christmas!" I squealed, backstepping against the trunk of the pine.

Violet snickered playfully, refusing to let me go. "I need your warmth!" she cried, rather fiendishly.

I watched the expression on her face, wondering how she could look so giddy and worry-free at a time like this. A crooked smile struck her lips as her hands slid further down into my trousers, rubbing against a sensitive part of me that was starting to rise from hibernation.

Then she stopped laughing. With her breast pressed against my chest, she kissed me on the neck.

The mood shifted abruptly from teasing to sensual, and the next thing I knew, we were both pulling our pants down in a frenzy of hot burning desire. And right atop the tree roots, in the midst of the wintry forest, we made love.

It was a raw and powerful affair that lasted only a few moments, but forever left the impression on me that Violet was a woman with promiscuous needs. That behind those innocent green eyes lurked a wild and unrestrained side of her that wanted to dance naked and set someone's world on fire.

When she was finished with me, she pulled her pants up and readjusted her gown overtop. She fixed her dreadlocks behind her ears, wrapped her blanket around her shoulders, and picked up her Colt from the tree roots. "I say we keep on hunting," she said, talking normally again. "I hate the thought of going back empty-handed."

She was acting like nothing had happened. Like love was just a game that ended whenever she felt tired of it.

But I played along anyways, because she had me wrapped tight around those long brown fingers of hers.

"I think we should split up," I said, fixing my hat and coat, re-buckling the gun belt, and tucking my shirt underneath. "That should increase our odds of stirring up something to shoot, I think."

I refocused my energy on the hunt, suddenly feeling this strong desire to make this outing a success, and thus prove my worth.

Show her that I was a man. And the only man she needed.

With the barrel of my pistol, I pointed to a distant strip of daylight where the forest ended. "You go that way," I instructed her, then turned and waved my barrel in the opposite direction, saying, "And I'll go this way, then circle back around. Hopefully, this maneuver will draw the animals towards you, so you can shoot em' dead."

Violet nodded. "Sounds like a plan," she said, then turned and quietly trotted away with her pistol at the ready.

And so we split up. But after five minutes of walking in the opposite direction, I ended up turning around and doubling back in a hurry, having completely lost sight of Violet and feeling a tad worried about it. I thought about shouting her name, but stopped myself short of doing so, dedicated as I was to the success of this hunt.

I moved quietly towards the strip of daylight at the edge of the forest where I had instructed her to go—but found nothing but trees and pine straw where I thought she'd be.

I continued moving along the edge of the forest, searching for her and growing ever more worried and disorientated, and thinking about what a stupid plan it was, splitting up like that. Then a strange rustling sound caught my ear. I froze in my tracks and turned my eyes towards the sound, spying movement in the low branches of a large pine tree about ten yards ahead.

"Violet?" I called out. "Is that you?!"

No response. I couldn't see anything, but something, someone was definitely hidden behind the green canopy of that pine tree.

A few heart-pounding seconds passed, then the branches rustled and shook again, and a low, animal-like growl resounded.

I tensed up with this terrified feeling that I was no longer atop the food chain, but a lowly human ventured out of his element and marked for easy prey. And as if to satisfy this feeling, a humongous bear dropped from the pine, landing on all fours with a heavy crashing thud.

My heart stopped dead. Pure absolute terror—no other way to describe it. I was face to face with a huffing monster in a silvery brown coat. It popped its teeth and licked its fangs, its front claws digging into the pine straw, long and sharp enough to slash me open and rip my heart out.

It was a grizzly bear, no doubt about it—its utter burliness and thick muscular body perfectly characteristic of the apex predator that Gaylord Hightower referred to in his book as 'the Giant of the Western Mountains'.

My first instinct was to flee. I briefly considered running out of the forest and into the open snow while screaming desperately for help, but then I remembered that bears run faster than humans, and surely this brute would run me down and tear my head off. To flee would be a terrible mistake, and besides, the black queen was starving, and she wanted meat.

Time to man up and provide.

I leveled my pistol and squeezed the trigger.

Nothing but a dull, empty click.

Misfire.

I squeezed the trigger again, frantically.

Click…Click. Click. Click. Click.

I turned the Colt sideways and glared at it. What the fuck! Did I load it wrong? Were the caps faulty? Meanwhile, the huge grizzly reared up on its hind legs and let out a deep, thunderous roar, standing three feet taller than me and slashing its deadly claws through the air.

I watched in awe, in horror.

Mostly horror.

The bear fell back on all fours, licked its teeth, a predatory gleam in its eyes that said this: I will be mauling you to death now, Pee-nuts, ready for it?

I wasn't. Pushing through the paralyzing fear, I turned on my heels to flee…

BOOM!

A sudden gunshot shattered the air and shocked me in place.

Violet. She came leaping out of the woods, firing twice more in full stride. The grizzly let out a loud, agonizing bark, then stumbled sideways and collapsed on its side, but quickly rolled back to its feet and dashed away with an awkward limp, letting out one final growl before vanishing into the dark bowels of the mountain forest.

The awestruck look on my face said it all. Violet's timing was nothing short of miraculous. She was my savior. A black Angel of Death. While Irwin's trusty Colt had utterly failed me.

I looked down at the gun. "What the hell is wrong with this thing?" I snapped open the cylinder to inspect what was loaded inside. A dash of black powder slipped out but no caps. *Good lord!* There were no bullets in the gun!

Feeling embarrassed by this, I quickly loaded five new caps around the cylinder with a measure of black powder, then slapped the cylinder into a clockwise spin like a gunslinger.

"Lesson learned," I said with a dumb shrug.

"Should we chase after the bear?" asked Violet, squinting distantly into the forest.

I hesitated to respond. My heartbeat was still coming down from the near-fatal encounter. "That thing probably weighed eight hundred pounds," I said.

"That's eight hundred pounds of meat," she replied.

"Okay," I said, puffing my chest out to hide my fear. "Let's go get it."

Violet brought her hand up and seized me by the back of the neck and kissed me hard on the lips. "I hope we kill it," she said.

Before I could get another word out, she turned and went on ahead, stalking deeper into the forest with her eyes low to the ground, looking for a trail of blood to follow.

I followed reluctantly, wondering which creature actually presented more of a danger to me: the monster grizzly bear, or that beauty queen of an ex-slave.

* * *

We searched the forest with our guns locked and loaded for another hour or so, despite losing the blood trail just minutes into the chase. Violet had twice shot the grizzly bear, we were both certain of that much, but that didn't stop the huge beast from getting away. Dead or alive, we never saw that bear again.

It was sometime around high noon when we emerged from the forest. The sun was shining through the clouds, but the air was crisp and cold. The snow was packed solid and the road through the pass was still nowhere to be found.

All said, we had spent the entire morning hunting in the woods and came away with zilch. No meat for dinner. But as far as my relationship with Violet was concerned, it had been a triumphant outing. A physical connection had been reestablished, and it was enough to inspire a pressing forth through the cold, rough patches.

But then we returned to camp, and those rough patches became miles longer and much colder. The entire party was gathered around my wagon and looking mournful. A few were visibly weeping. Irwin was dead. I felt it in my gut before they told me.

I walked by the dreary crowd without stopping and approached the tailgate. Irwin's ghostly head prodded at the far end of his buffalo blanket as it had for many days, but no breath passed through his lips. No rise and fall in his chest.

A snap of cold wind felt like a knife stabbing into my cheeks.

Now in the wake of death, most men fall to prayer. But not me. Because if there was a God, he was a real son-of-a-bitch for what he did to Irwin. And I simply had nothing to say to him. I merely stared at my brother's corpse. I didn't feel like crying, either. I just felt cold. Cold and hollow inside.

The crowd stammered in the snow behind me. Eventually, I turned to them and said, "I'm going to bury him. Here. Today. On the side of this damn mountain."

A grim silence followed. Nobody knew what to say to me. Then a hand fell on my shoulder and the ex-priest quietly said, "I'll help you dig, brother."

I looked around the snowy pass for a suitable spot to dig a grave. There was a low depression about twenty yards out, and as soon as the shovels could be fetched, that's where the ex-priest and I got started.

The digging was slow because the ground was frozen solid. It was hard work, made harder by the ex-priest, who did a lot more talking than digging. And the more he talked, the more deranged he sounded. His frock coat was torn at the shoulder seam, his face was rail thin, and the eyes behind the specs were as beady as ever. He twitched awkwardly, and babbled a bunch of nonsense about how Irwin's true journey had only just begun. Then he asked if I had any trail brew to spare, so that we might toast to Irwin's new voyage.

I stuck the shovelhead in the frozen dirt and stared at him, feeling this sudden rush of anger rising inside me.

I wanted to punch him in the face, and cocked my fist back to do so, but hesitated and gave him a chance to dodge it or at least remove his spectacles. But he just stood there like a sitting duck, so I slugged him.

He dropped like a sack of potatoes and sprawled out flat across the snow, the specs blown from his face, a stunned look in his eyes.

He looked downright pathetic, reaching out with a twitching hand, feeling around for her specs…and it made me switch tunes and feel sorry for him. I took his hand and helped him back on his feet.

"I'm sorry," I said. "I don't know what got into me."

"It's okay," he said, replacing his specs onto the bridge of his nose. "Anger is a natural part of grief." He swayed unsteadily and placed his arm around my shoulder for balance. A trickle of blood leaked from his lower lip.

"I got some trail brew in my canteen," I miserably resigned. "Wait here. I'll go get it."

He waited in the same spot, and was rubbing his bloody lip when I returned with the canteen.

He watched as I poured him a cup. He took a quick sip, gasped, closed his eyes, and smacked his lips together. "Awe, that's the stuff," he said.

"Feeling better?" I asked.

He took another sip, let out a pleasured groan. "Don't worry about the punch," he said. "I'm used to it. My wife hits me all the time. And the more disastrous this trip becomes, the harder she hits." He took another sip, chuckled, and said, "I'm starting to think she doesn't want to be here."

I humored him. "Women," I said. "They never know what they want."

Soon we were drunk and dragging Irwin's corpse across camp. We did our best to lower the corpse into the grave without dropping it, me at the head, the ex-priest at the feet…but the ground was icy, and halfway down the ex-priest slipped, and the corpse dropped and rolled to the bottom of the hole, coming to rest face down.

I glared at the ex-priest and balled my fist, wishing to punch his stupid face all over again.

As I bent down to roll my brother's corpse face up, a dark shadow crossed over the grave-hole. I looked up to find Boggs standing above the grave and holding a huge, half-cooked tomahawk by the bone and gorging on it like a savage. With his other hand, he removed his hat and held it in mourning. "I'd say something from the bible," he said with a mouthful of meat, "but I don't remember any of it."

He nodded his head at the ex-priest. "Go on priest," he said. "Say something biblical to send old Irwin on his way."

The ex-priest finished his drink and tossed the empty cup at Boggs's feet. "Amen to that," he said. "But first, I need another shot of firewater." He pushed his glasses up the bridge of his nose and stared aggressively more or less at Boggs. "On second thought, make it a double shot," he said. "Also, I'll take a bite of that beef."

Boggs dropped the tomahawk to the snow and stepped down into the grave. "You drunken shithead!" he shouted, lashing out and snatching the ex-priest by the neck. "Start preaching before I pound your face in!"

The ex-priest hung like a sad sack in Boggs's grip, too brittle to fight back. "I don't think Irwin was much of a religious man," he nervously whimpered. "What can I say? The old book isn't too kind towards non-believers when it comes to life after death."

Boggs slammed the ex-priest into a snow drift.

The ex-priest cartwheeled, lost his specs, laid out flat, twitched and quaked, and uttered a series of loud, manic groans. "Oh, Good God!" he blurted. "I don't know what I'm saying! I have a terrible headache! Please…just give me another drink so I can think straight again!!"

I stopped listening to this nonsense a long time ago, having sunken into an icy pool of feelings and grief inside my own head. My brother, the Wagon Master, was dead. And it hurt deeply. He was not just an older brother who guarded my best interest with an iron fist, but a brave captain who did everything in his power to save a party of decadent invaders from its own flawed ambitions and the 'every man for himself' mentality that ultimately prevailed. Irwin was a great man and a great leader, simply put, although history will not be kind to him on this point.

* * *

I was shoveling the last bit of dirt over the grave when the Crabtree brothers returned from their scouting mission. Calvin stopped above the grave and stared at the unpacked dirt. He removed his hat and brushed the snow from his wool overcoat. "I hate to be the bearer of more bad news," he said, "but the snow in the pass is ten feet deep. We barely made a half-mile before we were turned back. Looks like we're stuck here."

"Here?" snarled Boggs. "Hellfire. I'm going back downhill to that abandoned cabin."

Calvin looked miserably at his brother. "We were thinking the same thing," he said. "Ditch the wagons and fall back, hunker down inside that cabin, and wait for the snow to melt."

"This calls for a drink!" chimed the ex-priest, dropping his shovel and raising his empty cup to the air. "What do you say, Mr. Whiskey Man? Let's sample the latest batch of trail brew."

Chapter Fourteen

*"The remarks here made, in reference to the mildness, and uniformity
of California's climate, are applicable only to the valleys and plains, **for
the mountains present but one eternal winter.**"*
—Gaylord Hightower, *The Pilgrims' Guide to the West, pg. 94*

All were in agreement to ditch the wagons and withdraw downhill on foot and take shelter in the abandoned cabin until the snow levels were low enough for a breakthrough. It was a cumbersome plan and the timetable for our stay in the cabin was anybody's guess, for Mother Nature and her unpredictable weather patterns had taken control over our wayward odyssey.

I packed my essentials into an old saddle bag for the trip: spare clothes, a blanket, a few books, ammunition, a skinning knife, a tin can containing a handful of pine nuts (the last of my food storage) plus my whiskey canteen… and that was basically it, all that would fit in the sack, thus all I had left in this world.

Climbing out of the wagon, I caught a glimpse of the red leather cover of my diary lying at the very bottom of the cedar chest, and it gave me pause. I had this foreboding sense that I should chronicle my experiences from this point on, that our fantastic failures should be documented for permanent record, so that lessons might be learned by it—my contribution to civilization that I assumed would go on long after I was gone.

I decided that I would make a new diary entry once we reached the cabin, and stuffed the diary into the sack and slung it over my shoulder.

Glancing over the wagon bed one last time, I remembered when it was first packed to the brim with supplies, during those warm spring days at the beginning of our journey. Those days were long gone now, and the bed was empty, stripped down to the floorboards stained red with dry blood, with the ghostly presence of its former captain lingering between the walls.

An awful feeling arose in the pit of my stomach, and it felt like I was getting sick. I drank more trail brew from my canteen to perk myself up, then started on the downhill hike behind Cousin Wilbur and our lone sickly ox.

The Crabtree Brothers led the way, flattening a skinny path through the snow with their boots. Boggs followed behind them, huffing with exhaustion from hauling his essentials: two bloody raw slabs of beef and a ten-gallon vat of trail brew. The rest of us followed in a single file with our loads shouldered and our heads hung low like an army in defeat. After thousands of miles of grueling westward travel, to backtrack in the wrong direction was as disheartening as any tribulation we'd come up against thus far. Like the Myth of Sisyphus, we had rolled the big heavy boulder up the mountain, only for it to come tumbling back down.

The evening redness burned in the western sky as we descended into the high lake valley. A bitter cold wind howled and snapped our coats against our bodies. The snow was a foot deep, and the lake was halfway covered by a white sheet of ice. The unfrozen waters were dark blue, and the pine groves and beaches were all frosted white in snow.

Overall, the valley looked nowhere near as attractive as it had a week ago. The lake now looked like a small arctic ocean.

About Halfway down the mountain, I stopped along the edge of the path and waited for Violet to pass by. I was feeling warm and courageous thanks to the trail brew, and I had this pressing impulse to clarify the status of our relationship before getting wall-up together inside that tiny cabin with the others.

When she finally crossed before me, I sprang from the deep snow like a mountain lion and said, rather frantically: "Hey Violet, would you be my girlfriend?"

She looked at me sideways and trotted outside the beaten path to give me a wide berth. Her hands were gripped tightly to her gunny sack and the tatty wool blanket that wrapped her body. "Well, I *am* a girl, and I *am* your friend," she said in passing. "But being someone's girlfriend is…like…an official title, right? Like being married?"

I started trotting alongside her. "Um, no…" I stuttered. "No, it's *not* like being married…it's more like a verbal commitment to love somebody, and *only* that somebody."

"Sounds like being married," she flatly said, no eye contact, stomping downhill through the snow. "And I told you before, it's not a good time to be involved with someone."

Being that I was drunk and emotionally wrecked from the day's whirlwind of ups and downs, I didn't take this latest rejection quietly. "So you don't want to be my girlfriend?" I grumbled. "That's fine. Whatever. But thanks for the quickie in the woods earlier…and thanks for saving me from getting mauled by that grizzly bear. Hell, if you didn't shoot that damn bear, then *both* McEwan brothers might be lying six feet under the snow."

Violet kept stomping down the snowy path, saying nothing.

I rambled on. "Obviously, I would have shot that bear myself, had I remembered that the bullets in Irwin's gun were used to kill those Mexican scoundrels that wanted to gang-bang you."

Violet turned her head halfway back. "Maybe next time you should check your pistol before you go hunting," she coldly replied, then pulled her blanket over her head like a hood, shunning my view of her eyes.

Her words were icier than this winter hell we'd wandered into, but I took it in stride and kept on skipping behind her. "That's sound advice," I replied. "I've learned my lesson, and I'll be a better *man* for it."

"I thought you knew what you were doing?" she snapped. "What kind of idiot goes hunting with an unloaded gun?"

I stared at the back of her head, absorbing her insults like a punch-drunk boxer. "I'm not an idiot," I said. "Our next hunting trip will be more successful. I promise."

Violet grumbled under her breath, something about 'wasting time' and 'freezing my ass off', while her pace picked up to a stomping, angry speed walk.

I jumped off the beaten path and high-stepped through the deep snow to cut her off. "Want a drink?" I asked, holding out my whiskey canteen and shaking it in a tempting way, hoping that this might change the subject to something not so slandering of my intelligence or manhood. I spoke highly of the trail brew. "I find it helps me worry less," I said.

Violet surrendered her hands outward, as if a gun were aimed at her. "No thanks," she said.

"C'mon, just one drink," I said, fixing her with a persuasive smile.

"I don't feel like drinking," she snapped.

I lowered the canteen with a sigh. I could feel the onset of her bizarre mood swings, and to counter it, I tried, in desperation, to give her something to be enthused about. "Well," I said. "Since we're heading back to the lake, we can go fishing again."

Violet shook her head. "No," she said. "I'm going fishing with the Crabtree Boys tomorrow morning. They're good at catching fish."

I briefly stopped, floored by the sting of her words, then raced to catch up. "But Calvin Crabtree fishes with a net," I snorted, bitterly. "Any asshole can catch fish with a net."

"You should weave yourself a net then."

"I'm not weaving a *goddamn net*."

"And thus, the reason I'll be fishing with the Crabtree boys. My family is starving, and I can't afford to take chances with someone who claims to be an expert at hunting and fishing, but whose true goal is to get me away from camp just to *screw me*."

"*Screw you?!*" I loudly hissed, utterly outraged by her baseless accusations. All notions of compassion abruptly died in that moment. I fixed her with a hostile squint. If our conversation wasn't ugly enough, it was about to get a whole lot uglier. "*Just to screw you?!*" I wildly repeated. "The nerve of you! Where's your compassion? How can you be so mean and awful on the day my brother died? For Christ Sakes, Violet! What's wrong with you? I tell you what, if anybody's getting screwed here, it's *me!*"

With a swift, angry kick, I sent a drift of snow hurling down the mountainside. "God in hell!" I swore at the cold mountain sky. "First Irwin dies, then Violet turns into a real king-hell *bitch!*"

I regretted using that rotten word the moment it left my mouth, but what the hell? I was only speaking from the heart. A word sourced straight from the wellspring of cold blood flowing through me.

Without breaking stride, Violet turned her head back, pulled her hood down, and squinted those pretty green eyes upon me. *"Bitch!?"* she repeated in a challenging tone, her eyes stabbing knifelike into my very soul. "Oh, I'm acting like a *Bitch,* huh? Says a man who is walking *in the back of the line!* Says a man who needs to grow a pair of eggs and take some control over this party before we all starve or freeze to death! Like Irwin would'a done!"

I wanted to rip my own beating heart out of my chest and show it to her. Or maybe just snatch her by the arm and pull her face to face, look her dead in the eyes, and confess that I was simply not the man that Irwin *was*, but that I would do everything in my power to provide and protect her.

But I didn't snatch her. Nor did I say anything more. Because our situation was beyond human control. Because I couldn't do anything about the goddamn weather. And Violet knew this as well as anybody, because she was the smartest, bravest woman I had ever known.

The proper thing to do at this point, I thought, was to end the conversation before this hole was dug any deeper.

And that's just how this lovelorn scene concluded: me slowing my steps and quietly watching her storm off towards the snowy alpine lake, a brown-skinned beauty in a single-file parade of freezing, ragged pilgrims.

* * *

A fire was already ablaze in the fireplace when I entered the cabin. Somebody had tacked a dingy canvas hood over the entryway to break the wind, and the air inside was thick with woodsmoke and the smell of cooking meat. The cabin's roof was made of mud and sticks, and melting snow leaked from it, dripping into small puddles on the dirt floor. There was no furniture, nothing but a single hollow room congested with the sickly-thin human bodies of an entire wagon party. And once everyone was safely inside, twenty-five pilgrims by count of head, the room felt so overcrowded that I fell into a claustrophobic depression almost immediately, despite Violet's close presence, or, perhaps, because of it.

We all stared curiously at one another like strangers adrift on a lifeboat. Blank and bony faces illuminated in orange firelight. Everybody coughing and sneezing with a burning fever. When someone spoke, their voice echoed loudly between the log walls for everyone to hear, so people hardly spoke.

The Crabtree Family settled in the back corner by the fireplace, where patriarch Milt Crabtree laid out corpse-like on the ground, coughing up phlegm and cursing the 'evil snow' with such violence and antipathy that it frightened the children and generally added to the cramped damper and melancholy of the place.

The ex-slaves settled near the front entrance, and the ex-priest passed out face-down on the floor beside them. Boggs settled next to the fire, in the prefect position to seize a portion of every roast that went over the flames, like some fat greedy tax collector.

Calvin Crabtree mentioned something about organizing a fishing expedition for tomorrow morning, but Boggs shunned the notion, batting his eyes wearily and rolling his big grizzly head. "Ice fishing?" he groaned. "To hell with it. I'll stay here and keep the fire going." He snatched Calvin by the collar and pulled him close with a savage jerk. "But you go ahead and catch a fat salmon for me, my boy…and don't come back until you do."

With no floor space to spare, twenty-five pilgrims slept shoulder to shoulder that night in a dark, drafty vacuum of woodsmoke, mildew, coughing, and human reek. It was altogether disgusting. A tight heap of grimy bodies, all locked in one confined space like prisoners in a third-world jail cell. We had avoided freezing to death on the mountainside, to say the least, but it seemed we'd only traded one nightmare in for the next.

When all pilgrims appeared to be sleeping or close to it, I leaned into the flickering light of the fire to write my first entry in four months:

Mid-November, by anyone's guess, 1846

Christ, what a day...probably...no...definitely the worst day of my life. Our first attempt to cross the High Sierra ended in utter failure, we have few provisions to hold us over, and no food has been obtained through hunting or gathering thanks to the inclement weather...oh, and my brother just died...

But perhaps I'm being overly pessimistic about things...It could be worse. At least there's a fire in the fireplace. I'm warm and sheltered from the storms, and my section of the cabin offers a decent view of the pretty-eyed ex-slave and her heavenly body. And she is alive and well, physically...

But mentally, well, what can I say? She is black and crazier than all hell...and she deliriously believes that I take her fishing or hunting just to screw her.

Of course, she is halfway right about this, but I'll never admit that to her. My main concern with Violet is that she has no animals to slaughter, so when my bony ox (my last resort of meat) finally hits the chopping block, then, naturally, I'll have to share the meat with her, and her needy siblings, if I aim to keep her happy.

The ox is currently tied up behind the cabin, shivering and stammering in the snowy cold and probably wishing to be slaughtered sooner rather than later. And thinking about all those hungry black mouths feeding on that one scanty cow, it makes me wonder...What happens when the food runs out?

What the hell are we supposed to eat?

Our situation is preposterous! Yet our refuge/destination in California is only a mountain pass away! It is both incredible and bewildering how a sudden winter storm can transform a short distance into an insurmountable obstacle...No, it's maddening! Torturous! So close to living the dream, then halted, blocked, barred by the wretched Old Man Winter.

I see that I'm turning negative again, but that's okay. It's been said that diary writing is a useful tool in settling the nerves in stressful times. So, let's keep on rolling. Let's talk about the ex-priest and what a drunken crackpot he turned out to be. He has no animals to slaughter, save for the family dog, and I suspect that doggie's days are numbered.

The Crabtree Family, on the other hand, are better off than most: they have three living oxen between the twelve of them.

Then there's Boggs. That infernal skunk just slaughtered the remainder of his cattle today, and those two beef slabs won't keep him satisfied for very long. I hate to imagine what that fat screwball will do when the food runs out.

OK. I'm babbling. Let me cut this note off and try to get some rest. Hopefully, tomorrow will be a better day. If this cabin is as rock bottom as it feels, then there's nowhere to go but up.

The fire died out sometime overnight, and a bone-chilling cold settled in, the kind of cold that freezes you stiff in bed with your blanket pulled over your head and your hands tucked between your legs.

Calvin Crabtree was the first to rise that morning. I could hear him fidgeting about the room, fixing the snags in his nets ahead of the fishing expedition.

The rest of us seemed to awaken all at once in a drowsy flurry of coughing and groaning. Gradually, we bundled up in our coats and rags to follow Crabtree down to the icy shores of the lake—all except Boggs, old Milt Crabtree, and the ex-slave Daphne. The latter two had fallen too ill to rise from bed.

The cabin stood about a hundred yards from the edge of the lake, with a grove of tall pines standing in between. No apparent trails led down to the beach, so we hiked single file through the snow drifts, passing under frozen pines and the deadly sharp icicles that slanted down from the branches.

A subzero wind blew off the lake. The sheet of ice that fringed the shoreline glimmered like frosted glass in the early sun, dissipating some twenty feet offshore to dark and choppy waters. There were no other signs of life, no ospreys terrorizing the skies, no waterfowl flying in V-formations. All was frozen still. And the silence was towering.

Calvin Crabtree descended upon the snowy shores with a tin cup in his hand. He slowly sipped as he surveyed the lake for a favorable spot to fish. There was a real dilettante air about him. He explained his every move in a highborn tone and tossed his nets into the water like some local fishing pro putting on a demonstration to a crowd of tourists.

At some point, I realized that his cup was full of trail brew.

Christ, I thought, this bastard is taking this king fisherman act right to the edge, drunkenly prancing around the frozen edge of the lake and telling fish stories.

I fell to the back of the crowd, annoyed, shivering in my rags and cursing the freezing wind under my foggy breath. I had an eye on Violet, who stood in the middle of the crowd, another witness to the spectacle that was Captain Crabtree working over the lake. She was layered in every ragged garment in her possession, but her head was uncovered, and her dreadlocks swung like loose strings in the icy wind. Her body language seemed as irritable as mine; her arms were folded impatiently across her chest, paired with a frumpy look that very nearly creased the cuteness out of her face.

The jealous side of me wanted to see Calvin Crabtree catch nothing. That way, Violet might finally realize that Crabtree was nothing but a drunken fool.

And for reasons beyond Crabtree's comprehension or my own, I got my wish. Not a single fish swam into the nets that day.

We all returned to the cabin that night with frumpy, ugly faces, more or less. Come dinner time, we gathered around the fireplace to drink cups of melted snow and cook whatever was left. As usual, Boggs snatched from everyone's plate and drank trail brew until he passed out.

Another attack on the mountain pass was a popular point of discussion amongst the Crabtree brothers. They plotted a breakout for the following morning, but old man Milt Crabtree rejected the idea.

"I won't survive it," he groaned from his sick bed on the cold dirt floor.

Calvin argued with the old man. "Pappa, listen to me. We got three healthy oxen left. We'll strap you to the back of the strongest ox and plow our way through the pass."

The old man cringed his eyes shut to hold down a surge of cough. His whole body quaked in seizure, then went completely limp, as his breath slowly deflated from his lungs with a dying gasp. A few seconds passed…then he came trembling alive again, snapped his head up, and glared wide-eyed around the room. "Goddamnit!" he croaked. "You're not strapping me to the back of an ox!"

Calvin stood over his father. "Well, you're not dying here, old man," he said impatiently. "It's not ending like this."

Old Milt broke into another violent spasm of coughing and said nothing more. His wife leaned over him and patted the fevered sweat beading on his forehead. "I'm staying here with your father," she said, stubborn and angry, eyes quivering with fear and despair.

Calvin looked up at the rickety cabin ceiling for a long moment, then suddenly clapped his fists together. "I've heard enough of the weak talk!" he blasted in a fiery tone. "We Crabtree's die on our feet! Not lying on our backs! Now here's how it's gonna' be: Tomorrow morning, we're gearing up to sneak over the mountains once and for all." He sharply pointed a finger at her. "So help me, Mother! I'll strap you *both* to the back of a goddamn ox."

Indeed, Calvin Crabtree had every intention of crossing the mountains. But when the sun rose the next morning, it did so behind a white veil of falling snow that put all plans of escape on hold.

The rest of the day was a wintery nightmare of intermittent snow showers. And in the evening, the wind blasted with such force that the snow fell at a sideways slant.

Baffled pilgrims sat around the cabin waiting, watching, praying for a break in the weather.

But Old Man Winter had other ideas, and for the next nine days, it snowed almost non-stop. Nobody was going anywhere anytime soon. And for nine days straight, we hunkered down in a general state of paranoid isolation, closely watching over our meager rations and trying not to lose our minds.

Chapter Fifteen

O n the second day of the nine-day blizzard, the Crabtree brothers managed to shoot a small bobcat for supper. The meat was shared between all cabin dwellers.

On the third day they shot a single owl, too small to be shared.

On the fourth day, they shot nothing at all.

By the fifth day, the cabin was buried up to the roof in snow, and the Crabtrees spent the day shoveling out the entryway just to breathe fresh air and see the light of day.

On the sixth day, I ate my last handful of pine nuts. I was now down to my very last resort: the bony ox tied up behind the cabin.

And so, on the seventh day, the mounting hunger drove me to slaughter.

I was nervous about the whole thing, having never killed anything larger than a squirrel before. I thought long and hard about it and concluded that the two most sensible ways to kill the ox were to slice its throat or shoot it point-blank in the head. I thought the latter seemed more humane and less violent, but carried both a Colt and a knife as I ventured out into the storm.

To reach the outside world, I had to climb through a tunnel of snow. The tunnel ended near the cabin's roof, where the snow finally leveled off, five or six feet above the earth.

I saw the sky for the first time in days. It was dark, and the turbulence of swirling snowfall made it impossible to see more than five feet in any direction.

I started towards the backside of the cabin, a walk that quickly turned into a treacherous battle against the elements. I sunk my face into the collar of my coat, shivering against the biting wind and practically swimming through the deep snow.

As I rounded the back corner of the cabin, I spotted the onyx profile of a man climbing over the snowdrifts about ten yards out. He was coming in my direction, but the man was barely visible through the howling white wind, and I had no idea who or what to expect until he was a foot away.

It turned out to be Calvin Crabtree with a scarf wrapped over his mouth, a shovel in his hand, clothes encrusted in snow. He pulled his scarf down. *"Looking for the oxen?!"* He shouted.

"Yeah!" I shouted back, standing stiff with my hands plunged into my pockets and feeling a painful stinging in my toes from the wet snow seeping into my boots.

"They're gone!"

"What!?"

"I said, they're gone!" he shouted, then leaned into me and raised his shovel, so that the spade-shaped blade was an inch from my eyes. *"I've been digging through the damn snow all morning. Trying to find a frozen corpse."* He was shouting directly into my ear at this point. *"I figured the oxen were too weak to have wandered very far, that they laid down somewhere in the snow to die... But I can't find the bodies."*

"What about hoof prints," I shouted into his ear. *"Did you follow their hoof prints?!"*

"No hoof prints," he screamed. *"The storm has erased everything."*

I stared at Crabtree for a long second, letting the wind blast against my dumbstruck face. Well...I thought, now we're really screwed. That was the last source of meat. Gone.

I slowly turned my eyes over the whitened grounds around the cabin, noticing for the first time the hundreds of potholes were punctured into the snowdrifts. Holes all around me. Holes as far as the eye could see, where Crabtree had poked his shovel down in a frenzied search for a frozen animal corpse.

There was a hole near my feet, and I squinted my eyes down the shaft, but it was impossible to see what was down there. The snow was as dark and deep as an ocean.

I leaned back into Crabtree's ear. *"Let me borrow that shovel,"* I shouted.

He surrendered the shovel without hesitation. *"Keep it,"* he shouted back. *"I can't feel my goddamn hands anymore. I'm going back inside to warm up."* He pulled his scarf back over his mouth and began climbing through the snow towards the entrance tunnel. I watched him disappear behind the swirling snowfall…and then it was my turn to dig holes in the deep snow and poke the shovel down and feel for an oxen corpse, which I assumed would feel like a frozen lump of meat when struck with the shovel head.

I dug around for a good hour or so until the frigid conditions forced me to give it up. Wind burn had stung my face raw, and I nearly lost my toes to frostbite, only to learn what Calvin Crabtree had already confirmed, that the oxen were simply gone.

We never did find the corpses. At a time when we could least afford it, the blizzard effectively cut us off from our last reserve of food. From that point on, we all became sicker and weaker and more hysterical by the day. The atmosphere inside the cabin became ever more tense as the families amongst us became guarded factions, hoarding with extreme prejudice over whatever food could be scavenged.

The devil hunger. He would come to strain every incident, every movement, every breath.

Chapter Sixteen

Late-November 1846,

Trapped inside the cabin, which I have dubbed 'Starved Cabin', for eight days and eight nights now. Hungry as hell. No meat. Nothing to eat but snow and a few service berries scavenged from a frozen bush. They could be poisonous, these berries. I'll soon find out...because I must eat something.

I'm functioning on the most insubstantial of diets, and it feels like I'm slowly slipping away. My drive to seek out food is not what you might expect from someone who's starving. It's easier to just lay on the cabin floor, and count these poison berries, and stare up at the rickety ceiling and listen to the creaking of the log foundation as it takes a savage beating from the mother of all snowstorms...and let my thoughts drift beyond the cabin walls to a warmer place, some bright and peaceful small town with restaurants and bistros on each downtown corner, wholesome establishments with good hot food and decent people, a place where no low-down dirty Mexicans are permitted, and no sickly American refugees for that matter, no fat drunken bigots...just me and my gorgeous date, sitting in a booth across from one another, her pretty green eyes staring into mine, her hand on the table, my hand resting over top. I tell her the only thing that needs to be said: I love you. And then the waiter serves us. Something hardy. Gosh, look at that! A steaming bowl of chicken dumplings. And a fresh, hot loaf of cornbread. Dig in, my queen. Dig in.

I was snapped back to earth by the next round of madness…and the sudden shock of noise that attended the discharge of Boggs's firearm. He just stood up, drew his pistol, and fired across the room like a maniac, killing the Daulton family dog.

Using the firelight to line up his cuts, Boggs commenced slaughtering the dog with an axe. He chopped off the head, and a gush of blood spilled from the neck and made a dark red puddle on the dirt floor.

With an empty cup in his hands, the ex-priest staggered over to Boggs's side. "I believe we had a deal," he said, and dangled his empty cup in front of Boggs's face.

Boggs looked up, snarled, dropped the axe, raised his vat, and filled the cup. I laid my head back against my gunny sack and closed my eyes, trying not to think about how the ex-priest had traded the life of his dog for a measly cup of trail brew.

That's it. Just close your eyes. Lay back. Ignore that gruesome scene of blood and gore in the firelight. And ignore the empty void inside your stomach that had grown a voice…a voice that was asking questions about how roasted dog meat might taste, and another voice that claimed it tasted like roasted lamb, which tasted like roasted duck, which tasted like turkey, which tasted kinda' like chicken…

I tried to ignore it all. But then the savory smell of roasting meat grew thick and tempting in the air. Mutilated chunks of dog were hanging over the fireplace like Christmas stockings. Man's best friend would soon be devoured by man—and all the depravity that it implied was dreadful to ponder.

And I tried to ignore it.

Just go back to sleep.

But the voice.

The devil hunger.

He could smell the charred roasting smell.

Just then, I felt someone's boot jabbing into my thigh. I looked up to find the ex-priest standing over me with his cup, now empty again.

"Wanna' slice of dog meat?" he asked.

I perked upright. "I'll try it," I said.

"Let's make a trade," he said with a twitching grin. His face was shrunken and angular and colorless white, like a skull propped on a bony body. A talking skeleton in the orange flickering light, he said, "Fill my cup with some of that sweet joy juice…and help yourself to some ribs, maybe a paw or two."

I shook my head. There wasn't a whole lot of sauce left in my whiskey canteen. "I ain't got but a swig," I told him.

"I'll take it!" he eagerly replied. "So, we have a deal?"

I turned my gaze on the fire, feeling too ashamed to look the ex-priest in the eyes. The hanging dog meat was steaming black, and its grease dripped and hissed in the flames. It looked about as appetizing as a turkey at Thanksgiving dinner. The devil hunger was telling me to take the goddamn deal already.

"I'll try anything once," I said with a shrug, then tossed the canteen to Daulton. "And give me a few extra ribs to pass on," I added, nodding my head at the bundle of scrawny black bodies reeling in the dark corner near the front door.

Daulton agreed, stole a generous slab of rib, and handed it back to me, along with my empty canteen.

I tore off a single rib for myself. The meat was black and crispy, but bloody-rare against the bone. It looked savory. Smelled succulent. Eat, said the devil…. Eat.

No encouragement necessary. I closed my eyes and sucked a sliver of meat from the bone, chewed and swallowed it down my gullet with a groan.

No, not me, it was the devil who groaned.

And who knew?

Who knew that dog meat could be so rich?

So tender.

So wet and greasy.

Yeah. My mind was officially falling apart at that point. But my love was still strong. I rose to my feet and moved around the room to deliver the rest of the ribs to Violet.

She watched my approach with a focused look, her eyes tense and glossy with the twinkling firelight. She reached out to accept the meat before I could fully kneel down beside her. "Thank you," she said, eagerly tearing off a bone for herself, then passing the rest of the slab to her hungry-eyed siblings.

On the floor between them, Daphne was lying supine with a terrible fever. For five days and counting, she hadn't moved from this very spot.

Her face was skin and bone, her arms rail thin.

"How's she doing," I quietly asked.

Violet paused her chewing and stared vacantly down at her sister. "Still hanging on," she said.

"Damn," I said with my eyes downcasted. "I hope she pulls through."

Violet sucked the rib bone clean, stared blankly as she chewed.

I wondered what she was thinking about. Perhaps she was considering the strangeness of eating dog meat and nothing more, but then she turned her stare upon me, and her eyes squinted to study me: my bony face, my filthy beard, my sickly pale skin, and skeletal frame. For there I scarcely stood in the firelight, aware of my pitiful appearance, but helpless to do anything about it.

I felt embarrassed and looked away.

"Peter," she said. "You look terrible. Why don't you come outside with me and get some fresh air."

Me and the devil hunger, all we really wanted to do was go back to bed. But I humored Violet anyways. I pulled back the canvas hood tacked over the doorway and studied the snow tunnel that led outside. "It's colder than Christmas out there," I said. "Are you sure?"

She covered herself in her sleeping blanket and leaned into the tunnel. "C'mon," she said.

I followed sluggishly. The tunnel was dark and narrow, and we took to our hands and knees to crawl through it. After eight or nine icy steps, we surfaced our heads upon the snowbound wasteland.

The sky was uniform gray and dark with storm clouds, save for a warning red glow to the west, were the sun was falling away. A screaming wind stung our faces.

"Is there anywhere we can go to talk?!" Violet shouted against the wind, clutching her blanket tight around her shivering shoulders.

There was nothing but windswept dunes of snow as far as the eye could see. *"We're pretty well snowed in,"* I shouted. *"We should head back!"*

She pointed ahead. *"There!"* she shouted.

I squinted my eyes, realizing that she was pointing to a dark hollow in the snow that Calvin Crabtree had shoveled out in search of frozen animal corpses.

"Let's go," she yelled, then, like a soldier scrambling for a foxhole, she raised from the tunnel, ran across the snow dunes, and dove into the dugout.

I covered myself in my blanket and followed. The floor of the dugout was patted down solid like an igloo, and the icy walls partially sheltered us from the wind. Violet spread her blanket over the floor and motioned for me to sit overtop. I sat down and watched helplessly as she came plopping down overtop of me, adjusting her rump to fit comfortably in my lap. I smiled and wrapped my blanket over the two of us, then stuffed my hands under her bottom for warmth. Overhead, the outer dimensions of the dugout framed the dark, churning sky.

"Got any more trail brew?" she asked.

My head slumped. "No," I replied. "I wish you would've said something five minutes ago, before I give the last swig to the priest."

Violet shook her head. "Damn," she muttered. "I sure could use a drink."

She seemed disappointed in more ways than one. I asked her if she was okay, and this seemed to loosen a mountain of feelings and emotions she was holding back. And a rush of words came pouring out of her. She talked about her dying sister. Talked about her starving brothers. She grew frustrated over our bleak situation and rambled and ranted and cursed God, cursed the shitty weather, cursed the mountains, and all the uncontrollable things that were working against her.

She talked non-stop. We sat there cuddled up, and I listened for what seemed like an hour, but found it difficult to concentrate. I grew preoccupied with her plump little rear and the way it was nestled against my crotch.

A warm rush of blood and the throbbing sensation of lust kicked down below…but as Violet rambled on, this sensation grew softer and softer, and my joints began to ache from the cold. My feet were slowly going numb, and the dog meat inside my belly was starting to bubble up.

Was that howling of the wind or the howling of a wolf?

"It's time I told you the truth, Peter," I heard her say.

She paused and lifted her head from my chest to look at me, looking to see if I was paying attention.

"Me and my siblings are runaways," she said.

My eyes shot back from the fog. "What?" I gasped, glaring down at her. *"You're a runaway?"*

Violet tightened the blanket over her feet. "The story about Masta Beasley granting our freedom is all a big lie," she said. "The truth is—Masta Beasley's wife booted me off the plantation, on account of me having relations with her husband…and her son."

She paused for a moment"s breath. Night was approaching, a light snowfall was drifting down, and tiny wet snowflakes were gathering atop the blanket that covered us. I simply remained silent and frozen in place with my hands stuffed under her butt. I was eager to finally hear her true backstory, but was afraid to speak or move, fearing that the slightest interruption might cause her to second guess herself and withhold her confession.

Violet went on in a reminiscing tone: "It was late spring, early summer. Six or seven months ago. The day started out like any other. The sun was shining, birds chirping, bees buzzing atop all the colorful flowers and dandies that bloomed all over Masta's huge property."

"I was doing the laundry…hangin' wet shirts on a clothesline that ran across the side yard. I watched a stagecoach pull up the driveway, then Masta Beasley and young Billy came strollin' down the front porch steps of the big house to meet the stagecoach. They both wore straw hats and matching grey suits and black leather luggage cases, lookin' about as father and son as ever, all chipper and dapper. Young Billy said he was accompanying his father to the capital city, said they'd be gone on business for several weeks."

"Then the Lady Mistress came down the steps behind them. Nothing seemed out of the ordinary 'bout her. She was done up in a spot-less white summer gown, her blonde hair pressed into long, shiny curls. She hugged her son and kissed her husband goodbye, looking sad to see, then go."

"Oh, but she was putting on a show. Cus' as soon as Masta and young Billy were down the road and out of sight, she switched tunes, and I mean, she switched *all the way up*, and came storming into the side yard and kicked me right in the spine and sent me flying to the grass. Then she started screaming orders at me to pack my things and *GET OUT!*"

I broke in and said, "Wow. So, she literally kicked you out of the house?!"

Violet pulled the blanket tighter around her shoulders. "Told me to scat like I was some stray cat," she said.

"That's incredible," I said. "But what about your siblings? How'd they come to join you?"

"Well," she said, eyes distant in deep reflection, cheeks red with cold. "The Lady Mistress had it in her mind that every slave on the property needed to scat as well. Said she was done with our black asses......and with Masta and Billy gone on business, there was nobody to stop her from runnin' amuck on us."

"So, Master Beasley owned five slaves only?"

"Yes, just the five of us. My sisters were house servants like me. My brothers stayed in the stables, tended the horses."

"Masta Beasley didn't give a hoot about cotton farmin', or any other kind of farming', except for a flower garden and some fruits and vegetables here and there. Horses is what he cared about. The man had a different horse for every day of the week. Had a pair of Clydesdales that were the finest looking animals you'd ever lay eyes on."

"He sounds rich," I muttered. "How did he make his money?"

"The law of the land was a big thing with him."

"So, like a lawyer or something?"

"White folks called him 'Counselor.' He was a real man of the people, and the dinner parties he hosted brought in bigwig types from all over Dixieland. They came wearing fancy suits and big toothy smiles. They brought booze by the caseload, and young girls in silky gowns, southern belles with powder-caked faces. They'd lounge about the ballroom, drinking tall glasses of champagne and smoking tiny cigarettes, while the men got drunk and took to racing their horses all over the property, ripping the lawn right up."

"Sounds pretty extravagant," I admitted.

Violet shrugged. "For white folks, maybe, but not for a slave. My days were slow, mostly spent in the big house, passing the time with tedious chores. I never left the property, not once, in all my four years there."

"You didn't party?" I asked with a grin.

Violet shook her head. "No. On party nights, my duties changed to that of a cocktail server in a skimpy low-cut dress and a pair of wooden shoes that clicked like hoof beats against the hardwood floors. You could hear me coming a mile away."

"What color was the dress?" I asked for my own visual aid.

"Black," she muttered.

I pictured her in that skimpy black dress. "Wish I was invited to the party," I said.

Violet rolled her eyes. "Shut up," she said. "Anyways, once dinner was devoured and gambling on horses tired out, Masta and his most honored of guests would settle into the study lounge with fat cigars and chilled glasses brandy…and they'd drink and jabber loudly into the wee hours, plotting their conquest of all creation and how they'd split the wealth between them."

"The white man's favorite subject," I chimed.

"Clearly," she said. "And the more Masta Beasley would drink, the friskier he became with me."

"Frisky, how?"

"Well, I don't know. He'd say, *go on get me another drink, you little monkey,* then he'd pinch my thigh or slap my rump. He'd call me all kinds of names: *monkey butt, chunky monkey, foxy monkey, pretty-eyed monkey, hot tailin' monkey*…and whatever. I could go on for hours with these stupid names…but moving on with my story, eventually Masta' would creep into the kitchen and trap me against the counter-tops, or take me down into the cellar, always assuming that the ol' Lady Mistress was upstairs sleepin' in bed—or too drunk to give a hoot, heartless to her very existence, slaphappy to hump me like a cheap whore wherever he pleased."

"But the Lady Mistress knew it," I surmised.

Violet nodded sadly. "Of course, she knew it. And she knew about my nights in the barn underneath young Billy. She knew it all, for the morning she kicked me off the property, she says to me, *'Violet, I hate you. I have held knives in my hand with the intention of slashing up your pretty little black face…But it's wrong and misguided to blame you for the lewd behavior of the men in this house…for you, Violet, are nothing but a little negro girl, a subhuman creature sprung from some primeval jungle, whereas my son and my husband were raised to be decent and God-fearing.'*

"'Oh, but it is my duty—as the mistress of the house—to remind my husband of his marriage vows, and to humble my horny-toad of a son.'

"That's when she told me about California. Said it was a warm-weathered wilderness as dark and savage as Africa. Said that as long as we followed the sunset west and stuck to the main road, that even the dumbest slave could reach California in a few months. Said she read all about California in a book called the *'The Pilgrims' Guide to the West.'*"

"Written by the late great Gaylord Hightower," I said with a weary sigh.

Violet nodded. "Then the Lady Mistress pushed me into the barn. She pointed at a field wagon, which happened to be loaded with seven or eight bags of cornmeal. *'Take it and go!'* she screamed. *'Leave here! You little heifer! And if you ever come back, so help me god, I''ll carve those green eyes out of your skull!'*"

"She turned her fury on my siblings, shooing her hands at them and shouting: *'Go! Leave here! Take the road to California! Settle as far away from white people as possible!'* Tears began to run down her cheeks. She left the barn, ran back inside the house, but returned moments later with Masta's pistol in her hand. She stormed right up to me and pointed the gun at my chest. *'And take this,'* she demanded. *'This pistol was a gift to my husband from the Governor of Missouri. It will be a real kick in the pants to know that his favorite little black whore is somewhere on the other side of the world shooting rabbits with it.'*

"Then she sat on a bale of hay and wept like a loon. Meanwhile, we tied an ox to the wagon and packed our belongings in all haste. As we hurried about, she stopped crying, produced Hightower's book, and began reading passages aloud like they were instructions on how to build something. She was certain we'd survive the journey. She said things like, *"Ration your food to make it last,"* and, *"Never forget that California is still technically Mexican Territory, and slavery is **illegal** in Mexico, meaning that no white man can force you into being servants without paying a wage. Do you understand what I'm saying to you!? Do you hear me, Violet? You little slut! California is outside of American territory, at least for now, and thereby blacks are free."*

Violet suddenly leaned up. "Are you listening?" she asked.

I looked her dead in the eye. "Yes," I quickly answered. "Jesus, do you think I'm falling asleep? My chestnuts are frozen, wolves are stalking in the tree line, and I'm hearing the craziest story ever told."

"Well, what do you think?"

I stared thoughtfully. "Well," I said. "I think you lied about losing them freedom papers during a river crossing. Irwin's probably rolling in his grave right now."

Violet half-smiled. "Yeah," she said. "There was never any freedom papers."

"Now I understand why you're in such a big hurry to reach California," I said. "You're worried that Master Beasley had returned from his business trip, only to find his favorite slave and his precious Colt revolver gone missing— and so he gave the Lady Mistress a good walloping upside her silly head, then saddled one of them Clydesdales—and now he's comin' west to track you down."

Violet's smile suddenly collapsed. She tensed up and looked worried. "Do you think he's coming?"

I glanced up at the snowy skies and shrugged. "I highly doubt it," I said. "Nobody's going over these mountains until spring—and by then, we'll either be dead or on a faraway beach on the California coast, basking in the sun."

Violet looked satisfied by the notion. She relaxed her head against my chest. "A sunny California beach sounds nice. Can you live on the beach? Or build a house nearby?"

"I'd build a house for you," I quickly said, enthused by the notion. "Right on a bluff overlooking the ocean."

"Could you build a fence around it? So our kids don't run off into the water and drown?"

"Our kids?!" I said with a laugh.

Violet adjusted the blanket for warmth, nestled tighter against me.

"I feel so bad for Daphne," she said. "She's so close to freedom."

I shook my head. "Yeah, to die now would be such a pity."

A short silence followed. Violet stared straight ahead at the ice wall while I was busy building our beach house inside my head. Then she brought her hands above the blanket and rubbed them together. "My hands are freezing," she said with a shiver. "Can I warm them against your skin?"

I tensed up, sensing the cold touch that was coming. "No!" I screamed. "Get your frigid hands away from me!"

Violet jumped up and quickly attacked, shoving her hands under my shirt, and clutching her icy fingers around my bare chest. She laughed harshly. It was like being attacked by the abominable tickle monster. I squealed and squirmed and fought to free myself from her frigid grip, pushing off her and plunging back against the snow. "Freezing Jesus, Violet!" I gasped, huffing from the effort. "You're a real nightmare to be around sometimes."

She rolled onto her hands and knees like a playful puppy and pounced on me again. "Stop fighting it," she screeched.

I stopped fighting. She wanted it more. Tutoring me with her cold hands seemed to satisfy some strange pleasure in her, and I was too tired to fight back. Though a part of me wanted to pin her down and squeeze her breast out of vengeance, I simply couldn't muster the strength. Starvation had worn me thin. Even Violet grew exhausted from the horseplay and slowly rolled off me. She laid back against the snow, gasping and staring straight up.

A full moon shined through a break in the clouds. For a moment there, the half-buried starved cabin and the surrounding pines were visible, their snow-covered outlines glowing pale blue in the moonlight.

"Listen, Violet," I said. "No matter what happens…I love you."

Violet said nothing in return, but a faint smile stretched her lips.

I watched the moonlight trace the soft features of her face, features that were visibly thinner and sharper with bone. Starvation was putting a strain on her good looks. And yet the brightness of those pretty green eyes still put the moon and all the stars to shame.

* * *

Eventually, the cold became too much to bear. Violet and I returned to the warmth of the cabin, holding hands like lovers as we entered. But sadly, the scene we happened upon was so grim, so depressing, that I considered going back outside to sleep in the snow.

Old Milt Crabtree had kicked the bucket. His corpse lay stiff and grey across the center of the firelit room while his sons argued over what to do next. "What if we bury him, and he comes back to life?!" Brain declared. "I can't stand the thought of father suddenly awakening in his grave."

Calvin was standing over the head of the corpse and sullenly staring down at it. "We can't just leave his body here," he said in a calmer, more rational tone. "The sight of it will drive Mother insane."

Boggs rose snake-like from the darkest corner of the room. He stepped into the firelight, stood over the feet of the corpse, and made this curious remark: "Yes, we should take him outside and put him on ice immediately."

All activity in the room ceased. Calvin Crabtree looked up. His eyes narrowed on Boggs. "What do you mean by that?" he said.

A look of discomfort came over Boggs's face. His big, meaty fingers tapped anxiously against the top of his thigh. "Hell, I'm just saying what everyone else is thinking," he said and glanced around the cabin. His face was sweaty and glistening orange with firelight. His eyes shimmered red in his skull. He held his arms out innocently and said to the room: "If the snow keeps falling and we can't hunt or fish…well…we could starve."

"You don't look like you're starving, Boggs!" shouted Calvin, pointing a sharp finger at Boggs's plump belly. "Hell, only an hour ago, you were stuffing your fat mouth full of dog meat!"

Boggs grinned and rubbed his potbelly. "It was only one skinny dog, shared by twenty people," he said.

Everybody in the room was watching now. I half expected Calvin to throw his fist into Boggs's chin and knock him sideways. But Calvin only grumbled under his breath, then quietly went about the business of preparing his father's corpse for burial. Later on, he would venture out into the frigid darkness to dig a grave in the frozen earth while the rest of us stayed indoors, falling back to our half-mad thoughts. It was the first time that any sort of reference to cannibalism was openly mentioned, and the notion hung like a dark cloud over the cabin, slowly pervading upon our hunger-crazed minds as the cold starving hours dragged by and the snow piled up beyond the cabin walls.

Chapter Seventeen

I t was in the nineteenth year of eighteen hundred when the *Essex* sailed from Nantucket under the command of Captain George Pollard Jr. Two years at sea on a whaling voyage was in the forecast as the *Essex* sailed through the hurricane infested seas of the North Atlantic down to the South Atlantic and skirted Cape Horn. They made a resupply stop in the Galapagos Islands before sailing west into the vast seas of the South Pacific Ocean.

The *Essex* was positioned a thousand miles from land when the ship was charged and rammed by the very sea creature they sought to harpoon and butcher, a massive bull sperm whale some twenty fathoms in length.

The giant whale tore the haul apart and capsized the ship, and the captain and crew narrowly escaped.

The next ninety-six days were spent onboard three small lifeboats with no food or fresh water. The crew rowed south in search of islands, drank saltwater, and went insane beneath the ravaging sun. One sailor fell into horrible convulsions and died suddenly on the floor of the lifeboat, and the others, in feverish desperation, swarmed upon the corpse. The limbs were hacked off, and the spilling blood was poured into cups and gulped. The organs were cooked in the sunlight—all except the heart, which they justly tossed into the sea.

As the days drifted by, three more sailors died, their bodies cooked and eaten in the same gruesome fashion. But when ten days passed, and nobody died of natural causes, the men drew lots to determine who'd be eaten next.

The lot fell to Captain Pollard's first cousin, a young lad named Owen

Coffin. After a brief quarrel between captain and crew (Pollard offered to kill himself in Coffin's place, but Coffin refused the offer) a pistol was pressed against Coffin's head and the trigger was pulled. Captain Pollard eventually ate his own cousin.

A week after Coffin's sacrifice, a sail was spotted upon the horizon, that of the American cargo ship *Dauphin* coming to the rescue. Rather than celebrate their rescue, delirious sailors were observed snatching the broken pieces of Coffin's bones from the bottom of the lifeboat, stashing these pieces in their coat pockets, and were later observed sucking on these bones on the way to port.

* * *

Bright threads of daylight were shining through the tattered holes in the canvas tacked over the doorway. Laying there, studying the light, I slowly came to realize that the sky outside was clear and blue for the first time in nine days.

Inside the cabin, all was quiet and calm. Violet was sound asleep, lying in a tight pile of snoozing black bodies. The ex-priest was sleeping in the opposite corner, and Boggs was flopped beside the fireplace like a slumbering ape.

In the very back corner of the room, the Crabtree family was noticeably thinner in number. "Where's Brian and Calvin Crabtree?" I heard myself say.

"Gone," croaked a voice.

"Gone where?"

"Over the pass."

They'd left silently and without declaration.

"But why?"

"You know why," answered the voice. "Because they've been stashing food from the rest of us. Because they consider themselves the strongest climbers. They're efforts would only be hindered by the weak and starving. By women and children and runaway slaves dressed in rags and with no provisions."

"Yeah," I muttered. "Sounds about right."

"They'll rally help in Gayville, then return to the cabin with food and supplies as fast as humanly possible."

"Sure they are," I muttered, laying my head back and closing my eyes. "Those drunken bastards."

"Yeah," agreed the voice. "Bastards."

The Crabtree brother solo climb, ignorant, selfish, and thick-headed, though standard in emergency procedure, ended in complete failure regardless. A few hundred yards uphill from the cabin, they found the snow to be soft and extremely powdery, and their boots sank to insurmountable depths. Unable to advance beyond the first mountain ridge, they returned to the cabin without being absent a single night.

December 1846,

Another cold night trapped inside Starved Cabin. I'm so hungry that every recent attempt at diary writing has ended with me tearing the page out and eating it. Hopefully, I don't eat these words. Har-har.

According to the tally marks notched into the wall above my head, we've been snowbound for twenty-four days and twenty-four nights. I make the tallies with my knife, but its accuracy is debatable. I'm no longer certain of when the day ends, or when a new one begins. Everything's a blur. But hey, these tallies, they also mark the spot where I normally sleep, my share of the cold dirt floor, set halfway between the fireplace and the exit. A ladder of hierarchy has been established in regard to floor spacing. The exit, being the coldest and most undesirable portion of the cabin, is occupied by the lowly ex-slaves and the Daulton family, while Captain Boggs and the prestigious Crabtree family have permanently settled the prime real estate closest to the fireplace. As they should.

So here I lay, in the middle, between the whites and the blacks, a bastard of white skin but the deviant lover of a young black girl, which, accordingly, evens my balance on the scales of privilege. And I think I'm starting to prefer it this way... yes, I think I like my place in the middle.

If anyone tries to muscle in, I will stab them in the neck with this pencil, or pull a stick from the fireplace and light them on fire.

I get a good draft of frozen air that blows through the entranceway, which helps me sleep, and I have a good bird's-eye-view of who's cooking, or what's cooking in the fireplace.

Which is an interesting view on a day like this, because Violet's sister Daphne is dead, and I suspect that her flesh will be roasting over the open flames sooner than later.

The whole cabin is on edge over it. The drafty atmosphere is tense with expectations. Boggs is pacing around the fireplace with a skinning knife in his hand, licking his chops and rubbing his belly, eyes wild and fiendish for a taste of brown flesh.

On the other side of the room, Violet is pulling her sister's corpse by the arm, slowly inching towards the exit, trying to drag the corpse out of the room before Boggs can make dinner out of it. The corpse only weighs about sixty pounds, but Violet can hardly budge it. She's a bag of skin and bones herself, and she's really struggling. And looking at her now, I just want to close my eyes and fall back to sleep. Her arms are rail thin, and her face looks rough, and I suppose the laws of attraction can only withstand so much ugliness.

But I think that the right thing to do in this situation would be to go over there and help Violet drag the body outside and bury it under the snow. But on the other hand, I'm starving to death. Literally. I'm a dead man if I don't eat something soon.

I put the pencil down and shut my diary. I really wanted to give Violet a helping hand, but a sudden wave of vertigo came over me as I tried to stand up. My knees buckled, and I ended up crashing back down to the floor.

After the dizziness passed, I sat up and saw Violet now lying overtop of her dead sister with her Colt drawn and leveled.

I followed the line of her sights across the room. In the general direction of Boggs's face was where she was aiming. "Come any closer, and I'll blow your goddamn brains out," she said in a low, quivering tone.

Boggs laughed harshly. "C'mon, sis!" he said, pausing to glare at her, a fire raging in the fireplace behind him like a portal to hell. "She's just a coon, bought and sold at auction like any other farm animal," he said.

Violet put her thumb to the hammer and slowly, weakly, cocked it. "You're not eating my sister!" she cried out.

Boggs continued his erratic pacing around the fireplace, ignoring the loaded gun that was pointed at him. "What's so *wrong* about it?" he said, licking his crusty lips. "Hell, I bet it tastes like dark-meat chicken."

"Fuck you, Boggs," she hissed.

Boggs stared down at her. "No fuck you," he said matter-of-factly. "Stop fighting it. I know you're hungry. Your romp is skinny enough to dodge raindrops. And look at them other blackies over there. Hell, they look dead already. Now, give it up. Put the pistol away, sis, and let's eat already."

The devil hunger inside of me couldn't help but agree. Why fight it, indeed? Maybe I should crawl over there and talk some sense into her. Perhaps I should tell her the story of the *Essex*. Yes, tell her about how Captain Pollard ate his own cousin. Enlighten her to the wonderful history of survival cannibalism and how it has long been the natural degradation trip of the starving voyager. Sure, that should help her let go. Then maybe we can finally eat.

Christmas, 1846

Some people seem to think its Christmas Eve around here. But fuck those people. There's no Christmas tree decorated with paper whimsies and gold stars. No toys under the tree, and nobody's singing carols or decking the halls with bells of holly. Starved Cabin is about as Christmassy as a cave full of vampire bats. There is no joy here, no laughter, no lust for life, and certainly no sense of humanity. Only pain and starvation.

As I scribble this terrible screed, the entire Crabtree family is huddled in desperate prayer by the fireplace, but the drone of their prayers only makes me feel coarse and angry, rather than in need of spiritual refinement. I'm angry all the time now. I hate the world and everything in it. And the more I starve, the more hateful I become. I find the behaviors of my fellow inmates absolutely infuriating. I sense that certain men are hoarding meat, and it drives me into a violent rage. I want to murder every last one of them. Cut their throats open with a dull knife. Or set them on fire. Yes, stab them with a burning stick!

But I only seem to have energy for bickering and arguing with these bastards. And thus a dangerous amount of resentment stirs inside me that has no outlet for release. I am tormented by my own uselessness. I exist only in a terrible stupor of arrested frenzy, trapped between starvation and death, suffering through death's slow pervasion, waiting in angst for the darkness to engulf me, too feeble to fight back.

Now I know how Irwin felt. Oh, how meaningless and cruel this life can be. Oh Lord, tell me, how much longer?

For the record, starvation is a terrible way to go out. And if there is a God, well, he can kiss my bony ass for this.

On second thought, let's not curse God. A man only curses because he can't find the proper words to express his resentment in the moment. So instead, I shall consider my words long and comprehensively and save them for my face-to-face meeting with The Almighty in the land beyond this white hell.

I shall be there soon enough.

Anyways, here's the situation in the cabin: Yesterday, Violet finally gave into the devil hunger and allowed her sister's corpse to be butchered into neat little serving-sized cubes. But nobody bothered to go searching for firewood, so we ate the flesh raw, hunkered down over the corpse in our filthy rags like vultures, looking crookedly at one another, our minds gone completely over the edge.

By and by, it seems we shall pass the winter as prisoners of this here cabin, eating our dead, wallowing in filth and madness, waiting in the cold darkness for the snow to melt. Cannibals of a tribe of cannibals.

And so much for that. Cannibalism has become socially acceptable here at Starved Cabin. Everyone is doing it. Hell, even Violet got into the action and ate a piece of her own dead sister, knowing that if she didn't, she would die, and her corpse would be added to the menu.

I watched her shudder as she swallowed down the bloody cube.

Oh, my poor love, how far have the stars fallen?

How can such a beautiful woman be made to look so revolting?

Her eye sockets are ringed black, her skin hangs loose around her neck, and some of her fingernails have fallen off. She lays dormant on the floor for large portions of the day with her pistol resting across her chest, looking possessed by some demon that only wants to curl up and die.

...As if death is the only way out of this cabin.

Oh, but I still fantasize about her nonetheless. I imagine what might have been. The sunny California Dream we once shared. I see the white sand beaches and the lime-colored palm trees swaying in the warm blue sky. And look, there we are, relaxing together in the hot sand near the edge of the sea, watching the crystal waves crash and foam and surge across the surf. Our beach house stands on a sandy bluff behind us, a white picket fence around it. We are happily married. My child is cooking in her womb. And its everything I ever wanted. Life is a well-fed bliss of easy living and lovely baby making.

Violet is gazing at me and smiling. She looks as cute and innocent as the very first day we met, her golden-brown skin shining in the sun, her ropy locks fluttering freely in the cool breeze, the blue ocean, the soft white sand, her green eyes rendering me helpless, her lips begging to be kissed.

But no.

I can't block it out.

I hear a terrible scream coming from outside the cabin.

It"s Boggs—he's somewhere out there, staggering around in the snow, screaming insane gibberish at old man winter.

I wish somebody would go outside and shoot him already. Put him down like the rabid beast that he is. I watched that evil bastard cut the fingers and toes from Daphne's corpse with an ax, then stuff them into the pockets of his coat.

Then at night, when things are quiet, he chews on the fingers. He thinks we're all sleeping, but I can hear him, gnawing on the toes and fingers like a diseased animal, sucking the flesh clean from the bone.

That rotten scumbag. I hear him screaming again. Screaming at nothing. Somebody please, for Christ sakes, shoot him already.

Late December 1846???

There's no escaping Starved Cabin. The snow is ten feet deep outside. I have a great hunger for all the food in the world, but no desire to do anything at all. I want nothing and ask for nothing. I don't believe in God or anything else. My skin is rotting on the bone. My hair is falling out. I sit in the middle of a room full of lunatics, listening to their hideous whimpers and anguished cries about food. My pistol is loaded and within arm's reach. Extremely paranoid since eating Daphne. The hunger seems to turn good men into beasts and bad men into monsters, and now there's nothing left of Daphne to eat, so the monster is sharpening his knife again and the beast is waiting for him to make his move.

I'm just ready for it to be over with. I know what awaits at the end of this: Death. An end to the pain and suffering. And I'm ready for it. Take me now, oh lord, to me to that white sand beach in the clouds.

New Years 1847,

Happy New Year. Yes, I am still alive, and probably much to everyone's surprise, because according to Boggs, I'm not the 'burly' kind of guy who survives a tragic ordeal like this.

But fuck him. I outlasted the ex-priest, at least.

Yes, it saddens me to report that Eddy Daulton, the ex-priest from Pennsylvania who was traveling with his young wife and five-year-old son, is no longer with us. He is dead. Here is how it happened:

Daulton lost his mind completely and fell into a babbling trance in the dark corner near the entrance, trembling and mumbling over and over again about God's full cup principle or the Golden Rule or the Cup of Iniquity and all gibberish related so. He confessed to a 'litany of malevolent transgressions' such as being an atheist, a drunk, a cannibal—all of which he was certainly guilty of—and all of which had, metaphorically speaking, filled his cup of sin. And now, he, the ex-priest, would have to drink the consequences of his actions—and these manic notions boiled in his brain until he finally snapped and suddenly stood up and stripped out of his rags, saying that he needed to cleanse himself.

In the shivering nude, he walked right out the front door and into the snowstorm. Nobody had the energy to stop him.

Farewell, my friend.

I hope you found what you went looking for.

Chapter Eighteen

The frozen body of the ex-priest was tracked down and hauled back to the cabin for processing. Boggs took charge of cutting out the organs, chopping off the limbs, and dividing the parts among the families.

Every part of the corpse was consumed. Muscle and fat were entirely stripped away, and skin and bones were boiled down to a drinkable glue.

But once the corpse of the ex-priest was entirely devoured, then once again, we were out of food.

Then came the real evil. It was a young ex-slave named Rose who disappeared first, followed by her brother Rutherford. And in the days that followed these two disappearances, raw pieces of black flesh circulated the dark corners of the cabin.

Boggs gave a strong impression of being the man behind the butchering. I saw the blood on his hands and face. And I watched him creep erratically around the cabin, dealing flesh in secret to those who had something to offer in return.

The truth was rather obvious, but starving pilgrims traded for the harvested flesh without question, either unaware of the rapidly dwindling number of ex-slaves or ignoring it entirely, worried foremost about their own survival.

When Boggs took his third victim, he made no effort to be secret about it. He simply bashed young Donavon's head inward with the butt of his pistol for the entire room to witness.

I came awake to horrified screams. Slowly looking up and focusing my eyes across the dim room, I saw Boggs sitting on Donavon's chest, hammering down with his pistol as if chopping firewood.

In the ten or eleven hammer swings needed to break the skull wide open, poor Donavon never raised as much as a finger in his own defense. Blood was flung throughout the room, and Boggs became soaked in it.

Behind him, embers pulsed orange in the fireplace, no fire, no flames.

Throughout the dark room, others were sitting up, some covering their eyes, others watching in disturbed fascination.

Boggs sat back and stared down at the mess he made. "Fresh kidneys," he mumbled, a fiendish gleam in his eyes. He holstered his blood-soaked pistol and drew the skinning knife from a seethe on his belt. The blade was long and skinny, its shine dulled by old blood. He raised it high, then drove it down like a spike into Donavon's stomach. He carved and sawed, then dug his hands in and pulled out a small, purple-colored, bean-shaped organ.

He held the organ over the embers to study it, letting it dangle between his pinched fingers, a dark and slimy thing that looked like a rotten egg yolk. Then he sucked it through his crusty lips, swallowed it down with a slurp of the tongue.

It was horrible, but I was too weak to do anything about it. Same for the others.

But Violet. She came shuddering alive from her hunger coma with a hellish scream. She sat upright, eyes blinking rapidly into focus. She looked at her brother, looked at his crushed skull, then drew her pistol and leveled the barrel on Boggs's blood-splattered face and squeezed the trigger.

Click.

Misfire.

Boggs looked at Violet. He smiled at her, blood dripping from his beard. "Blackies shouldn't play with guns," he said, then cocked his left hand, swung forward, and smacked her in the mouth with an open palm.

Violet flew backwards. Her scrawny, rag-covered body sprawled flat across the dirt floor and stayed there.

Boggs laughed insanely, rubbed his hands together like a back-alley pimp. "I bet you guys think I'm completely nuts," he croaked, his eyes shifting around the room, looking at nobody in particular. "Ya'll think I have no restraint, eh?" he said. "Oh, but you've got old Boggs figured all wrong…I do have restraint. You see, I'm saving the best darky for last."

He laughed harshly. "How's that for restraint?!" he howled.

Violet made no response. She was out cold, but the assault on her had excited my blood enough to raise the Colt Paterson. This time, I had the good sense to check the load before firing. I snapped open the cylinder, confirming with a swift glance that it was loaded all the way around with five led caps and black powder, then lopped the cylinder back into place with the flick of the wrist. The Colt felt like a hundred pounds of iron balancing in my feeble hands, but I managed to level the barrel at Boggs's face and focused my eyes down the sights. My finger found the trigger and squeezed.

BANG!

The Colt kicked sharply, and the barrel punched me in the nose, flinging me backwards to the floor.

A splinter of wood blasted from the wall behind Boggs. He flinched, glared at the wall, then slowly hunched around to face me. A low growl rose from his lungs. Insanity burned in his eyes.

He jumped to his feet and crossed over me in a flash. The last thing I saw, before everything went black, was the bloody butt of his pistol hammering down towards my forehead.

* * *

I'm walking down a dirt road in the countryside. It's just me, alone, no other travelers in sight. The sky is grey, the day is cold. The black oak trees that line the road are barren of leaves, and the fields beyond are fallow, waiting for a warmer day to be sowed.

The road ahead leads towards a cul-de-sac ahead of a large, white-painted house. It looks like a plantation house. Huge white pillars, an elegant second-story balcony, a big shady front porch, all set upon vast acres of farmland.

I feel intuitively drawn to the house. I start jogging, then running towards it. As I approach the front porch, I notice that the second-story windows are burnt out and the roof is charred black and mostly caved in. Half-burnt toys are scattered about the front lawn: wooden toy boats, porcelain dolls, a charred-black rocking horse.

A rope swing hangs from the lowest branch of a big oak tree in the yard, but no children play. There's nobody. Not a soul exists here. Nothing to keep me at bay.

The front door is wide open, and I invite myself inside and quietly wander amongst the ashen ruins. The hallways are blackened down to the studs, and the floors are tarnished in ash and scorched remnants of furniture. I turn down a hallway. Picture frames still hang on the walls, but the pictures are burnt faceless, and the frames are charred black. I have no idea whose house this is, or how the fire started, yet I keep wandering down the hall until I come upon an open bedroom door.

I quietly enter. The room is cringing bright from the daylight beaming down from a burned-out hole in the ceiling. I pause and stare up into the light, squinting, blinking, imagining the molten torrent of flames that ripped this place apart.

There is a bed in the back of the room. It's oddly undamaged by fire. A queen-sized affair with a canopy that veils the entire frame in silky black curtains.

I get the strange feeling that I'm being watched by someone lying in this bed, hidden behind the curtains. I lunge forward and yank the curtains back to investigate. There I find Violet, lying comfortably over black silk sheets. She looks up at me and smiles. She's wearing a silky white nightgown that cuts away just below her hips, fully exposing her golden-brown legs against the black silk sheets. Her dreadlocks flow free and clean over the pillows. Her skin is oily and glowing. Her body is perfectly radiant. She looks like an absolute goddess. And like a lowly peasant, I knell before her.

"Did you do this?" I'm compelled to ask.

"Do what?"

"Did you set fire to this place?"

She smiles warmly, perfectly white teeth, green eyes twinkling like emeralds. "If I did, I didn't mean to," she casually says.

I sit down on the bed next to her and very gently place my hand atop her knee. I'm consciously aware of everything that's going on in the room, an integral world revolving around me in bright, vivid colors, and the sensations I feel are warm and sensual. I run my fingers up the smooth arch of her thigh. She giggles from the tickling sensation that is my touch, then throws her hands down to stop my advance.

"Wait a minute," she says, suddenly sitting upright in the bed and covering her parts with her hands. "First, you must do something for me."

"What is it?" I ask in a passionate whisper. "I'll do anything for you."

"Hide me," she says with an innocent blink.

"Hide you from who?"

She laid back in bed and stared up at the burned-out ceiling, looking vaguely frustrated by my line of questioning. "He's coming for me," she says.

I lean closer and grab her thigh with urgency. "Who's coming for you?" I ask. "Your former Master? That Beasley fellow!?"

Suddenly, my heart begins to beat painfully slow, like a bass drum fading out of rhythm. I fall over the side of the bed, sucking frantically at the air and scratching at my chest, then jumping up in a fit of panic, desperate to keep my blood circulating.

"What's the matter?" she calmly says.

I start pacing around the room, ignoring her question and clawing rigorously at my chest, expecting the painful stoppage of my heart at any moment. I drop to the floor and roll through the ashes, gasping, clawing, weak, and losing all control. I lose sight of the bed, lose sight of Violet. The daylight suddenly extinguishes, and I fall helplessly through the darkness.

* * *

I came awake suddenly.

My heart was slamming inside my chest.

Starved Cabin was all but empty. Everybody was gone except for Boggs, who was hunched over the fireplace, mumbling incoherently to himself and rubbing his hands together, though no fire was going, not a single smoldering coal.

Dumped on the floor beside him was Donavon's mutilated torso. The head and limbs were removed. The chest cavity hacked open and disemboweled.

A gust of cool wind fluttered through the old wagon canvas tacked over the entrance, pushing a rotten smell around the room. A streak of daylight flashed over the cabin walls, and out across a gruesome pigsty of blood, feces, fleshless bones, and half-eaten body parts spread around Boggs.

I patted my hands against my legs and feet—all there, thank god—then slowly leaned up on my elbow. My head was throbbing. Reaching up and touching my face, I could feel a crust of dry blood between my eyes. Then I remembered getting bashed in the forehead by the butt of Boggs's pistol right after he murdered Donavon and knocked Violet out cold with a swift backhand.

Violet.

Violet.

VIOLET!

I jolted upright and shot my eyes towards the dark corner where she normally slept. She was nowhere in sight. Her corner, and every other corner in the cabin, empty, vacated.

Bloody handprints adorned the walls like a violent crime scene. Worried now that Violet had been slaughtered for the feast, I studied the mess of mangled body parts on the floor. A couple of chopped human fingers were tossed about like cigarette butts. A single human foot stood on its heel, hacked off at the ankle.

I squinted. Studied the foot. Its skin was a dark shade, more likely to be Donavon's foot. I gasped a sigh of relief and touched the floor beneath me, feeling around for a pistol and thinking that I should shoot Boggs in the back of the head while I still had the chance. The dirt felt cold and wet against my hands, but no pistol, and no other human property for that matter, no weapons, no gear, nothing but my sack of books and clothes, and Boggs's vat of whiskey, overturned and empty.

It appeared that the last survivors of the McEwan party had bolted from the cabin while I was unconscious, fleeing from the flesh-eating maniac that was Boggs and leaving me behind to fend for myself.

Those selfish bastards.

I knew that Boggs was utterly deranged and that he would kill me next, and my desire to evacuate the cabin was growing more imminent by the second.

But it was painful to move, and my escape would be a sluggish performance, no matter how badly I wanted out.

I rose slowly to my feet and stood there, swaying for a moment. My toothpick legs trembled. I braced myself against the wall for balance as a wave of faintness came over me. Boggs paused his mumbling and slowly turned his head in my direction. I thought I heard him say something like: 'Oh, Pee-nuts, you're finally awake,' but his eyes were unfocused, and everything he said thereafter was incoherent babble. He became sidetracked by the slaughtered torso at his side. He reached out and dipped his fingers down into the open chest cavity to rummage through the blood and organs. His mind was clearly gone, departed from that fat greasy body of his.

With my eyes nervously peeled on Boggs, I started towards the exit. But it felt like I was walking for the first time in years, and my feet were reluctant to comply with my demands. With the wall serving as a crutch, step by painful step, I edged across the room and quietly passed through the canvas door.

A blinding white glare of sunshine threw me off balance. I fell back against the outside wall, blinking my eyes and feeling cold drops of water tapping against my shoulders, dripping down from melting icicles hanging across the cabin roof.

The day was seasonably warm and the air smelled so fresh that it made me nauseous. The sky was clear, the purest shade of blue, and the mountains were a mosaic of soaring white caps against it. The sun was hovering around high noon, and its warmth was toasting upon my face as I gathered the strength to step off into a world of melting snow.

Uncertain of my heading, or which direction my fellow travelers had gone, I looked east and studied the eastern pass over the mountains. Far off in that direction, the old, civilized world that I once played a minuscule role in was going about a regular day, another work-week in progress, millions of peasants grinding out an existence in the slums along the eastern seaboard.

It didn't seem like such a bad concept now, to have stayed home in the slums, to have a stable profession, to know where the next meal was coming from. And part of me wanted to start off in that direction.

But no. It wasn't my destiny. I was a dreamer. I was going to have Violet and that white sand beach, or I was going to die trying.

I turned my eyes west and slowly began lumbering in that direction, looking for a path to follow uphill for one last desperate run at the high pass, and determined, this time, to finally make it over the goddamn thing.

Unfortunately, my ambitions were stronger than my hunger-ravaged body. My thighs cramped up, and my knees snapped and gave out. I collapsed to the wet snow and rolled onto my bone bag of a keister, utterly fatigued.

I'd only walked a stone's throw away from the cabin. I could still smell the human rot coming through the doorway. Twenty or so steps was all a starved, weary traveler could do.

So what now? I wanted to continue, just a hundred miles or so, to sanctuary, but good God, I was exhausted.

I closed my eyes and was starting to doze off, when the sound of footsteps trampling through the snow caught my ear. I titled my head up, followed the sound with my eyes, and spotted a bouncing human figure coming down the mountainside, high stepping it in my direction.

It was Violet, or a hallucination thereof, wrapped in a dirty blanket and moving fast and full of purpose.

"Peter!" she called out, locking her eyes on mine.

I cleared the phlegm in my throat to speak.

"Violet?!" I called back, my voice weak and raspy.

As she came closer, I saw that she was holding something small and metallic in her hand. "The pepperbox," I muttered upon realizing what it was. "Oh, no, Violet. Not the pepperbox."

Violet tried to stop, but slipped over a slushy-wet rock and came crashing into me like a human bowling ball. We both tumbled haplessly into a snowbank. The pepperbox dropped from her hands, but she quickly recovered it and wrapped her blanket around it, wiping the wet ice from the triple barrels in a hurry. "I'm gonna' shoot that fat rotten son-of-a-bitch," she said, a clear edge of pure hatred in her voice. "Then I'm gonna' cut his heart out and eat it."

Ignoring her crazy-sounding plans, I rolled onto my hands and knees, sucking at the wind that'd been knocked from my lungs. "Where are the others?" I gasped.

Violet staggered to her feet and glanced uphill. "Calvin Crabtree led the party towards the high pass," she said. "But when we came upon the abandoned wagons, I couldn't help but stop and climb into your old Studebaker. I only meant to say a prayer for Irwin, but then I happened to look inside the cedar chest and found the pepperbox at the very bottom… right where you left it…and all I wanted to do was return to the cabin to shoot him."

I shook my head. "Forget Boggs," I said. "C'mon, let's get the hell out of here, keep moving West until we get somewhere—anywhere on earth but here."

I wanted her to agree, and take my hand, and walk side by side towards a brighter future together. But Violet wasn't listening. She was staring dead at the cabin, the pepperbox trembling in her hands, vengeance boiling in her eyes.

I grabbed the back of her thigh and tried to stand up. "Violet. C'mon, let's go," I pleaded with her.

But she refused to listen. Her aim was locked on Starved Cabin. She was still trapped there inside her mind, fixated on a homicidal redemption, and there was simply no reasoning with her.

With no energy to physically stop her, I simply gave up on the matter and sat back in the snow, thinking that if the enormous prospects of escape and freedom wasn't enough to keep her from wanting to kill Boggs, then clearly nothing would.

Utter madness. Meanwhile, Boggs was standing at the entrance of the cabin and no longer wearing his coat or a shirt of any kind. A large and extremely psychotic-looking man, half-naked and soaked in blood like an evil butcher.

"Dinner is almost ready!" he called out. "Come on back inside and wash up."

He took a step forward, drew his skinning knife, and waved it wildly in the air. His head bobbled with a giddy chuckle, then he glared dead at Violet. "I said get back inside! Right now!!"

Violet leveled the triple barrels in the general direction of Boggs and squeezed the trigger.

Of course, the pepperbox misfired.

Nothing but a dull, wet click.

"Goddamnit!" she screamed. "What the *fuck* is wrong with this thing?!"

Frantic, she squeezed the trigger again and again.

Click. Click. Click. Click.

Boggs uttered a mouth full of crazy laughter, then took a step closer and slashed his knife in a half-circle, his eyes feasting upon her.

The big crazy pilgrim was on the verge of his most anticipated meal, but then his laughing suddenly ceased, and his grin collapsed, and his eyes turned distractedly to the south-east, trying to focus on a distant profile of a man edging around the lake and moving rapidly towards the cabin—a small black figure against the whitened landscape, growing larger and larger with each step.

It seemed an unexpected bystander was about to unknowingly enter the deadly slaughter grounds of our little cannibal society.

What a pity, I thought.

The man's swift approach was aided by a pair of snowshoes, which, at a distant glance, made him appear like a rescuer sent by some government agency to deliver food, medicine, and news from civilization.

Boggs's face twitched with confusion. He stared blindly in the general direction of the approaching man. "Who in tarnation are you?!' he called out.

The man walked briskly within ten yards of the cabin before finally slowing his steps. He came well-outfitted in winter clothes and climbing gear, tall and well-balanced on his feet, with a white pearl-handled pistol holstered on his hip. His coat was black, his hat was black, and a black scarf was wrapped over his mouth, which, when pulled down to speak, revealed a white American face with gentlemen blue eyes.

"The name's Jack Beasley," he said with an unmistakably Southern accent. He turned his blue eyes on Violet and grinned a rotten slaver's grin.

Violet looked utterly mortified. She stiffened against the breeze, and the pepperbox dropped from her hand, splashing in the icy slush at her feet.

Well…I thought, why the hell not? Our situation was so ridiculously fucked up that the slaver's sudden appearance was hardly surprising. And I simply sagged backwards on the snowy sidelines to watch how things would play out, too weak to be much of a factor,

Beasley reached for the canteen slung around his shoulder. He took a slow sip and wiped the access water from his mustache with a gloved hand. "You look like hell, Violet," he said.

Violet sat down in the snow beside me, saying nothing, a dejected look on her face that was something similar to mine.

There was an extra pair of snowshoes hanging off Beasley's backpack. He reached for the snowshoes and tossed them at Violet's feet. "Put those on," he said in a calm but commanding voice. "And for Christ sakes, let's get moving. It's taken me three months to track you down, and I lost two good horses along the way."

He paused and gazed bitterly over the snowy highlands. "I've had about enough of the cold. I want a hot bath and a hot meal served at a decent restaurant…and I want it by the end of the week. Now tie those goddamn snowshoes on your feet and get your black ass *up*—"

Beasley suddenly cut himself off mid-sentence and jerked the pistol from his belt holster. He swung around sharply and aimed the barrel at Boggs, who was lurching towards Beasley's blindside with his skinning knife raised to strike. "Hold your horses right there!" he shouted. "Come any closer, and I'll put a bullet between your eyes!"

Boggs slowed and lowered the knife. He stared, dumbfounded, more or less at Beasley, his eyes a bottomless pit of blackness and lunacy.

Beasley looked suspiciously behind and around Boggs. "Say, what the hell is wrong with you, fella?!" he said. "And where's your shirt?" He turned his blue eyes on Violet while keeping the barrel trained on Boggs's forehead. "Who the hell is this man, Violet?" he wondered. "And why does he smell so bad? And who's that scrawny fella sitting beside you?"

For a withering moment there, it felt like a spotlight had been turned on me. It was my turn to speak, but my response was slow, and Boggs cut in before I could formulate an introduction in my head. "The names Boggs and that Little Black Piece of Meat is coming with me tonight." He laughed manically and pointed his knife at Violet. "We have dinner reservations!" he howled.

An uncomfortable look flashed across Beasley's face.

"Violet? What the hell is this man talking about?!"

Violet shook her head. "Just shoot him already," she said in a cold, dry tone.

Beasley shrugged, then leveled his pistol point-blank at Boggs's forehead and pulled the trigger.

BANG!

The deafening blast echoed sharply between the mountains. A beautiful pink mist sprayed from the back of Boggs's head. He reeled back a step, his eyelids fluttering like butterfly wings, then his body went limp and collapsed into a shallow pool of slush with a heavy splash.

Beasley holstered his smoking pistol. "OK, Violet," he said with a testy sigh. "We're done here. Put the snowshoes on. Time to go."

Violet stared vacantly at Boggs's floating corpse. She gradually rose to her feet and took a trembling step towards the corpse as if entranced by it, then squatted down and pried the skinning knife from Boggs's dead-stiff fingers, completely ignoring the snowshoes.

Beasley watched her. He folded his arms impatiently across his chest, but appeared rather unthreatened by the gesture, as if things were never that far out of his control.

"Violet. What are you doing?" he asked.

Violet ignored him and straddled her legs over Boggs's bloated belly. She raised the skinning knife over her head. The blade swung downward like an ax, stabbing into Boggs's chest cavity. A savage grunt seemed to vent from her very soul. She began sawing back and forth, cutting through bone and organ.

"Christ almighty," muttered Beasley, squinting his blue eyes over the cabin. "What the hell happened up here?"

Violet continued slicing into the chest cavity with an insane focus in her eyes. She was cutting out Boggs's heart, this I knew, because she had her own vengeful reasons to do so. It was a horrible thing to witness, yet I felt vaguely aroused by it. I couldn't help but encourage her. "Are you going to cook that heart?" I asked. "Or just eat it raw?"

Beasley looked annoyed. "Hey!" he snapped at me. "Shut the hell up! Cooked or raw or fried in chicken grease—in the name of God, she's not eatin' that heart!"

I shrugged and laid back in the snow, and closed my eyes.

Violet tossed the knife aside and dug her hands frantically into the bloody chest hole. She severed the arteries, using her overgrown fingernails, then lifted the heart from the body—a slimy black ball of blood that she raised above her head and squeezed, allowing a spurt of blood to drip over her mouth and chin.

She looked at her master and licked her lips in a crazy, suggestive way.

"Is this what you want?" she asked him in a sultry voice, smiling psychotically, teeth glistening red.

Beasley lunged forward and smacked the heart muscle from her hand. "Get a grip on yourself!" he scolded her.

The heart muscle flew through the air and bounced off a snowbank like a tennis ball, rolling to a stop near my feet. I stared down at the bloody ball for a long moment, half-expecting it to suddenly start beating again.

"Enough of the craziness!" shouted Beasley, pointing his finger sharply at Violet's blood-soaked face. "If you're *that* hungry, I got plenty of smoked beef and cheese and a few biscuits that you can eat...but if that don't straighten you out...then...well...goddamnit, Violet! Maybe I need to go upside your head for a quick readjustment!" He opened his palm and made a smacking gesture, then half-turned and dug inside his backpack, removing a wad of smoked jerky wrapped in wax paper. He unfolded the paper and presented it to her. Food, normal human food.

Violet's eyes snapped into focus. She stared at the jerky, lips trembling with longing hunger.

In the way a man would toss food at a wild animal, Beasley tossed a piece of jerky at her. The jerky landed in her lap and balanced there for a moment, before Violet snatched it into the palm of her hand.

"The snowshoes," he insisted. "Put them on. Now."

Violet shoved the piece of jerky into her mouth with a grunt. As she chewed, she quietly grabbed a snowshoe and began fitting her foot inside. Beasley squatted down and laced the shoes for her.

I was still sitting in the snow, watching her every move, and trying to match her eyes, so she could recognize the hurtful protest in mine. I didn't want her to leave me, and I certainly didn't want her to leave with *him*, that slaver/lawyer of a white man whose very existence seemed to represent everything that was greedy and wrong in human nature. But once her snowshoes were laced up, Violet rose to her feet, staggered momentarily from the awkward feel, then half-stepped over to her master's side, looking broken and humiliated like a beaten dog, waiting for further instruction. Beasley nodded west, then began walking in that direction. Violet followed obediently, her head down, eyes shunned away from me.

I was trying to think of something quick and meaningful to say, but my spirit was broken, and my mind and body were ravaged, and before I could think of anything, they were shuffling away from me. In desperation, I reached out and tried to grab Beasley by the snowshoe, but he anticipated the move and quickly stepped out of my reach.

"Wait!" I weakly cried. "Can I have a piece of jerky?"

Beasley sighed, then tossed two small strips into my lap and sent a biscuit bouncing off my forehead. "There," he said. "Now don't go eatin' that damn human heart…it will make you sick." He nodded at the dismembered heart lying in the snow nearby, glistening in the sunlight like a bloody meatball.

Fuck you, I thought. I'm already sick, and I'd rip your heart out and eat it if I could.

"Where are you taking her?" I asked.

"I think we'll go to California," he said, squinting his blue eyes westward. "See if it's as beautiful as they say."

"We're technically still in Mexico," I said. "Slavery is illegal here."

Beasley shrugged. "So," he simply said.

"So…. You're gonna' let her walk freely, right?"

He eyed me wearily, then grabbed Violet by the back of the arm and pushed her along, ignoring my question.

"I love her," I cried out, one last Hail Mary from my pathetic position in the snow. "I'm gonna' marry her!"

I said this as loud as possible and could hear myself echoing off the mountainsides. I listened for a reply, but Beasley only laughed and kept on walking.

Violet turned her head back to look at me, but Beasley quickly yanked her arm, and she looked away before any sort of sentiment could pass between us. I was hoping to share a burning, star-crossed lovers' gaze with her, or catch a flicker of sadness in her eyes, a distressed signal of her desire to continue fighting for those dreams we strove for, but failed to obtain, in our journey west…a yearning to have that beach house and that white picket fence, or simply Love and Freedom.

But nothing. Nothing from her at all.

But I know the feelings were mutual, I know she desired those things as badly as I did. I could feel it in my very blood, but the slaver Beasley had no patients for love, and certainly no patients for freedom, and just like that, Violet was hustled away and walked out of my life without saying goodbye.

I merely laid back in the slush and watched her go with one eye squinted. Not a single ounce of hero was left in me. No energy for a last-ditch effort to save her. And the fact that Beasley had tracked her down seemed so inevitably fated that, in that moment, I simply accepted it, as if she was never really mine to lose in the first place, and as a reunited Master and Slave disappeared over the high ridge, I slowly closed my eyes and slipped away.

Sure, in the days to come, there'd be more suffering in store for me, but as far as the terrible saga of the McEwan Party was concerned, our disastrous crusade essentially ended here, with Boggs's demise and Violet's capture. The dance was over. The Lords of Trailblazing had decided to terminate the party just one hundred miles before reaching our treasured destination, and for perfectly logical reasons: because we were arrogant, because we were drunks and atheists, because we lusted inter-racially and humped in the woods like wild dogs, because we were pale-skinned and overprivileged and greedy, because we were brutal American capitalist, land-snatchers, self-seekers, thugs, pillagers, and oppressors. Because we bullied the natives. Because we stretched ourselves beyond our means. Because we foolishly rolled our wagons too high into the mountains, too close to the clouded winter sun, then plunged headlong into a twisted orgy of self-preservation and flesh-eating madness, all in the crusade for wealth and power.

And when the winter snows do finally thaw, a story will emerge that is neither worthy of legend nor tragic, because the McEwan Party never rose to the heights for which a real tragedy must fall to merit such glory. Because our transgressions were so grossly evil that our story deserves to be forgotten, denied, erased from the record. No monuments or statues were erected in our memory. No landmarks renamed by future generations in tribute to our fantastic failures. No McEwan Lake. No Boggs Mountain. No. We deserve none of it, because our crowning achievement will go down as one of the most rotten and depraved animal acts in the history of humankind. Because cannibalism is downright disgusting.

In the end, I lost everything, and it almost felt poetic in its appropriateness. The ghastly ordeal in the trapping snows of the Sierra Nevada had left me all alone, heartbroken, penniless, lost and ashamed, and perhaps permanently fucked-up in the head.

And maybe I deserved every last strike. But then again, I was a survivor of the McEwan Party Disaster. God kept me alive, and there had to be a reason for it, perhaps because the final incredible truth of the matter is this: I yearned to salvage something from the ugliness. Something wholesome and righteous. Something beautiful. Because love was the driving force behind my survival.

Chapter Nineteen

I was coming down the mountainside, reeling through knee-high snow and searching for a path to follow out of the highlands, when I spotted a horse standing atop the crest of the next ridge. It was Ringo, my brother's runaway nag, easily recognized by its light-brown coat and powerful breast, and the black leather bridle still strapped around its nose.

To find Ringo alive and healthy was about as shocking as anything thus far. I eagerly called his name, but instead of healing to my call, Ringo snapped his teeth at me and trotted away. This rude gesture all but cemented the fact that it was Ringo in my mind, and I started cursing at him with a familiar grudge in my tone, like old foes reunited. *"Ho! Ringo! Stop! You stupid horse! Ho! Stop!.... Ho! It's me, Peter...I know you remember me.... Goddamnit Ringo! Stop walking away!!!"*

I pursued Ringo to the bottom of a snowy ravine where a rushing mountain spring flowed. Ringo stopped along the rocky banks and dropped his snout for a drink, giving me a chance to walk up and stand beside him. His mane was wildly overgrown from his time in the woods, and long brown strands of it fell like women's hair over his eyes. I reached out, pulled the mane from his eyes, and slicked it behind his ears, but Ringo, unappreciative of the gesture, snapped his teeth and leaped away and continued upstream at a trot.

I cursed him again, then followed.

We came upon the headwaters, where the spring became a graceful series of waterfalls cascading down the snowy mountainside. Ringo seemed oddly fixated with the waterfalls and began climbing uphill, following the spring's course. I stayed after him, and one after the other, we stepped up icy wet boulders and crossed into a narrow gully where the snow was mostly thawed. Here, the spring became a stagnant interval of small pools carved in the bare granite, each pool a step higher than the previous and steamier on the surface. I squatted down to test the water temperature with my finger—it was warm—and a good indication that a hot geyser was gushing somewhere nearby. Ringo jumped over the spring and landed with a thunderous clap on a high ledge above the gully, then disappeared from sight behind a strange wall of churning white steam.

Where was this darn horse going?

I pressed forward, jumped over the spring, climbed up the ledge, and stepped blindly into the churning wall of steam. On the other side, I discovered a big kidney-shaped pool of steaming hot water. A wall of mountain edged the back side of the pool, while the other side opened to a grand sweeping view of the white highlands and a low green valley beyond. A single tree sprung from the rock and hung over the hot pool like a huge beach umbrella. Apple-sized fruit dangled from its leafy green branches. Ringo was standing beside the tree in a haze of churning steam and glaring back at me as if leading me to this spot was his plan all along.

And I was grateful for it. Hot Damn, I thought. What a wonderful place! Finally, through all the suffering, heartache, and terrible fortune, it seemed some good karma had fallen my way. A little golden nugget of food and sanctuary that I desperately needed.

I picked a fruit from the tree and studied it against the misty sunlight. The fruit's skin was waxy and smooth and yellow-green in color, like a lemon, but larger.

I sunk my teeth into it. And Sweet Mercy! It was so sour and juicy and sugary and scrumptious that I coughed and choked on it.

"That's good," I said to Ringo, nodding favorably at him while sucking fruit juice down my gullet. "Sorry for cursing at you, old pal. Can we put the past behind us and be friends?"

Ignoring my apology, Ringo stretched his long, mangy neck into the branches and picked a fruit with his teeth. I shrugged and turned my attention to the hot pool. The water was crystal clear down to the silver-colored bottom. White steam swirled snake-like upon the surface, gradually rising and dissipating into the calm breeze.

I stepped to the pool's edge and stared down at the face looking up from the surface: a pale man-child with ratty, overgrown whiskers and eyes as bloodshot and beady as ever. "Hey there, handsome fella," I whispered. "Wanna go for a swim?"

I stripped out of my rags and limped naked into the pool. The water was the perfect temperature, hot and relaxing, and a good hour was spent washing my body clean of three months' worth of human grime while eating sugary lemon fruit. Then I felt tired and wrapped myself in my ratty wool blanket and lay poolside. I gazed and brooded over the view of the mountains and the distant green valley...until my eyes became too heavy to keep open.

* * *

A strange commotion startled me awake. The first thing I saw was the sun, glaring down from the apex of a cloudless blue sky. I wasn't sure how long I'd been out, but was fairly certain the moon had waxed and waned at least once, and the day was a new one.

The clicking sound of a hoof tapping against rock caught my ear. I lifted my head and saw Ringo standing beside the fruit tree, flicking his tail and mindlessly chewing on fruit.

A bog of steam sat over the surface of the hot pool, slightly hindering my view of the three naked squaws standing on the opposite side, staring back at me.

And Holy Smokes! I rubbed my eyes, wondering if it was all just a dream. But the breeze was cool and misty, the midday sun beating hot, and the smell of minerals boiling in the hot pool was thick in the air... and it was all too real to dream up. This was actually happening. Three young native gals in the lovely nude were actually standing on the far side of the pool. Gorgeous faces...remarkable bodies...matching hazel eyes...sun-kissed golden skin... long coal-black hair that laid perfectly straight down slim, delicate shoulders.

It was a stunning picture. Sisters perhaps. Maybe triplets. Maybe sirens from a Greek tragedy. Whatever the case, they seemed undeterred by my presence and continued to just stare in my general direction, naked.

One squaw stepped to the edge of the pool and extended her leg to test the water with her toe. She smiled, then subtly waded in.

I couldn't help but watch. The strangeness of it had me frozen in place, naked but wrapped in a blanket along the pool's edge.

The other two squaws joined the first in the pool…and the three of them started giggling and splashing one another, paying no attention to me. And if things weren't strange enough, a dark-skinned elder suddenly appeared out of the misty air, standing along the pool's edge where the sisters had first appeared. The old man was only half-naked, no shirt, no shoes, just a loincloth and a myriad of beaded necklaces hanging down his wrinkled chest. He held a walking stick to steady his gait.

The old man surveyed the hot pool with a reposed air, then squinted vaguely in my direction. Our eyes connected, then he started shuffling around the pool's edge, coming in my direction, tapping his walking stick against the slick table stone as he went.

He crossed before me, eyes squinted hard as if he couldn't quite see me. And as if invited to do so, he sat down beside me and crossed his legs.

I sat up to study the old man. There was genuinely nothing to be alarmed over. His wrinkly half-naked body looked absolutely harmless, and three squaws seemed completely at ease, floating and giggling in the hot water like womenfolk on a spa date. I stayed wrapped in my blanket, the morning stiffness setting in, feeling groggy and resigned to share the hot pool oasis with the natives.

"Are those your daughters, old man?" I asked, not expecting the elder to understand the king's English.

"Yes. Those are my daughters," he responded in a native accent, and one that made him sound wise beyond his years. He laid his walking stick across his lap. One end of the stick was shaped like a bowl, and he began packing the bowl with a greenish-purple-colored herb. When the bowl was fully packed, he held the stick out like a musical instrument, struck a match, and held the flame above the bowl. He short-puffed on the skinny end and tamped the bowl with his thumb, then blew a thick cloud of white smoke over the pool.

The smoke had an earthy smell to it, but with a strangely intoxicating quality, like opium, but not quite.

The old man waved the skinny end of the pipe near my face, gesturing that I take it. I leaned away out of instinct and shook my head, unsure if I was ready to trust this peculiar old man and the strange bohemian substance burning in his pipe. I turned my eyes on Ringo, just as the big Quarter horse lifted his head to match my stare. I started wondering, *why didn't these Injuns steal such a splendid horse?*

"Not all of us are horse thieves," said the elder, as though reading my mind.

Again, he held out his pipe. "Don't be yellow," he said with a grunt. "It's a good smoke."

I stretched my arms and legs with a groan. "If you insist," I said.

I brought the pipe to my lips and sucked a dash of smoke into my lungs. But the potency was devastating. I was flung to the ground in a seizure of coughing and hacking. It felt like a ball of hot ash was stuck inside my lungs. "Sweet. Mother. Of. God!" I squeaked, choking, straining to suppress the convulsions.

Meanwhile, a wet, naked, rosy-red squaw climbed out of the hot pool. A curvy, womanly figure against the steamy sunlight, she drew my eyes magnetically with her slow rise and titillating walk. Distracted from the harsh burning sensation in my throat, I rolled onto my back and stared up at her, watching the beads of water drip down her slim waist and fleshy thighs. I felt paralyzed by the sudden sensual ambiance of the moment, unable to hide the superior but tolerant grin plastering across my crusty face.

"Roll over," said the old man. "My daughter will make you feel strong again."

He held out a small glass vial containing an oily golden-colored liquid and passed it to the squaw. She took the vile and kneeled beside me. "It's Okay," she softly assured me, blinking her amber-colored eyes.

She dabbed a drop of golden oil onto her finger and reached out. I nodded and closed my eyes, feeling her wet fingers glide across my neck and dig into the stiff muscles. She started rubbing, and it felt good…too good.

My guard suddenly triggered. I jerked upright. "What's happening here?" I cried.

"Relax, my friend," said the elder, his ancient face without expression, his deep-set eyes gazing distantly over the white peaks, where scattered grey clouds took mystifying shape against the warm blue sky. "If it's a reckoning you seek," he said. "Strong you must be."

I glared at him, half-suspecting that he was practicing some sort of native voodoo on me.

Then I felt lightheaded, and a strange cotton-like feeling was growing in my arms and legs.

The wet-naked squaw reached out and pushed against my shoulder, coaxing me back down to the ground.

"Relax," grunted the old man. "Lay down."

Confused but intrigued, I stretched out and made myself comfortable, lying face down against the cool rock while the squaw sat over my hamstrings and locked her knees against my hips. I could feel her walking down the naked ridges of my spine, finding the sore muscles of my lower back, rubbing vigorously, and pushing the tension right out of my mind. Her sisters came up from the pool and fell on either side of us, and an orgy of caressing my pain away commenced, that was, by far, the most exotic rub-down of my life.

What a pleasant surprise, indeed. All my worries seemed to drift into the cool breeze. I closed my eyes, feeling intoxicated, moaning and taking gulps of air, my mind sensually drifting…drifting…drifting…and falling back to those long hot summer days of trailblazing, those fantastic moments when we were the masters of our own destiny for a change, pilgrims of a wagon party slowly trudging down the lonesome road through the wild west, the rugged beauty of the desert, and Violet, the pretty-eyed ex-slave, a lusty brown figure in a dingy gray gown, walking out in front of her wagon and lashing her ox with the flick of the bullwhip, the high wheels creaking onwards towards those unexplored horizons that promised a better life to those of us who desperately needed it.

Then I thought about Beasley. Master Beasley. And the thought was sobering. "That jackass of a slaver!" I screamed, jumping suddenly to my feet. "He can't do this to her! She deserves to be free!" The naked squaw on my back yelped and fell backwards into the pool. I turned to the elder and eyed him intently, no longer feeling groggy or sore, but riding an incredible burst of energy and sudden determination. "Have you seen her? Which way did they go?!"

The old man was calmly packing his bowl with more green-purple-colored herb. "Sutter's Fort," he grunted, distractedly. "It's the first stop for all the white American colonizers."

I leaned into the old man's space. "Sutter's Fort?" I repeated intensely.

"They'll issue your passport," he said, striking a match, puffing on his bowl, tamping it with his thumb. "Remember, California is still Mexican Territory…for now."

"And slavery is illegal in Mexico," I muttered bitterly.

He blew out a huge cloud of white smoke. "But she's still his slave," he said.

I stood up and punched my fist into my palm. "Not if I can help it," I wildly shouted. "Now, what's the fastest way to Sutter's Fort?"

Squinting through the smoke, the old man turned his eyes over the sweeping view of the down-sloping mountains and the virgin green valley in the distance. "Follow the flow of water downhill," he said. "The river leads to the road; the road leads to the Fort."

I nodded and turned away. My winter rags lay in a messy heap under the tree, and I was eager to get dressed, rushed by this sense of precious time being wasted.

Meanwhile, the three naked squaws appeared to have forgotten all about me. They had returned to the steamy waters of the hot pool—but no matter, I was done fooling around with them anyways. All I could think about was Violet and the beach house.

I got dressed in a hurry, then turned my sights on Ringo, thinking that I could go searching for Violet one of two ways: by hobbling on my own two trodden feet, or booming on horseback like a White Knight in shining armor.

I snatched Ringo by the bridal and pulled him face to face. "Look here," I said aggressively. "You need a rider, and I need a horse. We're a natural pair. Now let me on your backers, and don't get no ideas bout' bucking me off."

Ringo flicked his ears and shuffled his feet. The look in his eyes seemed agreeable enough, and I threw my blanket over his backside like a saddle.

Before mounting, I turned back to the hot pool to say farewell to the lovely Injun sisters.

But they were gone.

And so was the elder.

"Old man!?" I called out.

My voice echoed hollow over the empty hot pool. No response. Nothing but the lingering smell of the old man's burning bush and the sound of a cool wind whipping up the mountain.

I shrugged, then mounted Ringo and fixed my sights on the down-sloping mountains and green valley beyond.

I was in love…and that's what love will do to man. Get him up on that horse and send him down that dusty road through uncharted territory, striving and suffering day after day, giving it all to reach that fabled promised land.

Acknowledgements

The Nevada Public Library System, the wonderful people of Las Vegas, and Gwyn Jordan of Gold Dust Literary Agency, the one and only agent a struggling writer could ever need.

About the Author

Sean Tyler is a novelist, journalist, freedom fighter, U.S. Coast Guard vet, and father of two. He holds a bachelor's degree in history from Youngstown State University in Ohio. In order to fully immerse himself in the subject matter of White Hell, Tyler spent a winter in a log cabin along the shores of Donner Lake, California, where deathly starving members of the Donner Party feasted on human flesh some 175 years ago. Tyler currently lives in a fortified compound near 'The Strip' in Las Vegas, Nevada.

SOCIAL MEDIA HANDLES:
  Facebook: https://www.facebook.com/sugarseanh
  TikTok: https://www.tiktok.com/@theseantylerexperience
  X: https://x.com/SeanTExperience

AUTHOR WEBSITE:

212

Also by Sean Tyler

Sean Tyler - The Nevada Independent